HOLE IN THE HEART

MARK MOSCA

A MYSTERY

For Gayle,
But not her children's
book list!
Hope you enjoy...

Mark "Mosca" Jenkins

Hole in the Heart is a paperback original mystery published by OTTER B BOOKS, March 1994. Information concerning rights to reprint this book or portions thereof in any form except as provided by the U.S. copyright law may be obtained by contacting the publisher at 1891-16th Avenue, Santa Cruz, CA 95062; (408) 476-5334.
Printed by arrangement with the author.
Manufactured in the United States of America.
ISBN 0-9617681-7-7

Grateful thanks to the estate of García Lorca for use of the lines from his poem *La Guitarra* on page 67.

The cover illustration and design is by Jane P. Miller.

FOR D.P. VERNEUIL

ONE

There were three men in the small kitchen. One was naked and taped onto the gray formica table. Several thicknesses of gray duct tape ran across his stomach and forearms and under the table, which was too small for him. He strained to hold his head up over one end of the table. His eyes were wide and he was gagged with more duct tape. At the other end of the table his legs were spread and his knees bent over the corners. His ankles were taped to the metal legs of the table.

On the triangle of formica formed by his spread legs there were an egg, a pack of Camels, a half-empty bottle of Orendain tequila and a stone salsa bowl. The bowl, from a Mexican restaurant, held the remains of several joints, and one that was still lit. A long thin wisp of smoke rose straight up into the airless room, like incense. Which was what it was supposed to look like when they started shooting it. Copal or whatever those guys used.

There was a burlap sack on the floor under the table. It moved every few seconds. There was a large poster of the Sacred Heart of Jesus over the sink, held there with duct tape. On the counter next to the sink was a large kitchen knife.

There were two other men in the room. One stood at the end of the table between the naked man's legs. He had a jaguar mask pushed up on his forehead. He looked to the third man, who was leaning against the kitchen door. He was dressed all in black and was loosely holding a camcorder in his right hand. The man on the table looked back and forth, from one man to the other. His muscles were flexed from his neck to his shoulders, the veins stood out.

The man in black said, "Rehearse it again. Slowly, no mistakes."

The jaguar-man shrugged and reached for the joint to show he was in no hurry to obey. He took an elaborate drag, held it down, offered the joint to the man in black, who took it and smoked. The jaguar-man lowered his mask and picked up the stone bowl. He stood facing the man in black, who said, "What are you waiting for?" The man in black didn't let out any smoke as he spoke and his voice sounded choked.

"My incense. You always tell me to do it right, so I'm waiting for the fucking incense."

The man in black exhaled with a relieved sigh and put the joint back in the salsa bowl. The jaguar-man slowly extended the bowl in front of him, over the naked man, whose eyes followed the bowl with terrified interest. The tape held his mouth wide open.

The jaguar-man turned slowly to his right and held the bowl out to the Sacred Heart of Jesus. Then he rotated back until the bowl was over the naked man again and raised it over his head, lifting his masked face heavenward — to the low ceiling. He lowered the bowl again and looked to the man in black.

The man in black nodded: That was it. He put the camcorder to his face and without recording looked through the viewfinder at the jaguar mask. It was better than he'd dared hope for. Straight out of a nightmare, via a garage sale. It would make a perfect close-up: orange with black jaguar dots; the mouth, open in a snarl, had wooden pegs for teeth; a snake curled around the forehead; its head pointed down between the eyes to make the nose.

He lowered the camcorder to his side again. The jaguar-man raised his mask and wiped his face. He was wearing clear latex gloves and one of the fingers flapped loose where he was missing a finger. Even the man on the table relaxed for a moment, letting his head fall back. Almost immediately he struggled to lift it again and look at the two men. The bag under the table moved spasmodically, squawked and then was still again.

The jaguar-man picked up the bottle of tequila, took a slug and offered it to the man in black, who took a drink and put it back on the table. "Okay," he said, back to business. "Do the shit with the egg now."

"Oh, come on man, I already know how to do it." He took the joint out of the bowl again and smoked. He stubbed it out and took a fresh one out of his pocket.

As he was lighting it the director explained it again: "Knowing it in your mind is not the same. You still have to rehearse." He went to the jaguar-man, took the joint out of his mouth and put it back in the bowl. "Do it right. And put the mask down."

"Yeah, yeah." He put the mask down and began to quickly pass the egg over the naked man's limbs.

"No. Do it *right*."

Jaguar-man slowed down and continued. He began to laugh. "I seen my grandmother do this lots of times," he said through his laughter, then tried to stop laughing, forcing himself to finish the job. He was still shaking with silent laughter and the egg trembled just above the naked man.

It made the man in black want to laugh too, which pissed him off. He shouldn't have to deal with this kind of shit when he was trying to concentrate. With exaggerated flatness he said, "What the fuck you laughing about?"

The jaguar-man held up the egg, lifted his mask and giggled, "Just thinking, man."

His face seemed to be melting with laughter, as if his face wasn't solid anymore. It *was* funny. The man in black clamped his throat to hold down his own laughter and hissed, "What the *fuck* is so funny?"

"My grandmother used to do this, you know?" He struggled to get the words through his laughter: "To *heal* people." He dissolved again.

The man in black said, "I don't think it's going to work this time."

The jaguar-man fell against the counter, writhing with laughter.

The man in black hadn't meant it to sound like a joke. But it was funny. He felt bubbles of laughter filling his chest, pressing behind his eyes, in his sinuses.

It wasn't what he goddamn meant. He wouldn't let himself laugh. He said, "Get a fucking grip on yourself."

The jaguar-man sniffed a few times, trying to stop laughing. The man on the table was watching them, straining forward, drenched in sweat.

The jaguar-man sniffed violently and said, "Sorry, man. I just mean, it don't make a whole lot of sense, the egg shit."

"It doesn't have to make sense," the man in black said, word by word. "It just has to look like we're into some weird shit."

"Weird shit?" The jaguar-man fell apart again. "Weird shit!

Oh don't worry, it gonna look like some weird shit all right!"

The man in black couldn't stand it, he was going to lose it. "The chicken," he shouted, "just do the goddamn chicken!"

The jaguar-man held his hands out in front of him in a calm-down gesture, heaved himself off the counter and bent down to the burlap sack. As soon as he picked it up it exploded with motion and squawks. He held it at arm's length, shaking with laughter, and trying to undo the string. A chicken's head popped out of the sack and then the wings burst free. He pulled it out and held it upside down by its tied feet. Batting wings, squawking, twisting. Jaguar-man shook with laughter, the man on the table was going crazy, the man in black knew he was losing it too.

The jaguar-man managed to say, "*Pinche gallina.* Don't think this fucking bird *wanna* rehearse!"

It was impossible: the blur of the bird, his melting friend, the bug-eyed man on the table, everything. The man in black leaned against the wall and the million bubbles of silent laughter floated free.

The jaguar-man threw the chicken on the floor. "Fuck the fucking chicken." It flapped its wings helplessly.

The man in black closed his eyes. There weren't any more shapes. There was just a field of laughter, rolling through him.

Then the waves were less violent, they slowed down, he was coming back.

"Shit," he said when he could.

He'd fucked up. Let things get out of hand, lost control. Smoked too much so things were striking at funny angles. It wasn't him, it wasn't... professional.

He went over to the man on the table and patted him on the thigh. "Take five, fucker."

No, that wasn't the way. He couldn't say funny things, things that could strike him funny after he'd said them.

He raised the camera and looked through the eyepiece, to cut out what he didn't want to see, cut out his friend, concentrate, take charge.

He found the various objects and zoomed in on them: the knife, the bowl, the poster of Jesus.

It didn't matter much what order he did it in. He'd just use a few jump cuts. Save the editing. He wasn't worried about rhythm or building it up or any of that shit. The subject matter would be plenty compelling, no problem there. That thought zinged in at a funny angle. No, he told himself. Don't react.

The poster of Jesus: the simpering eyes, the hair-do. Don't react. He'd taken it from the wall above his aunt and uncle's bed on a trip north the week before. Did they actually make love under that poster? The pressure in his chest started again. No. He zoomed on the heart: The heart was flame-licked, crowned with thorns, a gory, gaudy Mexican Sacred Heart. Thick lips of flesh opened to reveal the red heart. It struck him. In tight like that, zoomed in on the flesh lips, the Heart looked like a... just like a.... The quivering laughter started again and he dropped the camera to his side.

It didn't take as long this time. The jaguar-man was laughing again and looking at him expectantly. The man in black said, "No. Nothing. Never mind."

It was finished now. He went over to the table and put his hand on the naked man's shoulder, slippery with sweat. The man struggled as if he was trying to do a sit-up and made a noise through his nose.

"I'm sorry," the man in black said. "We botched the rehearsal."

The man made a desperate sound against the tape.

"You cool?" the man in black said to the jaguar-man.

He nodded.

"I mean it."

He nodded again.

The room had changed, the field was different. "This time we'll shoot it. Give up on rehearsing."

The jaguar-man nodded again and the man on the table made another desperate sound.

The man in black patted the naked man's shoulder. "I just don't think you get it, Domingo. It's not your fault, I know. You're not a professional actor. We told you the script and naturally you thought you should play it for sheer terror. But that's really not it. You can be frightened, sure, but the role also calls for great dignity."

The man in black kept his hand on Domingo's shoulder. Domingo's wide eyes didn't seem to be taking anything in.

The man in black sighed. "Let's go through it again. Just relax, okay?"

Domingo let his head and shoulders fall back, obediently. He kept his eyes on the director.

The director said, "Okay, first: motivation. The motivation is

you fucked with me and you got caught. Right?"
Domingo weakly nodded his lolling head.

The man in black put his finger on the elaborate scar on
Domingo's chest — lines radiating out from a circle, a keloid
sunburst — and began to trace the hard spokes. Domingo tried to
suck his chest into the formica table.

The man in black said, "You forgot what this means."

He stepped back, put down the camcorder and undid the
buttons on his black shirt, revealing a similar scar. "See? The sun.
El sol. But you forgot what it means and you fucked with me,
Domingo. Didn't you?"

Domingo gave a helpless nod, confessing.

"Oh, I can understand. It was partly my fault. You guys
couldn't take it seriously when I started the film program. You must
have thought I was out of the picture...."

Domingo shook his head vigorously.

"But I wasn't. It was just something I had to do. To *express*
myself. You know?"

Domingo was straining up again, nodding.

"And you have to be punished, Domingo."

Domingo fell back against the table again, sobbing through
his nose.

"You have to help me with this film."

Domingo lay back, swinging his head from side to side.

The man in black stepped up to him again and studied his face
with compassion. "Jesus," he whispered with disbelief. He turned
to the jaguar-man. Domingo strained forward to watch them.
"Jesus, he thinks we really mean it. He thinks we're really going to
do it."

The jaguar-man looked confused.

"Domingo, it's just a *film.* We wouldn't... it's just art."

Domingo's eyes were streaming with tears.

"You'll help me with my art, won't you?"

Domingo nodded, bleary, weeping with gratitude.

The man in black patted his shoulder again. "So, your
motivation: you got caught, you're scared. But the bigger picture
is... dignity. You're preparing to die a glorious death, an Aztec
death. When your soul leaves your body it will help the sun climb
to its zenith and then your soul will turn into a hummingbird. A
great honor, *verdad?*"

Domingo nodded uncertainly but energetically. The director

patted his shoulder again and stepped back. He picked up his camcorder again.

"Let's get it right this time, Dedo," the director said to the man in the jaguar mask.

Dedo began to rearrange his props and got the chicken back in the sack. When he was ready he looked to the director.

The director put the camcorder to his shoulder and set the viewfinder to his eye.

He said, "Action, Dedo."

Dedo said, "You got it, Fausto."

Dedo picked up the salsa bowl. The wisp of smoke curled up.

Fausto was entirely focused. Himself again. Filming from out of a clear, deep silence.

He held himself still as his muscles and bones melted.

TWO

The plane from Mazatlán to Tijuana landed and taxied to a stop. Fausto looked at the two babies on the seat next to him. They were still sleeping peacefully in the special seats provided by the airline. He hesitated before waking them and beginning the whole rigmarole again. A smiling flight attendant appeared, to help him with the babies. One thing about babies, people sure treated you different.

He leaned over and unbuckled one of the babies and handed him — her? it? he couldn't even remember — to the stewardess. The baby began to howl. Fausto and the stewardess smiled at each other again. Babies are something else. He got the other baby out of its seat and got the bag full of baby stuff over his shoulder. The stewardess handed him the first baby so he had one in each arm. The baby in his right arm messed his diaper with the familiar burbling sound and Fausto closed his eyes. When he opened them the stewardess was smiling even more sympathetically. He shrugged his shoulders and began to work his way down the aisle.

It was almost over, he reminded himself. The last run.

In the terminal he found his girlfriend and his uncle, who had been in different parts of the plane. Each of them was holding two babies. They caught a cab.

"All yours?" the driver joked, referring to the six babies.

Fausto, in the front seat with him, nodded and looked out the window, leaving the driver with the impossible arithmetic.

When they got to the motel Socorro got out with her two babies and Fausto had the driver drop him and his uncle off at a little restaurant a block away. It wasn't necessary: The motel wouldn't have cared if they'd showed up with a hundred babies.

But each time Fausto insisted they do it this way. It focused them, put them in a border-crossing frame of mind, got them to start paying attention to details. The first time they'd done it his uncle had asked him why and he'd said it was a rite of passage. His uncle had just nodded. Since Fausto's brief stint as a university student his uncle hardly listened, just nodded no matter what he said.

They had a cup of coffee without speaking. His uncle held the cup in both hands as if to warm himself. His thick fingers, permanently bent from a lifetime of holding tools, fit the cup perfectly. He had a flat face with broad indio cheekbones and, like Fausto, a strong nose. He had coarse indio hair that stuck out so straight from the sides of his head you could see right through to the surprisingly white skin. Everywhere else he was nut brown. Fausto looked away, unable, as always, to believe he shared any genes with the man.

After a few minutes of silence Fausto told the old man to go and Tío gathered up his two babies. They were quiet. They always were. Something about the old man calmed babies.

As soon as he was gone one of Fausto's babies started to make a fuss and he realized he still had the one with the dirty diapers. He'd meant to give that one to Tío. He held out for a couple more minutes, finishing his coffee, and then walked to the motel, a baby in each arm. When he got there Tío was on the balcony in front of a room so Fausto would know where they were. When Tío saw him he went into the room, leaving the door open and Fausto went up the stairs and into the room.

The four babies were laid out in a row on the carpet against the wall and he added his two to the line. Socorro had the Huggies, pacifiers, Similac and bottles already out on the table. Fausto fell onto the couch and said, "Jesus." He got out a cigarette. "Socorro, you better change that one on the end."

She gave him a tired-angry look.

He laughed and said, "Don't try it. Just go back to being a long-suffering Messican woman. That plays better, right Tío?"

His uncle didn't understand. Fausto lit the cigarette and closed his eyes. Maybe they'd all go away.

But they were still there when he opened them. Socorro was changing the babies and his uncle was just standing there. The man could stay in the same position for hours; sitting, standing, it made no difference. It was some kind of indio thing, Fausto figured, but it drove him crazy. He took another drag and leaned back, blowing the smoke at the ceiling.

"What time is it, Tío?" he asked without looking down.

"Two."

They had all the time in the world but he couldn't stand his uncle just standing there, or sitting there, silently worrying whether they were doing the right thing.

"Better get going, Tío."

"Already?"

"It's better. Socorro will be about half an hour behind you."

Fausto looked down from the ceiling to his uncle. The good thing about people who never understood anything was they never asked any questions. They were used to not understanding.

Two of the babies were crying now. Fausto pointed to one of them and said, "Better take that one."

The old man went over to pick him up and then went to the table to get his shoulder bag.

"Socorro," Fausto said, "let's do the passports."

Socorro went to her bag, opened an inside zipper and took out nine passports held together by a rubber band. Fausto found the one of his uncle and then found one that matched the baby boy Tío was taking across. There was always a reasonably good match because they picked the babies each time to go with the passports. The age was all that really mattered anyway.

He gave two passports to his uncle. "Okay, Tío. Remember, you're Miguel Higuera, you live in San Diego on Acacia Street. There's no stamp in your passport because you just walked across for the day. This is your grandson. His name is Jose Higuera. Right?"

His uncle nodded and in his maddening way repeated everything he had just been told.

"*Andale*," Fausto said, slapping him on the shoulder when he'd finished and guiding him to the door.

When he'd gone Fausto threw himself back down on the couch and said, "One down, five to go."

Socorro was mixing bottles and giving them to the babies. One was still crying, punching the air with his fists and his feet.

Fausto went out onto the balcony to smoke another cigarette. This was the last run; soon there wouldn't be any more babies, just the money, which he would parlay into real money. It wasn't an easy way to make a living but someone, he reflected grimly, had to do it.

He went back inside. The baby was still crying and Socorro was just going into the bathroom.

"You ready?" he said.

She looked at him. "I can go to the bathroom?" she said angrily.

He made a magnanimous gesture and she went on into the bathroom.

As soon as she came out he said, "Those two," pointing at the one who was crying and another one that was starting to look unhappy.

She looked at the babies and then smiled with satisfaction. She pointed at the one who was making all the noise. "I can't take that one, not if I'm supposed to be taking twins."

"Why not?"

"Oh, come on, Fausto, you can figure it out. He's twice as big and twice as old as the others. Twins are supposed to have something in common. Like the same birthday."

He made a beaten gesture. "Just pick two, get them across and get back here to save me from that one." He pointed again. The baby was arching his back against the floor with each scream.

Socorro went through the passports, got the right ones, repacked her bag and put it over her shoulder. She went to pick up two quiet babies and went to the door. She turned and said, "Three down and three to go."

"Go, go. And get *back!*"

"He needs to be burped, Fausto." She left.

Fausto went over to the crying baby and picked him up. He sat down with him and bounced him roughly on his knee, speaking in time with the bounces: "Shut-up-*hi-jo-de-la-chin-ga-da!*"

The baby roared louder as if he'd understood the insult to his mother, threw his head and shoulders back and then suddenly burped with a sound like a hollow clap. They looked at each other with surprise. The baby subsided and some milk ran down the corner of his mouth. Fausto tried patting him on the back the way he'd seen mothers do and the baby gave a couple smaller burps.

Exhausted from his efforts, the baby went limp and his head lolled off to one side. Fausto hesitated and then brought him against his chest.

Sounds came to him from the tunnel of the distant past. Soothing sounds that were almost words but weren't. He wanted to hear them, he knew they were important. He stopped trying because he knew they'd never come if he tried. But he stayed alert to surprise the words if they came back on their own.

When they did it was his mother's voice from the beginnings of his memory: *Duérmete niño/Duérmete solito.* Sleep child, sleep alone.

He jumped up and paced with the baby. It had been a mistake. He didn't want that voice, his mother's words. He paced and rocked the baby, blocking the image with activity. But he saw the blood, the arm rising and striking, again and again, and he heard her screams.

THREE

When Socorro got back he left and caught a cab to the Cañon Zapata. It would be several hours until the shift changed on the border and they could risk taking the last three through. And he wasn't going to spend those hours with babies.

The trip to the Cañon Zapata had become part of his personal crossing-over ritual. The first time he'd come out of simple curiosity — he'd heard about it in prison — but he kept coming back. Something about all that desperation braced him, focused him. It was a kind of meditation.

As the cab got closer to the Cañon everyone seemed to be carrying something: suitcases, bolsas, plain cardboard boxes tied with string. But most of them carried something light, an Adidas bag or something like that — something that wouldn't slow them down when they ran.

The cab went as far as it could and he walked the rest of the way down the rutted path into the cañon. People were already gathering, though they wouldn't try to cross for hours. The waiting, scared, was part of it and every afternoon and evening a temporary society formed in the cañon. People milled until they found their coyote — if they had enough money for one — and then stayed close to him, ignoring outsiders.

The people who had no money, or had been robbed clean before making it to the cañon, would have to cross on their own. Everyone avoided them and their bad luck.

Vendors worked the little society, selling chiclets, blankets, tequila, running shoes, switchblades, religious medals and rosaries. Women cooked on braziers to feed the people before they dropped down into the cañon.

Across from the cañon was a strip of no man's land and then the fence. On the other side of the fence was Gringolandia, patrolled by the Border Patrol. Out of sight, they too were getting ready for the evening.

Fausto bought a plate of tacos and a cup of coffee and settled against a fragment of stone wall, left over from some building that no longer stood. He ate and watched.

The people in that cañon had drifted north a thousand, two thousand, three thousand miles, all to end up pressed against the border in Tijuana, getting ready to try their luck. Other people's desperation, so thick you could almost taste it.

He leaned against the wall and let one of the stones dig in under a shoulder blade. He smiled: desperation! In prison he had taken a community college course — it would look good when he came up for parole. The course had a kind of symmetry: They'd found a kind, plump, blond woman to teach enraged, hard, brown and black men. One day she'd told them about a guy who'd felt so desperate about the life he was living that he decided to go live by a lake and grow beans. It had been a revelation to him.

If they thought that was desperation, he had a real edge on them. He was prepared to go much, much further than that. He owed the teacher, la maestra, for the insight and for the image that had helped him through the three years of prison: the image of the blond hair, the red lips, of the blouse pulled tight over her full breasts as she held a book up to make a point, her finger marking a page. That image had served and served, floating between him and his prison partners. The blond hair would spill through his fingers, the moist red lips....

All in all, though, prison had been good for him. He'd been losing control. They'd got him on armed robbery, but if they'd got him on some of the other things he'd done.... He'd cooled down in prison. Got some ideas. Met some people. Even a simple thing like the passports, that was a prison connection.

But the real thing was, one taste of prison and he knew he'd never go back. He'd gladly die first, and that gave him a real edge on people who thought you grew beans if you were feeling desperate.

He looked at himself in the full-length mirror on the bathroom door. His black hair, long and oiled, was combed straight back. He had the same hawk nose as his uncle but everything else in his face was lean and narrow. He didn't have the broad indio cheekbones or that look his uncle had, like he'd just been hit between the eyes with a hammer. He took off his clothes and fingered the scar on his chest, ran his fingers over his muscles.

He took a long shower and dried. He put on his asshole outfit — couldn't cross over in black: teeshirt with broad blue and white stripes and upside down feet stitched over the heart; bluejeans and docksiders without socks. He dried his hair with Socorro's blow drier until it was soft and fluffy. He could almost pass. He looked whitened.

They got the last three babies ready and caught a cab to the border. They went into the Customs building at almost the same time but headed for different lines. Socorro's line moved faster than his and he watched her take through her second batch of twins that day. When he got to the Customs agent in his line he handed her the two passports and fussed with the baby in his arm. The agent had a boiled face and looked like she was exploding on the inside.

She looked at the passport and said, "Just over for the day?"

"Just over for some dinner." He smiled and tickled the baby, who cleverly held out his hand to the woman.

She smiled without much feeling and held out her finger for the baby to grab, already looking at the person behind them in line. She handed back the passports and pulled her finger free.

He walked the couple hundred yards to the parking lot they always used and found the huge Silverado with Tío standing next to it. Three of the babies were already in their carseats and Socorro was leaning in the open door getting her two strapped in. The interior light illuminated the mesh covering over the back window, which showed an eagle circling over mountains. When Socorro finished he handed her his baby and she bent in again. He got in the front passenger seat and Tío got in behind the wheel.

He looked over the back of his seat and watched Socorro making the last preparations like a stewardess on a special baby flight. This was the last run. What was he going to do with six carseats?

In a few minutes they were on the freeway to San Diego. Fausto leaned back and watched the taillights, waiting for his uncle to start in.

In a few minutes his uncle said, "You coming with us this time?"

He shook his head. "I have to fly."

"It's a lot of work for Socorro."

"I have a meeting with my parole officer tomorrow morning."

"We can make it."

"I have to fly, Tío."

His uncle nodded and drove. He always said the same thing but he always dropped him off at the airport. Fausto wasn't going to risk going back to prison because of an act of God like a flat tire and a highway patrolman who might wonder what they were doing with six babies. And he didn't need another eight hours with babies anyway.

His uncle never asked for explanations. He drove carefully, had a little statue of the Virgin of Guadalupe on the dashboard and a picture of the Sacred Heart above the rearview mirror, and never really expected answers.

In a minute his uncle cleared his throat and Fausto got ready for the next part.

Tío said, "Are you sure we should be doing this?"

Fausto waited to be sure he could answer without losing his temper. He said, "Tío, I know it's hard to trust me after my... problems, but Jaime wouldn't lie to you."

"You wouldn't lie to me either," the old man said.

"Jaime explained it all, didn't he? We're *saving* these babies. Think of the lives they would have down there. Jaime will put them up for adoption. They'll have good homes."

Tío nodded and Fausto relaxed. It worked every time but he had to be sure he got through it all without getting angry or laughing. He just had to keep it on a level his uncle would understand, referring to poverty, invoking the sainted son, Jaime.

He looked at the old man one more time and then closed his eyes. They'd needed him for his contacts in Old Mexico but now he knew too much. True, he didn't know what he *knew,* but if he were asked the wrong questions, he wouldn't know enough to lie.

Fausto opened his eyes and looked out the side window. He was too tired to think all that through now.

One step at a time. Place these babies. Get Dedo out.

FOUR

Fausto walked down Ocean Avenue in Carmel-by-the-Sea, a rich tourist town that called itself a village. The street was lined with boutiques that were too small.

He floated through the tourists: head back, oiled black hair, dark glasses, earring, black silk shirt, loose black pants, kung-fu slippers, aluminum photographer's case.

Between a bar and a bakery he found the passageway he was looking for. The lower half of the wall was Mexican tile; the upper half was plastered rough to look old. At the end was a small fountain with a trickle of water. The stone was greenish where the water slipped over it.

He went up the stairway next to the fountain, read the brass plaque next to the door, and went in without knocking. The receptionist looked up from her computer screen. "Sir?" she said without losing her poise.

He gave her a minute to take in the small drill bit he wore for an earring, the tips of his scars visible where the silk wasn't buttoned. He said, "I'd like to talk to Mr. Newkirk, please. I don't have an appointment but I think he will see me if you will tell him Jaime Sanchez's cousin is here, on rather urgent business."

He took off his dark glasses and smiled politely, certain he had the password. Jaime.

"Just a moment, sir." She got up and slipped through the door behind her.

He looked out the window next to her desk. There was a patch of blue — the sea in Carmel-by-the-Sea — a few hundred yards away between two stands of Monterey pine.

The door opened again and the receptionist came out with a

man who smiled warmly — a relaxed smile in a tan face — and
held out his hand. He was slender and had the silver-templed
look that took the sting out of middle age. He was the way Fausto
expected from talking to Jaime: rich, confident, didn't have to wear
a tie to the office.

"I'm John Newkirk," he said as they shook hands.

"Fausto Sanchez, Jaime's cousin."

Newkirk gestured to the interior of his office and put his
hand on Fausto's elbow as he went in. The office was a long room
with a window along most of one wall, showing rooftops, more pine
and sea. Against the opposite wall there was a large fieldstone
fireplace; the stones were blackened around the mouth. Above the
fireplace there was a painting of a man and woman in their Sunday
best. They looked as if they'd been inflated with bicycle pumps
and the air had smoothed out any expression on their faces.

Fausto took in the rest of the room quickly: beams on the
ceiling that looked like they could have been hewn by Father
Serra's indios, a small table with a comfortable armchair on each
side, and at the far end of the room a more serious hardwood desk
which was empty except for a computer and a framed photograph.

Newkirk pointed at the comfortable armchairs and then at
the desk to give him a choice: "Business or pleasure?"

"Business, I'm afraid."

Fausto followed Newkirk to the desk and took his seat across
from him. The wood was like a mirror between them.

"Nice place," Fausto said, looking around again. "Interesting
painting."

"Thank you. It's a Botero."

Fausto nodded, then looked out the window.

"Jaime didn't tell me he had a cousin," Newkirk said when it
felt like it was time for someone to say something.

Fausto smiled slowly. "I don't suppose he did. Jaime has come
up in the world and I've been in and out of jail, so...." He shrugged.

"I see."

"But Jaime told me about you. I guess you met in connection
with his adoption agency."

"That's right. We adopted through his agency a few years
ago, a baby girl."

"Jaime thinks the world of you."

"I have a high opinion of him too."

"From what he's said I guess you must be about the best lawyer in this part of California."

"I doubt that."

Fausto didn't say anything for a moment and watched Newkirk, who didn't seem especially nervous. So he wasn't one of those people who went to pieces at the mention of prison, which would make it more fun.

"Do you need a lawyer?" Newkirk prompted.

"It's not me, but I have a friend who has a parole hearing in a couple weeks."

"I'm afraid I don't do that kind of thing, Mr. Sanchez."

Fausto looked at him. "You will do this one, John. In fact it will be the most important case in your life."

Newkirk swallowed and studied Fausto, as if he hadn't really been looking before. "I'm afraid you don't understand. I don't do *cases*. I do investment things, corporate things."

"You will do this one, John."

Fausto reached over to the framed picture on the desk and turned it to him. It showed a woman with delicate features. Her blond hair was cut with bangs; the sides were cut so the front ends were longer than the back and curled up under her jawline. She wore simple pearl earrings and her smile showed small moist teeth like more matching pearls. Her eyes were blue.

"Blue eyes," Fausto said thoughtfully. He looked at Newkirk, who still hadn't flinched but was paying complete attention. "This must be Alison. No pictures of Billy and Maria Elena?"

Newkirk didn't answer. He swallowed slowly, still in control, but it was getting to him. A blue vein stood out on each temple.

Fausto opened the aluminum case on his lap and took out a switchblade and sprang the blade. "Don't push a button, don't move." Tiny points of sweat appeared on Newkirk's forehead and Fausto thought, unless he was imagining it, that the veins had begun to throb. "You will do this case, John, or I — or one of my associates — will kill you, and Alison, and Billy, and Maria Elena. You do see now why it's the most important case of your life, John?"

Newkirk nodded again. He had staying power but a drop of sweat broke loose and ran along a blue vein, then down his temple and onto his cheek. Fausto reached for the picture of Newkirk's wife and lay the point of the knife on the glass. He squiggled the point back and forth and it made a thin squeaky sound. He watched Newkirk watch the knife. He didn't crack but something in the face changed, his inner conviction, Fausto thought, that things necessarily turned out right for people like him. Fausto squiggled the point on the glass again and then thoughtfully closed the knife.

Fausto let out a sigh. "You're thinking, of course, that if you can just get rid of me, you can do something, like call the police. But I've told my associates that if anything happens to me — I get arrested, disappear, die — anything at all, they have to kill you. And Alison, and Billy, and Maria Elena, and the goldfish if you have one."

"I understand," Newkirk said.

"I hope so. These, uh, associates of mine... I met them in prison and they're not, uh, the crême de la crême, know what I mean?" He held the picture of Alison in front of him and cocked his head admiringly. "Some of them even have like sex problems, I don't know what all. No, you'd rather just deal with me."

Newkirk held his gaze but an eyelid was dancing now. That was good. He hadn't just folded. You didn't want someone you couldn't respect working for you.

Newkirk slowly — so Fausto wouldn't object — put his hand on a drawer, opened it and reached in. He came out with a legal pad.

"Super, " Fausto laughed. "A *legal* pad. "

"Tell me about your case, Mr. Sanchez."

"My friend has a parole hearing on August 14. You have to make sure he gets out."

"I've never done this before. I can't promise."

"If he doesn't get out I kill you and... etc., etc."

Newkirk swallowed. "You can't entirely control things like this."

"A man like you can control it. Just buy them off. That's what I'd do, play it safe. But I won't tell you how to run your case."

"What's your friend's name?" He looked down at the pad.

"Dedo."

Newkirk looked up. "D-e-a-d-o?"

"No, D-e-d-o. He lost a finger and got a nickname. *Dedo* means finger."

"He has another name?"

"Alfonso Gutiérrez. He's in for armed robbery, aggravated assault, severe bodily injury."

"Same thing you were in for?"

Fausto nodded.

"But you're out and he isn't?"

"Dedo's not so smart. He doesn't know how to ingratiate himself with people, like me."

"Tell me about the crime."

"We robbed a bunch of camera and video stores and subdued one of the clerks a bit excessively."

"You didn't kill him?"

Fausto shook his head. "Do I look like a killer?"

"Has Dedo killed anyone in prison?"

"Not that they know of."

"Is this his first time in prison?"

"First time in real grown-up prison."

Newkirk relaxed slightly. He wiped his forehead with his hand. "It should be possible."

"That's what I told myself," Fausto said enthusiastically. "He just needs good counsel, someone, uh, entirely committed to his case."

Newkirk said, "Mr. Sanchez, how do I know you won't kill... us, after he's out?"

"Kill my lawyer!" He took the knife out of the briefcase again, popped the blade and put the point on the polished hardwood desk. He pushed the knife across the desk and a thin strip of wood curled away from the point. "I sort of think of you as being on retainer, know what I mean?"

Newkirk nodded again. Fausto lay the open knife in the aluminum case and unbuttoned the black silk shirt. He picked up the knife again. He placed the point under his left nipple and pressed until the skin was taut.

Fausto said, "The bottom line is we have to trust each other. You'll do what I say because you believe me when I say I'd do anything. And in exchange I won't kill you. There's no reason for me to."

He pressed the point until it popped the skin and a thin line of blood ran down to his stomach. "You have to trust a man who'll do anything."

FIVE

Calvin Main walked up Greenwich; at the corner of Grant he turned and looked across to Russian Hill. It was a warm evening and he was putting off getting home to an empty, wifeless apartment.

He'd worked late finishing his report to an insurance company on a fraud case he'd investigated for them. He'd had dinner and half a bottle of wine. He'd considered going to Gino and Carlo's for a couple of drinks and the baseball game but decided to go home instead. Since his problems had begun — or come to a head — a month ago he had made a point of being orderly and moderate, to compensate.

He went on up Grant to Edith and then down to his apartment building. He went through his mail quickly in the lobby. Nothing from her. He went up the stairs to his apartment. A few steps from his door he saw a yellow Post-It stuck on the door. When he got there he peeled it off and stuck it in his jacket pocket, being careful not to read it. His hand trembled with anger as he got his key into the lock.

The note was too short. He'd written her a three page letter — since she wouldn't talk to him on the phone — and she'd written her response on a two inch piece of paper. He'd asked her to believe him and forgive him, which she couldn't possibly have done in two inches. It would have taken a much, much bigger piece of paper.

He got the dead bolt open and resisted the urge to kick the door open. He took a deep breath. This whole business was making him want to do things, like kick doors open, that only someone he despised would do.

Inside the door he hesitated for a moment, trying to locate

what had changed. It was the blank space above the fireplace. She
had taken the Guatemalan weaving when she came by to stick the
tiny note on his door.

His weaving. No, that wasn't true. He had given it to her
about ten years ago. It had been one of his first gifts to her. So it
was hers, in the sense that it was... hers. But still it was his in the
sense that she never would have had a Guatemalan weaving if he
hadn't given it to her. All her interest in those things had come
from him.

This whole business was making him that way about
everything. He worried everything to death, argued whether it
was his or hers, from him or her, his fault or hers.

He went to pour himself a glass of wine, less interested in
being orderly and moderate now. The wine was in a little oak barrel
with the word *rosso* painted above the spigot (a gift from her to
him, that she'd found in a little shop on Columbus). He took the
wine over to the couch and watched the last soft yellow sunlight.

He took the little note out of his pocket and read: *You should
have thought of all that before you started sleeping with her.*

She'd been able to fit *that* onto a Post-It.

Bitch.

He leaned back and closed his eyes. It would have been funny
if anything struck him funny anymore. He was furious with Ingrid
for leaving him when *he* had been the one caught in bed with
someone else. He was thinking what a bitch she was when *he* was
the one who had written the ridiculous letter full of lies.

But logic had nothing to do with it. Today he was having an
angry day, so everything made him angry. Yesterday he'd been
having a guilty day so if he'd gotten the note yesterday it would
have been like a kick in the stomach. The day before that all he'd
felt was relief it was all over. If he'd gotten the note then he would
have been glad.

But today was an angry day. He finished his glass of wine and
went to get another. He sat on the couch again. Why in the world
should his wife have forgiven him? The letter had been full of lies.
There *had* been other women. The only special thing about this one
was he'd got caught this time. If he'd been Ingrid he'd have been
furious with him.

The real problem was there was no way to make himself look
good to himself. That's why he had angry days.

But the anger was starting to drain. It always did, fortunately.

This anger cycle was ending and he might have a few hours of peace before the next cycle, whatever that would be, began.

He stayed that way, head back against the couch, for a few moments longer, then got up and went to his answering machine. Part of his orderly routine was not letting things pile up on him.

He waited for the machine to play.

Tone: *This Van Duc Mr. Calvin. Definite clutch. Please you call me.*

First thing in the morning, Van Duc.

Tone: *Mr. Main, Harry Langstrom here. I was just wondering... Have you found anything yet?*

Yes, Harry, I have. Your wife *is* having an affair and I have pictures. But... I know it's awfully squeamish for a private investigator and all... but the way things are in my life right now, I haven't had the stomach to return your calls.

Tone: *This is Ingrid, just in case you've forgotten my voice. Is Dan Wilcox going to handle the legal stuff for you? I'm assuming he is and am advising my lawyer to contact him. Please advise otherwise. P.s.: I took the Guatemalan hanging.*

I noticed, Ingrid.

It sounded like she was having an angry day too, and sarcastic. Which of course was her right and what he had to expect, in all fairness, and there had been other women. Etc.

He filled his glass again. Why fight it, it was turning out to be an immoderate day. He went to stand at the window. The anger was gone; even the phone message didn't bring it back. He just felt tired.

There had been other women.

He said out loud, "Okay, Ingrid, divorce. Let's get it over with."

He toasted his reflection in the window. "Here's looking through you, kid: womanizer, drinker, door kicker, out-loud talker."

His reflection in the dusk light was slippery. If he tried to look at it it disappeared; but out of the corner of his eye it was clear: broad face, short thick hair, heavy even features. The face Ingrid had once called uneventful.

Maybe that's why there'd been other women — too many comments like that. You see, it was her fault.

Other women: He thought of Carmen as he did almost every day.

That's what this was all about. Carmen, not the woman he'd

actually got caught with.

Carmen had been the only real betrayal and even if it had been over for years, it was coming back now in the form of a divorce.

Maybe this was the beginning of a new cycle. What would be a good name for it? Justice? Paranoia?

He watched the lights begin to go on on Russian Hill and thought of Carmen with morose pleasure.

SIX

Carmen was about to leave for a meeting. Richard had just gotten home from work late and was settling into the couch with a large drink. Carmen reminded Richard what to do when Josefina woke up. He watched her in her crib, smiling and looking forward to giving her a bottle.

There was a knock at the door and they looked at each other and shook their heads. Carmen shrugged and went to the door.

There was a young man dressed all in black with an aluminum case. His hair was combed straight back and he had an earring and dark glasses. His head moved up and down as he looked Carmen over. Richard came up to her side. The two men looked at each other without speaking.

Richard Mannock was in his late thirties and it was starting to show through the middle. He had a red face and thick blond curls that were beginning to look too young. He was big and expensively dressed. He spoke first. "Yes?"

"Señora Mannock, Señor Mannock?"

They nodded.

"I'd like to speak to you about Josefina. It's rather important. May I come in?"

"What do you mean?" Richard said, not polite, not quite rude.

"It's just routine. If I could have a moment."

Richard and Carmen looked at each other. Perhaps it was an unannounced home visit, if there was such a thing. Like other adopting parents they could hardly believe their luck, and had a superstitious fear it wouldn't last. They couldn't risk offending an official, no matter how unroutine he looked. They stepped out of the door to let the young man in.

He took off his dark glasses and walked into the middle of the living room. He nodded slowly as he took in the Spanish Colonial antiques. Carmen and Richard looked at each other again. She gave him a look that encouraged him to be polite.

The young man walked over to the fireplace to look at the painting above it. It showed a little girl standing stiffly in a heavy dress with a tight bodice and a bell skirt. It was very old. The young man nodded again and walked over to look out the picture window at the field of artichokes that ran down to the dunes that hid the ocean from sight.

The young man was nodding to himself when Richard interrupted his thoughts: "What was it you wanted to talk about exactly?"

Carmen put her hand on his shoulder. He got angry too easily, and they didn't know who this young man was yet.

The young man turned and walked back to them but spoke to Carmen instead of Richard: "*Hablas español, verdad?*"

She nodded uneasily. There was no reason for him to speak Spanish. And if there had been he wouldn't have used the familiar register.

He mumbled, so Richard wouldn't get it, "*Híjole, chiquita, que bueno que te casaste con un rico.*"

No official could possibly talk like that. She felt her face flush and forgot to breathe for a moment. The young man smiled, walked over to the couch and sat down.

Richard looked at Carmen: What did he say?

She shook her head. Even if she could have spoken out loud she wouldn't have translated: The young man had complimented her on catching a rich Anglo husband.

But Richard had caught the tone. He went over to the couch and warily lowered his large body onto the end opposite the young man. He picked up his whiskey, took a sip, and, confident his voice conveyed easy authority, said, "You wanted to talk about my daughter."

Carmen went to the armchair at Richard's end of the couch.

The young man opened his aluminum case, positioning it on his knees so the raised lid blocked Richard and Carmen's view. He took out a manila folder. "I'd like to get your reaction to this." But instead of giving it to Richard he opened it and looked, nodding to himself.

Richard put out his hand. The man looked from the folder to

Richard's extended hand. There was an expensively thin watch on the thick wrist. Blond hairs curled over the edges of the gold wafer.

"That's a beautiful watch, man. What kind is it?"

Richard lowered his hand. "What do you want?"

"Oh, nothing man. But the watch is so incredible, I just wondered."

Richard took a deep breath, swelled with it and let it out. He said carefully, "It's a Philipe Patek." He put out his hand again for the folder.

"Patek? Hmmm. Guess I got some gaps. But I'm about to come into some money. First thing I'm going to do, get me one of those watches." He shook his head at the beauty of the watch and leaned forward to give Richard the folder.

Richard opened it and looked at the single photocopy in it.

The young man put his hand back into the case and put his fingers around the grip of a .22 target pistol with a silencer. He waited. This was a trial run — he would be doing this many more times — and he had to find out if it would work. It was an experiment. More than anything he was curious. Richard took a long time....

The young man undid the top two buttons of his black shirt and ran his free hand over his chest. Carmen watched him. His chest was covered with scars.

Finally Richard looked up and said, "What is this?"

Carmen reached over and took the folder from him.

The young man said, "It's a birth certificate. From Mexico."

"So what?"

Carmen put the folder down and went to the crib to pick up Josefina. She stood next to the crib holding the baby.

The young man smiled. "I think the Señora has figured it out. That is little Josefina's birth certificate."

Richard leaned forward, shoulders tensed. "Josefina was born in San Bernardino county. Not Mexico. We have all the papers."

"You don't have the right papers."

Richard's fingers were white around his whisky. He put it back on the coffee table and curled his fingers into a fist.

The young man said, "Yes, Josefina's birth was *registered* in San Bernardino." He inclined his head slightly to concede the point. "But she was born in Mexico. The document you have is a birth registration, not a birth certificate."

"It was a home birth. The birth was registered when she was a month old. Her mother was... she didn't..." Richard stopped.

Fausto finished for him: "Her mother was a poor Mexican girl. She was afraid to go to a hospital. She wasn't married. She was illegal, blah, blah, blah. You see, I know the script. I wrote it."

Richard's hands were hard fists, the knuckles were white. He was breathing hard.

Carmen said, "Richard, don't do anything." Her voice was exaggeratedly calm, as if she were telling someone not to move because a rattlesnake had just slithered under him.

She spoke to the young man: "How much?"

"Ten thousand."

"Like hell!" Richard started to get up.

At the same moment Carmen told him to sit down and the young man took the .22 out of the case and pointed it at him.

"What the... what the hell's going on?" Richard sputtered.

"You really don't get it?" the young man laughed. "Your adoption is illegal. The most superficial investigation will reveal that that baby" — he moved the gun from Richard's forehead to the pink bundle in Carmen's arms — "isn't from San Bernardino."

Richard started to get up again. "And you actually think..."

The young man casually held his arm out in the direction of the fireplace and pulled the trigger. The gun made a spitting sound and a hole appeared between the eyes of the stiff little girl in the painting. "Yes," he said, "I *would* use it. Now sit down."

Richard subsided again.

Then he began to fill out. He said, "The adoption couldn't possibly be illegal. We adopted through an absolutely respected agency."

"Nevertheless...."

"I think you're full of shit," Richard said.

"Richard!" Carmen hurried over to the couch and stood behind him with one hand on his shoulder. She pressed Josefina to her with the other.

The young man shrugged. "Check the footprint on the Mexican birth certificate with Josefina's foot."

"Fine, I'll do that."

Carmen said, "How can we get the money to you?"

Richard wasn't going to give up. "Like hell."

"Darling," Carmen said in her emergency voice again, "shut up."

The young man smiled and relaxed his aim, letting the barrel of the gun rest on the lid of the aluminum case.

His curiosity was satisfied. The results were disappointing, of course, but he'd learned what he came to learn. His act wasn't convincing enough. The show wasn't ready to take on the road yet. Of course he could get the money out of the Mannocks — Carmen was ready to hand it over — but that wasn't exactly the point. The point was he had to do the same thing ten times all in one night and even a couple people like Richard Mannock would cost him valuable time, essential time.

"How would you like us to get the money to you?" Carmen repeated.

"Oh never mind," he said, letting out a long sigh. He got up wearily and looked around the room again. "Nice things. Nice furniture, nice view, nice wife, nice baby... "

Carmen interrupted: "What do you mean *never mind?*"

Richard flung a thick finger in the direction of the door. "Get out!"

"Right. And you might want to check out that footprint before you decide to call the police."

"Out."

The young man walked slowly to the door and stopped.

"You're one lucky fucker, Mannock."

"Yeah, yeah." He was talking down the punk.

"This'd been real life, you'd be dead."

Richard nodded: Right, asshole.

"Guess that's a wrap," the young man said and floated out the door.

Richard thought he'd scared him off.

Carmen had no idea what had just happened.

SEVEN

Carmen drove fast but forced herself to breathe slowly, not to give in to the panic she felt. Richard had insisted she go to her meeting, to show how little he was affected by what had just happened, how in control he was. Every instinct told her to stay with Josefina, but she had agreed, for a very different reason.

She had to talk to John Newkirk, who knew something about her adoption. He was on the Board of Trustees of the community college where she taught, but their meeting, every week, was in a motel room, not at the college.

John opened the door with his usual ironic smile and stepped aside for her to enter. Then, like every week, he took her in his arms and kissed her. But this time she left her arms at her sides and turned her lips away from his kiss. She could have been made of wood.

He relaxed his embrace and stepped back, surprised, still holding her by the elbows. He looked at her but didn't say anything. Normally — always — they made love before speaking. The first time it had just happened like that, and since then they had done it consciously, as a tradition, or a sign to each other.

She looked away from his eyes and he said, "What is it darling?"

He sounded like a star of silver screen. She shook her head. She had driven fast and now that she was here, she wasn't ready to talk.

He asked her if she wanted a glass of wine and she nodded. He went to the imitation-wood counter that held the TV, the ashtray, the plastic card with the motel regulations and the bottle of wine he brought. He was a connoisseur and every week he brought a bottle of red wine worth its weight in gold.

As he poured her glass she knew what he was thinking. It hadn't breathed enough. He always uncorked the bottle when her car pulled into the space in front of the room and it had time to breathe just enough while they made love and dreamily chatted. He wouldn't say anything though.

She took the glass from him and swallowed half at a gulp. He didn't wince; he looked at her inquiringly.

She shook her head and went to sit in the armchair next to the bed.

He knew she needed a moment. He went to the window and drew the curtain to start his ritual with the wine. He poured a bit, tilted the glass one way and the other in the light, studying the color. Normally, after sex, she found this seriousness amusing, endearing. Tonight it irritated her and she looked away.

She thought of Josefina in her crib. She shouldn't take it out on John, the perfect lover.

She looked at him again. He was tasting the wine, making rinsing, chewing motions. He belonged to a French organization that had been drinking wine since the Crusades, or something like that. He got newsletters. She couldn't stand it, watching him concentrate on the different tastebuds on different parts of his tongue.

Meanly she wondered if he got mistress newsletters, that provided him with those wonderful ideas he executed on her. She resented even the perfect pleasure he gave her. How did she seem to him: herbaceous? Full pepper in the nose? She knew he must enjoy her tremendous finish.

She finished her glass in a slug and held it out for more. He filled it and watched her with concern. She wanted to say something harsh: it was too perfect the way he cared about her, just as the way he made love was too perfect. She wasn't ready to talk yet. He took another sip of his wine, with the concentration of a neurosurgeon.

She knew what was happening. The present crisis was disturbing the treaty between the warring voices within her. For years her deepest voice — the voice of the Mexican grocer's daughter — had agreed to barely whisper: only whores had lovers. The militant voice had been allowed to speak much louder: Richard's sexual attention had wandered and she had certain needs, certain rights, as a woman. Lately she'd caught a faint new voice she called the rich woman — thirteen years of marriage to Richard had changed her. The rich woman thought like someone in a novel. She didn't care about rights, she Took Lovers. The rich woman was more fun than the others. She actually thought you could do something because you wanted to.

But the crisis tonight was amplifying the original, deep voice.

It was funny really. If she'd divorced Richard, she would have been like everyone else. Instead she'd saved her marriage, by means of lovers. A *string* of them. That still had the power to shock.

Perhaps the deep voice had been in charge all along. The grocer's daughter was adamantly opposed to divorce. She had proved that to herself when, years ago, she had broken off with the one lover she was truly beginning to love. Divorcing Richard would be denying part of her own life, no matter how mistaken it was in some ways. The sunburst of love she had felt for him was an essential part of herself, even if the light and the heat had dimmed. Richard was her husband, inseparable from herself.

John was the perfect lover — kind, consummate, connoisseur of her body — because she loved him only when she made love to him.

"John," she said. Her voice was loud and startled both of them.

He waited for her to speak again.

"Something awful happened tonight. A man came to the house. What do you really know about that adoption agency you steered us to? He said Josefina wasn't really ours, I mean, the adoption is illegal. With phony papers, he wanted money. But he left, I mean, wait I'm sorry, let me start over."

She wasn't making sense, the words seemed to be bouncing around the room.

But John seemed frozen, not confused.

He said, "What did the man look like?"

EIGHT

A pig and a duck were parked on the shoulder of a country road, getting ready. An overgrown hedge hid them from the house down the dirt drive. Fausto was ready — a pig mask and blue rubber gloves — and Socorro was almost ready. She had her duck mask on and was working her fingers into a pair of pink dishwashing gloves. Fausto watched her and made some oinking sounds. "Socorro Duck," he laughed behind his mask.

She scowled at him behind her rubber mask, forgetting he couldn't see her face. Then she pulled her mask up so it rested on her forehead. "I don't see nothing funny about this. Nothing."

"Ay Madre de Díos," he groaned through his pig snout. "Not again."

"You never said nothing about nothing like this. We bring the babies north, put them up for adoption, collect a little commission, that's all I ever heard. Nothing like this."

"Shut up," he said almost patiently. "This is part of the commission business. That's all you need to know. Don't worry about the details."

He reached over to the aluminum case in the back seat and got out the .22.

"That's a detail?" she said, scared. "You *promised* no one would get hurt."

"No one gets hurt." He tapped her thigh with the gun. *"Vámonos."*

When the pig crashed through the door the old woman froze and clutched the baby tightly to her breast. The pig was in a crouch, holding the gun straight out and holding his right wrist with his other hand like the old woman had seen them do on television. A duck came in the door behind the pig.

Out of old habit, the woman looked to her husband seated in front of the television. She'd forgotten the strokes. The man continued to nod at what the talk show host was saying. The wrinkles on the back of his bald head looked like a giant thumbprint. A toddler braced himself against one arm of the old man's armchair and a crawler explored the carpet near his feet.

The old woman looked back at the pig, who seemed to understand. He straightened up and half lowered his gun. "Yo, fuckhead," he said to the man watching TV.

The man turned, smiled at them and returned to his show.

"Must be used to pigs and ducks," the pig said to the old woman, then looked back at the duck. "Which one is it?"

The duck pointed to the baby in the woman's arms.

"Well get her."

The duck went up to the old woman, who just squeezed the baby tighter, angry and afraid. The duck looked to the pig for help. He made a disgusted sound, went up to the old woman and put the barrel of the gun against her temple.

"No," the duck shouted.

The pig pressed the end of the barrel against the old woman's skin. Her head tilted slightly and her eyes grew round. She relaxed her grip on the baby.

The duck gently took the baby girl in her arms but she started squealing anyhow, terrified by the mask. The duck rocked her and whispered to her in Spanish. The baby stopped crying as suddenly as she had begun and watched the duck face with round, fascinated eyes.

"Go see if there's a phone in any of the other rooms," the pig said to the duck.

When she left he went over to the phone on a small table against the wall and took the wire out of the wall jack and the back of the phone. He set the gun on the table to roll the wire into a ball and shoved the ball into his pocket.

The duck returned and shook her head.

"That's it then," the pig said. "It's a wrap." He went over and put his hand on the old man's shoulder. He was still watching TV. "Hey, you're a lot of fun, man. Hang in there."

The old man turned and smiled benignly at them.

The pig nodded to the duck, who headed to the door. He

followed her, stopping at the door and raising his arm to point the gun at the old woman again. Her confusion returned. The pig smiled behind his snout and lowered the gun. He went out.

He followed the duck up the long dirt road to the hedge and the car. He turned and took one last look at the little white house with clumps of geraniums all around the base. The garden was waist high in weeds. Everything around the house had gone to seed. A hundred yards off neat fields began that ran all the way to the sea, obviously worked by someone other than the old man. They were empty now. It would take the old woman a good fifteen minutes to get to a phone.

He went on to the car, where Socorro was getting the baby into a car seat. It was a good thing he hadn't gotten rid of them all after the last run. The baby had the duck mask in her hand and was happily chewing on the bill. He took off his pig mask and passed it over to the baby, who seemed confused now that she had two masks to choose from. She smiled and picked up the pig mask, giving the snout a bite. "Atta girl, Josefina," Fausto said.

He made a U-turn so the old lady wouldn't see the black Riviera go past her drive if she'd come out of the house, though he doubted she was in any shape to notice anything.

When they got to the freeway a couple minutes later he lit a cigarette and exhaled contentedly. He turned and winked at Josefina, then picked up the car phone. He pushed some numbers with his thumb. "KMST-TV? A baby has just been kidnapped from her daycare at 23113 Nuñez Road. The police don't know yet so if you're fast you can get a real scoop.... No, I assure you this is for real.... If you don't believe me just tune into the police frequency and you'll hear all about it in fifteen minutes or so, 'course by then it'll be too late for your scoop... Me? Just a concerned citizen."

He laughed and set the phone down.

Twenty minutes later he was in the living room of Socorro's house smoking a joint to unwind while Socorro took Josefina over to another woman's house for safekeeping.

He took a drag and sniffed through his nose. He looked around the room. Socorro had extraordinary taste. She had a shelf of books in imitation red leather, a wood carving of Don Quixote, silk flowers, a painting of surf hitting rocks.

He looked at his watch, gathered some saliva on his tongue, dipped the burning end of the joint in the saliva and swallowed it.

He picked up the phone, dialed and got a receptionist. "Put me through to Mr. Mannock please. It's urgent. His daughter has had an accident at her daycare."

It had been two weeks since he'd gone to the Mannock's house. For a week Carmen had taken Josefina to work with her. Then they'd relaxed and put her back in her daycare. Now she'd had an accident.

In a moment Mannock said, "Yes?" He was steeled for bad news, but hoping it wasn't too bad, maybe just a cut or a bump.

Fausto didn't say anything.

"Yes? Mannock here."

....

"Is anyone there? Who is this?"

....

"Hello! Who is this!"

"Mr. Mannock," Fausto said softly. "It's me."

"Who?" The question trailed off and there was a very satisfying silence. Fausto imagined Mannock's face.

"We have Josefina, Mr. Mannock." Mannock made a sound.

Fausto laughed. "Words do fail, don't they? But just listen. Carefully. We need to be clear on this. First, I'm not planning on hurting her — she's so cute — but really that depends on you. Clear?"

He heard Mannock breathing. Mannock made another sound.

"Good. You will be hearing from me again about the financial aspect, but not for a week or so. Is that clear?"

"Yes." This time it was soft, almost whispered.

"In the meantime you talk to no one about our... visit. That is the key to Josefina's, uh, well-being. And, as I said last time, you really don't want people looking at the adoption too closely."

"I... understand."

Fausto hung up and savored the moment.

NINE

Deputy Clare snuck quick looks at the massive Lieutenant Victoriano Huerta on the passenger seat next to him as he drove them, lights flashing, to the reported kidnapping. He'd seen Huerta many times — who could miss him? — and he'd heard stories about him — who hadn't? — but he'd never actually worked with him. He was curious and a bit uncertain how to behave. He was vaguely uncomfortable.

He felt better when he realized what it was: Huerta was so broad he took up the space of two people. His shoulder was too close, he was in his space. Clare relaxed and snuck another look.

Huerta had a mitt of a hand on each knee. The fabric of his suit was stretched tight over his thighs. His hair was thick and curly. His face was broad, flat and expressionless. His nose and lips were fleshy and seemed stuck onto the plane of his face as an afterthought. He was very dark and the skin on his neck was pitted. The pits were darker than the rest, like little pools of pigmentation. He was ugly. Deputy Clare squared his shoulders and concentrated on driving, feeling guilty, as if the thought itself was insubordinate. But he couldn't help it — the man was ugly. Even his clothes were ugly. He felt another twinge of guilt: A man that shape — nearly as wide as he was tall — probably had to shop at special stores. Maybe all they had in those stores was cheap dark suits. But surely, he thought, sneaking another look, they had shirts that weren't pink; and no one made him wear a brown tie with the pink shirt and the black suit.

People talked about Huerta's clothes. Clare had heard the other stories too: Huerta never smiled. Huerta never got angry. Never swore. Rarely talked. Went to six o'clock mass every morning. Carried a rosary in his pocket. He seemed slow — he *was* slow, because of his size. But he solved cases.

People didn't know Huerta very well but they told stories about him.

Clare are kept his eyes on the road and wondered what Huerta was thinking.

Lieutenant Huerta was thinking that Deputy Clare was sneaking looks at him and he was remembering the other kidnappings he'd worked on in his career. Most had been cases of one divorced parent taking the child from the other one. That wasn't so bad, but two of the cases he'd never forget. In one an eleven-year-old girl had been taken, and molested, for a week. They'd found the girl; arrested the man; the case had been solved. But the girl would never be the same. The other case, a two-year-old girl, had never been solved. They'd found the tiny skeleton, but never found a suspect or made an arrest. Just a skeleton he still thought of every time he saw a picture of a missing child that said, Have You Seen Me?

Huerta had seen them and he hated kidnapping. He hoped this would be one of those custody kidnappings or even a ransom kidnapping like on TV, where the kidnappers weren't necessarily sick. He'd never actually worked on one of those.

He raised his right hand and tapped his chest four times above the heart, making an abbreviated sign of the cross. He supposed the deputies had figured it out and the gesture was part of the Huerta lore. Or maybe they hadn't.

He put his hand back on his knee and they pulled into a dirt drive. Clare slowed down the car. At the end of the drive a young woman in a fashionable linen suit was talking to an old woman in a housedress. A man in bluejeans, his face hidden by the camera on his shoulder, taped the interview. A heavy young woman in a lime and raspberry spandex exercise suit stood a few feet from the group. A toddler lunged through the tall grass fifteen or twenty feet away from the group of adults. A car parked near the group said KMST-TV.

Clare looked at Huerta, who without changing his expression somehow looked even grimmer. "TV?" Clare said.

He stopped the patrol car behind the TV car. Only the woman in spandex looked at them.

Huerta opened the door, turned on his seat, got his feet out and leaned forward, pushing on his knees as he rose. Clare watched him, then got out himself.

Huerta went up and stood behind the elegant young woman, who paid no attention to him.

The toddler re-emerged from the grass with his hand in the air, making a gun of his fist and forefinger and throwing bullets wildly into the sky. Huerta noticed another baby on all fours trying to work up the nerve to crawl down the porch step and into the garden.

The old woman was saying something about masked people and the reporter was translating her broken phrases into articulate news story language: "Two masked intruders broke into your daycare, ma'am, just a short while ago, and took a baby girl right out of your arms?" She had the voice all news people on TV had, full of sympathetic humanity.

Huerta took a step forward and put his hand over the lens of the television camera. "That's all," he said.

The TV people finally turned to face him, angrily, but lost some of their steam when they saw what they were up against. They recovered from their surprise and there was some discussion of rights and complaints, but in five minutes they were gone.

Huerta looked at the baby, who had gotten down the step and was crawling after the toddler in the grass. The first thing, as always, was to create order.

"Your name, ma'am?" he said to the old woman in the housedress.

"Jane Dimaggio." She made her name sound uncertain.

"You have a daycare here?"

"I just take care of three little ones," she said defensively.

"And one was kidnapped."

"Two people came in, they broke through the door, they...."

He put his heavy hand on her shoulder and nodded reassuringly — they would get to all that.

"And you, ma'am?" he said to the woman in spandex.

"Helen Howard. I live in the next house up the road. The kidnappers took out Jane's phone so she walked to my house and called you from there. I drove her back."

The woman seemed capable and sensible in spite of her outfit. "Mrs. Howard," Huerta said, "could I ask you a favor?" She nodded. He looked at the children in the grass. "We will try to get these children's parents over here as soon as possible. Do you think you could keep an eye on them for a few minutes, see they don't hurt themselves?"

"Of course."

Huerta turned to the old woman. "Could we go in the house now, Mrs. Dimaggio?"

She looked to Mrs. Howard for guidance. Mrs. Howard nodded and Mrs. Dimaggio started up the path, a little unsteadily, Huerta thought, for a woman who had managed to hurry up a country road to get to a phone. He wondered if the shock had been delayed by her activity and was setting in now. If so, questioning her was going to be hard.

Huerta and Clare followed her into the house and looked at the man in front of the television with momentary surprise. The man turned and smiled at them and they understood.

Huerta asked the old woman to get the children's emergency phone numbers. She got a notebook out of a drawer in the kitchen and gave it to Huerta.

"What is the name of the child who was taken?"

"Josefina," the woman sobbed, crossing her arms over her breasts and holding herself tightly.

"Last name?"

"Mannock. Josefina Mannock."

Huerta had been looking through the notebook. He looked up at the name and hesitated. He only knew one Mannock. "Any relation to Richard Mannock?" he asked.

"His daughter," she sobbed. "Brand new. I mean they just adopted her. Their first child."

He looked through the notebook until he found the page about Josefina. He looked at the address. It was the old farm, which Richard must be running now. He looked at Richard's wife's name, Carmen, and remembered. Richard had married a Mexican girl, which had surprised everyone. That had been a long time ago, maybe ten years ago, no, more.

"I know Richard Mannock," he said. Deputy Clare looked at him and he elaborated: "I hiked a football to him for four years." It was a lot of personal revelation for the Lieutenant and he shook his head as if he'd been wallowing in nostalgia.

He turned to the old woman. "What are the names of the other two children?"

She told him and he told Clare what to do: Call the parents of the children in the front yard. Call Richard and Carmen Mannock and tell them to go to their house, where Huerta would meet them as soon as possible. Call in to the Department and get someone to begin the paperwork for a tap on Mannock's phone. Maybe this would be a ransom kidnapping — Mannock was rich after all — and he wanted to be ready.

Clare left to use the radio in the car since the phone was out.

Huerta was alone with the old woman, unless he counted the husband. She was still sniffling and holding herself.

"Let's sit down," he said. He put his hand on her shoulder again and they went to the little table in the kitchen, which was divided by a counter from the living room, where the old man was communing with the television.

Huerta sat across the table from her and waited for her to stop sniffling. He saw there was a half-full pot of coffee on the stove. He got up and poured the coffee into a saucepan and turned on the burner. He waited for it to heat up and then poured it into two cups. He asked the woman if she wanted milk and went to the refrigerator when she said she did. Deputy Clare came back in and watched him pour milk in Mrs. Dimaggio's cup and give it to her. She cupped the coffee between her hands without thanking him, as if she was always being served coffee by lieutenants from the Sheriff's Department.

Huerta set his own cup on the table and turned to Clare, who was watching him with interest. Huerta realized Clare was probably wondering what would be the most effective way to make something trivial into a Huerta Story: Huerta Makes Coffee for Witness.

"Yes?" Huerta said.

"I made all the calls but I couldn't get Mannock or his wife. He was out of his office."

"Does he have a car phone?"

"No."

Huerta nodded. "Thanks, Deputy. You want to go keep an eye on those kids now? Let Mrs. Howard go home."

Clare, an accomplished bachelor who wore a heavy gold chain around his neck under the uniform, didn't look too happy.

Huerta said, "Be good for you," and went to the table and his coffee.

Huerta and the old woman sipped their coffee for a moment. Huerta thought it would be time well spent. It would give the old lady time to calm down, and let her get used to the way he looked. What he thought of as the ugly-Mexican-factor could be a problem with people her age.

He said, "Everything will be all right," and the woman nodded. "It wasn't your fault." The woman shook her head.

He didn't say anything else for a moment. They were like a couple after a party when everyone has left.

When he did begin, he began with small questions with easy answers. It would be slow with the old woman who didn't know how much she knew. But he was good at questioning and would, eventually, get it all.

It took about fifteen minutes. There wasn't much to get. A man and a woman wearing a pig and a duck mask had broken into her house. They had taken Josefina Mannock. They had known which baby they were after. The woman had spoken Spanish. He knew how they were dressed. Not much to feed into the computers in Washington.

He patted the old woman's hand once more and excused himself. He went outside and saw Deputy Clare standing in the tall weeds, which were moving. The kids, he supposed, were under the movement.

They would leave as soon as the kids' parents got there for them. Until then he could do some thinking, though the Story was that he solved cases by staring, not by thinking: They didn't think he was too bright but he solved cases so they had had to make up a Story to cover the discrepancy. He couldn't complain. He knew he secretly enjoyed the Stories.

He went around to the side of the little house and looked out over the artichoke fields to the dunes. He supposed it looked like staring but this time it was simpler. He was remembering Mannock, or as he'd been called in those days, "The Man."

The Man had been tall, handsome, rich and — as if all that weren't enough — the star quarterback. He had effortlessly run, thrown, danced and seduced his way through high school. The Man had had nicknames for him, Huerta, too: The Mass, an allusion to both his religion and his size; and Buns, a simple reference to what the quarterback saw of his center.

Mannock would make his jokes and then slap him on the back — one of the guys — to show it was just in fun. Mannock danced his way through life and the heavy people got a slap on the back.

The force of the memories surprised him. He hadn't suspected there were memories that still burned if he dug down twenty years. At the time he'd never resisted or tried to explain. He'd felt so different that explaining was useless. What could they understand of his different shape, different color, different people, different God?

And there was a another reason. Mannock may have gotten to him with his jokes but at the same time Huerta had never really respected him. People like Mannock didn't really know what mattered and what didn't. Even then Huerta had known that if he had strength it wasn't in the body he lugged around; it was in knowing what mattered and what didn't.

The fact that Mannock had just started a family proved his point. A serious man didn't wait until he was thirty-eight. He himself had a daughter in San Jose State and another with one more year of high school to go.

As if to further prove Mannock's frivolity a sleek red Mercedes pulled into the drive and raised a plume of dust before dramatically braking. Huerta knew it had to be Mannock.

He took a couple of steps toward the car and waited for Mannock to get out and appear through the cloud of dust. Mannock looked around quickly as if there were decisions to be made on the spot. His glance ran over Huerta and then returned to him.

Huerta watched Mannock realize it was him, watched the surprise on his face. If he'd been a person who smiled, he would have smiled at that moment. Instead he walked over to Mannock and stuck out his hand.

Before Mannock could recover from his confusion and say something, Huerta said, "We weren't able to get you on the phone. How did you know to come?"

TEN

Fausto smoked a cigarette, replaying the conversation with Mannock in his mind.

He sighed and shook his head — the brief moment had been perfect. He got up and drove into some fields a couple miles south of Salinas. He dug up the box he'd buried there three years ago when he'd felt the circle tightening around him and drove back to Socorro's house.

He put the chain on the front door. This went beyond Socorro's need to know.

He opened the metal box, undid the plastic wrapping and took out the cassette. He put the tape in the VCR and sat on the edge of the couch — nerves, he wasn't even sure the tape was still good. When the tape began to play he sat absolutely still, skin tingling. It was about the same as he remembered but with the passage of three years also different, more distant and beautiful.

He rewound it and played it again. Perhaps the tape had deteriorated just a bit. The image wasn't quite as sharp and the colors had bled a bit and become more lurid. He liked it. Maybe it was better that way.

He got up and fiddled with some buttons until the image was in grainy black and white. He liked that too, very vérité. Noir.

He rewound and watched it again. He'd forgotten how effective all the mumbo jumbo with the mask and the chicken and the incense had been. Dedo was perfect and Domingo, well, you could say he'd been into his role.

He took out the tape, put in a blank one. He looked at his watch. He still had three hours to kill.

He went to the kitchen and made two bologna sandwiches. It struck him funny that in some ways this was the most important day of his life and he was making bologna sandwiches.

After he ate he stretched out on the couch. He'd be up most of the night. If he could sleep now, it would be good.

He drifted in and out of sleep but kept bringing himself back, worried that he'd sleep too long and miss it. He gave up and turned on the TV to KMST-TV and stretched out again. He half watched an old movie, not quite asleep or quite awake. Then he watched an old sitcom. After the sitcom, it was time and he sat up. Before commercials a voice said, "Stay tuned for today's lead story: a kidnapping here on the Central Coast."

"It worked!" He jumped up. "It goddamned worked." He went over to the VCR and put his finger on the record button, waiting for the commercials to end. He pushed the button and went back to the couch to see what they'd done with it.

The newswoman welcomed everyone to the program and then the screen held a shot of the little house surrounded by the clumps of geraniums. The newswoman gave the essential story in a voiceover. The house, cut out of its surroundings, framed by the TV, seemed desolate, a place where real bad things might happen.

When the voiceover finished the camera cut to the newswoman interviewing the old woman, who wasn't making much sense.

The camera cut to another house and Fausto murmured, "Yes, yeeessss." It was, as the voiceover said, SeaMist farm and the "Mannock residence." It was a huge old Victorian with a deep veranda around the ground floor. Above the verandah the second floor rose rather simply until the roof broke into a number of gables. It was an eloquent contrast to the old woman's run-down place.

The camera cut again, to the same newswoman, this time interviewing Richard and Carmen Mannock. Fausto whooped. It was better than he'd dared hope for.

When they moved on to their next news story, he ejected the tape and went with it, and his three-year-old tape of the sacrificio, to the garage where he had some used editing equipment.

He worked with concentration for about an hour, to get his sales pitch just right.

When Socorro got back he was in the bedroom pretty much asleep, though it was still light.

He woke up when she dropped her shoulderbag to the floor in

a gesture of dramatic exhaustion. She leaned against the wall opposite the bed, tilting her head to one side so her hair fell onto her shoulder. She was wearing a halter top and jeans. Her stomach was bare and she was standing off balance with her hip cocked to draw attention to her shape.

"Hard day at work?" Fausto laughed.

She nodded and shoved off the wall. She went to the bed and sat on the edge next to him. He moved over a bit, still lying flat.

"Got everything?" he said.

She nodded.

"Let's see," he said, businesslike.

She got up to go get her bag off the floor. She opened it, reached in and brought back an inch-thick bundle of bank passbooks held in place with a rubber band. She sat next to him on the bed again.

He began to look through them. She had opened each account with twenty dollars.

"You checked to be sure they can wire money to the bank in Mexico?"

She nodded.

"By the day after tomorrow each of these accounts should have just under ten thousand dollars in it."

She nodded.

"First thing day after tomorrow, make the rounds and have the money wired to Mexico."

"You've explained it to me a hundred times, Fausto."

"Just don't fuck it up."

She put her hand on his chest and the touch seemed to startle him. He started to get up, then relaxed under her hand.

"When do you leave?" she said.

"Couple hours."

"Will I see you again?"

"What do you mean?"

"You know what I mean."

He looked at her. She was giving him one of her serious soulful looks, that he hated.

He looked away. "Course you'll see me."

"Don't lie to me, Fausto. I'll send you the money, no matter what. But I have a right to know what you're planning."

"A right! What is this shit?"

She was rubbing his chest. He reached to her hand and

removed it.

"When will I see you?" she persisted.

"Not until Mexico, *mi alma.*"

"How will I know where to meet you?"

"I'll get in touch."

"When you get down there with Dedo, you sure you're going to want me?"

"Would you please, please shut up." He looked at her again. Her eyes were wet. "Oh God," he groaned.

"You leave right from the Bay Area tonight?"

He hesitated, not sure how much she needed to know.

"I'll be back here tomorrow, briefly, to talk to Tío."

"Why?"

"After tonight they'll connect me to this. I'll be gone but he'll be here. I have to, uh, brief him, make sure he'll keep his mouth shut."

"I can help. Stick with him."

"That's okay. I'll be very convincing. You just worry about transferring that money."

"Will I see you tomorrow?"

He groaned again. "Not until Mexico. I'll be in a rush."

She put her hand on his chest again and carefully began undoing the top button on his shirt. He closed his eyes and his jaw muscles tightened. She undid the other buttons and separated the two halves of his shirt. She put her hand flat on his stomach. His muscles flinched, then he relaxed. She had never known a man like him. Sometimes she thought her fingers burned his skin.

She traced his scars with her fingers, waiting for his breathing to get deeper. She bent over to kiss his chest.

Her hair grazed his chest, delighting his skin and making it crawl.

ELEVEN

It was about eight when Calvin Main got home. He'd met with his lawyer that afternoon and that had put him behind with his work.

He poured himself a glass of wine and went to rewind the tape in his VCR. Since his problems with Ingrid he'd been recording the news every night to watch when he got home. It was part of his new orderliness. As if the economy, the Republicans and Democrats suddenly mattered to him.

The international and national news seemed about the same as usual. Then there was a story about a big fire in the Richmond District. There was a shot of firetrucks on a wet street with a smoking house in the background. A reporter was talking to someone next to a pile of limp canvas hoses.

He went to the refrigerator and got out a tupperware container with cold ravioli. When he got back to the living room the screen held an image he recognized, a large Victorian farmhouse at the end of a palm-lined drive. A voice was saying, "... SeaMist Farm, the Mannock residence." Richard and Carmen. He took a breath and held it. He stood next to the couch.

The camera cut to a group of three figures on the porch of the farmhouse: a newswoman and Richard and Carmen. The newswoman pulled a strand of hair from the corner of her mouth and said in a grave voice, "It happened this morning?"

Carmen nodded. Her face was lined and swollen. Richard looked vacant.

"I know how painful this is for you, but if you could tell us what happened, in your own words...."

Carmen looked at the woman with an expression of tired

distaste. "This morning our daughter, she's five months old, was kidnapped from her babysitter's house two miles south of here. By a man and a woman."

There was a pause while the newswoman waited for Carmen to elaborate. She didn't and the woman said, "I believe we have a picture of the child." The screen filled with the picture of a baby girl.

Main put down his ravioli and remained standing next to the couch.

When they came back on the screen the woman asked, "You have no idea why anyone would have done this?"

Carmen shook her head.

"And you've had no word from the kidnappers?"

Instead of answering Carmen said, "My husband would like to say something."

The newswoman turned to Richard and pointed the microphone hopefully in his direction.

Richard opened his mouth and started to say something, then cleared his throat instead. He was heavy and inarticulate, with the sheepish look of a victim. It wasn't the Richard he knew, the sun they'd all circled.

Richard tried again. "If you think you have seen this girl... " He stopped, looked at the ground, then tried again: "I am willing to pay a sizable... reward. No questions asked." His voice gave out and he looked away from the camera, unable to believe this was happening, to him.

The newswoman made some commiserating remarks and the anchorman gave the number of the Monterey Sheriff's Department but Main wasn't taking it in any more.

Richard and Carmen! His oldest friends, on TV, packaged as a minute of pathos, offering a reward... their baby had been kidnapped. What baby?

His oldest friends, and he didn't even know they had a baby. But now "oldest friend" was an official status more than anything real. He'd only spoken to Richard once in the last five years — a few meaningless words at Richard's father's funeral.

Richard would think it was just the drift of time that kept them from seeing each other.

But it was his wife, Carmen, the one woman — yes, Ingrid — that he'd loved more than any other.

Main had loved her in college — he'd met her before she knew

Richard. He'd loved her when they'd had their affair, at a time of strain in her marriage. And he supposed he loved her still. It was hard to say. She'd broken off the affair, before Richard found out, to save her marriage, even though, he was almost sure, her feelings were as strong as his, or almost. Very tragic stuff.

He'd reworked those feelings until they weren't quite real anymore, until they were bittersweet and even enjoyable.

Probably it wasn't an unusual story. He didn't know. But it had felt unusual for years. And now, seeing them on TV the day he'd talked to his lawyer, that certainly felt unusual.

He picked up the ravioli and the fork and went to stand at the window and watch Russian Hill. Some lights were going on.

He tried to eat — orderliness — and put down the container.

He couldn't even tell what he was feeling, except unusual.

Should he call them? How many oldest friends would they have who were also private investigators? No, he shouldn't. If they wanted help, they'd call him. And if they did, what would he say?

Was he ready to see them — her — in his present catastrophic state of mind? If they called he could give them the names of a couple of people in Monterey, impartial people.

He put on a record and went back to the window.

The record had ended and he hadn't moved when the phone rang. He wasn't surprised.

He went to stand next to the phone. When it had rung two more times he heard his voice on the answering machine: "You have reached, etc...." It didn't sound like him. Or he didn't sound like it.

Tone: "Cal... I'm sorry, Cal... I know I'm the one who said we shouldn't even communicate, but... "

He picked up the phone.

It certainly *felt* unusual.

TWELVE

At a few minutes before midnight Fausto pulled quietly to a curb in Orinda, across the bay from San Francisco. He turned off the engine and the lights. On the seat next to him he had an accordion file with ten manila folders in it. He took out the first one and checked to make sure the photocopy of the Mexican birth certificate was there. He looked at the plan of the house he'd drawn a couple weeks earlier when he'd been by posing as a confused meter reader. The sketch indicated he should go in by the side door to the kitchen. The top half of the door was glass.

He got the canvas book bag from the floor and made sure everything was there: the .22 with the silencer, the flashlight, the glass cutter, the cassette, the gloves. He took out the pair of transparent latex gloves and held them out in front of him. They looked like ectoplasm in the moonlight. He worked them on. They gave his fingers a smooth, dead look — a nice effect.

It was all for effect really. It didn't matter if he left prints everywhere — he'd be in Mexico by the time they had it figured out. For that matter, it wasn't really necessary to start so late, and put himself on a tight schedule, but there was nothing like a surprise visit in the middle of the night to create an effect. It wouldn't be Operation Sheer Terror without the sheer terror. And terror depended on attention to detail, to effect.

The terror wasn't just for fun: he had to be sure no one would call his bluff like Richard Mannock — poor Mannock — had.

He looked at the house. There was a light on upstairs, so he'd have to be very quick. Even so, it was ridiculous how easy it was to break into a house when the purpose was to find the owners rather than evade them. He just had to get in quicker than they could

figure out what was happening, dial 911 and get out their address.
He got out of the car, closed the door very quietly and hurried
around the side of the house to the kitchen door. He stood still for a
moment listening for a dog, though he'd seen no sign of one when
he'd wandered around looking for the meter. It was so quiet he could
hear faint voices from a television upstairs. He got out the gun and
held it in his left hand.

He looked through the window. His eyes were accustomed to
the dark and he thought he could find the stairs without the
flashlight. He took out the glass cutter, drew a deep breath, and
scored a square in a corner of the pane of glass. He pushed it
through with the palm of his hand — it made no more noise when
it broke on the linoleum than a dropped glass — and quickly
reached in and turned the knob. He opened the door, hurried
through the kitchen, the dining room, into the hall with the
stairway. He raced up the stairs three at a time. At the landing he
took two leaping steps to the door with the slit of light
underneath, put his back against it and opened it in one continuous
motion. He swept the gun across the room as he rode the door into
the room.

It had been unnecessarily dramatic but the effect was nice:
they were frozen. The wife in a nightie was sitting propped up on
pillows; the husband in pajamas had thrown off his covers and sat
up but gotten no further. Their expressions of surprise were changing
to fear. Arsenio Hall was assing off on TV. There was a crib in the
corner of the room with a sleeping baby.

Fausto leaned against the wall and took a few deep breaths.
He kept the gun on them and their expressions jelled into wide-
eyed fear. The husband snuck a look at his wife and reached across
to her hand, then looked back to Fausto.

Between breaths he said, "Peter and Julie Telford," as if
announcing them at a ball. "I won't harm a hair on your heads. If
you do what I say."

He was in a hurry but he watched them for a moment longer, to
enjoy it. They were between thirty and thirty-five — prime
adopting age. The woman had a clean scrubbed face and a sensible
banged haircut. She was blond and blue-eyed. He imagined she was
one of those good women who wore denim skirts and drove a Volvo.
He thought there would be a heavy blue vein under the white skin
of each breast.

He looked at the husband — getting heavy, going bald,

wearing pajamas. He looked back at the woman. He couldn't look at a man who would let himself go bald. He wondered if she was wearing panties, then went to work: "That's little Leif." He pointed the gun at the crib.

The woman shuddered and managed to say, "What are you going to do?"

Fausto shot a disgusted look at the man — why was he making his wife ask the questions?

He handed the man the manila folder. "Open it."

The man opened it, looked at the Mexican birth certificate and showed his wife.

"I don't understand," he said.

Fausto explained: that their adoption was illegal, that they couldn't go to the police because they'd lose Leif, that they would have to deposit just under ten thousand dollars in the bank and account noted on the inside of the folder, that they had thirty-six hours to make the deposit, that the consequences would be grave if they didn't.

"Do you understand now?" Fausto concluded.

The man nodded uncertainly. Fausto went over the baby smuggling-home birth scheme again to be sure they understood they would lose Leif.

"Let's go into consequences in a little more detail," he said.

The man and the wife exchanged quick looks and Fausto went to slip his cassette into the VCR.

He smiled at the opening shot: Dedo in the jaguar mask holding up the stone salsa container, a wisp of smoke. The husband and wife didn't smile.

cut: Domingo tied on the kitchen table, his head hanging off the end, all his muscles tense with the effort to hold his head up. Close up, so close you could see the sweat running down the sides of his face.

cut: The old woman on the evening news. She said, "They were wearing masks, a pig and a duck. They kicked in the door. The pig came in with a gun." The husband and wife both looked from the screen to Fausto with the gun. He shrugged: What can I say?

cut: The jaguar-man holding up a knife, slowly turning from side to side with it.

cut: The newswoman saying, "I believe you have a picture of the baby."

cut: The screen full of Josefina.

cut: A long shot of the Mannock house with voiceover: "This morning there was a bold kidnapping in this beautiful Central Coast community."

The man and the woman looked quickly at each other.

cut: Dedo slowly lowering the knife to Domingo's chest; Domingo straining up, watching wide-eyed, opening his mouth against the gray tape.

cut: The newswoman saying, "And you don't have any idea why this happened?"

cut: Richard Mannock looking at the ground.

cut: Dedo pushing the knife through the muscles of the solar plexus. Domingo arching back in a spasm.

cut: Richard Mannock saying, "I am willing to pay a sizable... reward."

cut: The picture of Josefina again.

cut: A close-up of Dedo's hands holding the heart. The empty latex finger hanging down. Blood dripping.

cut: Blank screen. Voiceover: "...a bold kidnapping... a bold kidnapping... a bold kidnapping..."

The man and woman were staring at the empty screen. The woman looked at him first. Her eyes were wide and her mouth was opening wider, too wide. He pointed the gun at her in case she was getting ready to scream. Nothing happened for a moment.

Fausto said, jauntily, "So do we have a deal?"

The man finally looked at him but didn't say anything.

"Am I getting *through*?" Fausto said. He waved his hand in front of the man's face as if checking for signs of consciousness.

The man nodded.

Fausto went to the machine and rewound his tape. The man and woman just watched him.

THIRTEEN

Calvin Main pulled into the long drive and stopped for a moment. The view hadn't changed much since the last time he'd been there. For that matter, it hadn't changed much since his childhood. It was the same view the camera had held on TV, only wider and deeper.

To his right was a sign that said, "SeaMist Farm, R. Mannock." To his left were the remains of an old wooden cart from the time of Richard's grandfather. Main remembered when Richard's father had had the old cart hauled from behind the barn to the entrance of the farm because it would be picturesque. He had been a child.

He let the car idle and looked down the drive lined with hundred-year-old palms. It ran straight to the fine old house where the newswoman had interviewed Richard and Carmen. What he couldn't see, hidden behind the house, he could remember clearly: the barn, the worksheds, farm equipment, piles of irrigation pipes. Further on, nearly to the dunes would be the little rust cabins where the farm workers stayed at harvest time. They had usually been empty and he and Richard had played in them.

He rolled down the window and took a breath: the ocean and artichokes, the odor of the end of a warm day.

He put the car in gear and slowly went down the drive. It was all the same but somehow it wasn't exactly. Halfway down the drive he realized what it was and stopped again. What was different was there was no activity, no pickup trucks, no workers. And there was more. The shape of the farm had somehow changed. It had shrunk to the small fields of artichokes immediately surrounding the house. The outer fields had been plowed under and beyond the empty fields, where there had been nothing but dunes, there were buildings. They looked like condominiums in gray, weathered wood.

Richard was developing most of his land instead of farming it.

He drove the last fifty yards to the house and stopped in front of it. He got out and went to the door. He was reaching for the doorbell when he heard raised voices inside and hesitated. Richard and Carmen were arguing. The voices stopped. He waited another minute to be sure and rang the bell.

Carmen opened the door and looked at him without saying anything. She smiled weakly and stepped forward to greet him with a hug. He held her stiffly, aware, in spite of himself, of her shape under the clothes. He stepped back and held her at arm's length by the shoulders.

"I'm sorry it took so long," he said and mumbled the excuse about his court appearance that he'd already told her about on the phone the evening before.

She shook her head that it didn't matter. "You came."

Her face had been changed by anxiety and fear. There were dark wedges under her eyes but the rest of her face was drained of color. The lines in her face were deeper, the lines from her nose to the corners of her lips, the line from the bridge of her nose up into her forehead. They broke her beautiful face into planes.

She started to say something else but her lips trembled and she pressed them together. She took his hands off her shoulders and led him by the hand into the house.

"What is it?" Richard said from somewhere upstairs.

"Come and see," Carmen said. She dropped his hand and her voice sounded unnaturally cheerful.

Richard appeared on the landing wearing nothing but a towel around his waist. He'd put on weight and his strong shoulders and chest rose out of a shapeless gut. He looked like an unfinished statue. His face couldn't have registered more surprise if he'd been miming the word in a game of charades.

Main stepped to the foot of the stairs and said, "Richard."

Richard's face clouded up and he looked to Carmen. "What the hell is the meaning of *this*? I thought the subject was closed."

"You were wrong, Richard. We do need him."

Richard came halfway down the stairs. "Maybe *you* need him. I sure as hell don't."

Main stiffened. "Richard, I'm sorry, but — "

Richard looked back to him as if noticing him for the first time. "My dear fellow," he said in a preposterous drawing room voice, "absolutely delighted, don't you know, but — " he dropped his voice to a stage whisper — "just a spot of trouble, eh, may not be the best of all possible moments, what?"

He turned and went back up the stairs, taking them two at a time. His strong calves popped with each step and his haunches rolled under the towel.

Main looked at Carmen.

"He's leaving for Mexico," she said. "Can you stop him?"

They both knew he couldn't. He started to say something but went up the stairs instead, dutifully.

He went into the master bedroom without knocking and tried to ignore the confusion of images that met him there: fat Richard squeezing into a pair of bikini briefs next to the salmon king-size bed where he, Main, had once made love to Carmen.

Richard said, "Skip it, Cal."

He dug an old pair of jeans and a denim shirt with plastic cowboy buttons out of a drawer and began putting them on.

Main spoke softly. "Richard, give me five minutes. I don't know what's going on."

"Can't. I'm racing to catch a plane." Main noticed a half-full duffel bag on the floor next to the bed. Richard went to the dresser and began to load up his pockets with wallet, keys, handkerchief, comb. He put on an expensive watch that didn't look anything like cowboy gear.

"I'll drive you to the airport," Main said.

"Skip it, Cal."

"Richard, I might be able to help. I know more about this stuff than you do. It's my job." He'd never worked on a kidnapping but Richard didn't know it.

Richard picked up his duffel bag and left the room. Main followed him down the hall to his office.

Richard removed an oval-framed picture of a Mannock patriarch from the wall, exposing a wall safe. When Richard got it open after a couple false tries, he took out a passport, a roll of bills and an envelope. He shoved the roll of bills in his front pocket, folded the envelope and put it and the passport in his shirt pocket, buttoning the flap.

"Kidnappings are very dangerous," Main said.

Richard ignored him and picked up the phone. He dialed

information and asked for the number of the Mexicana ticket counter at the San Jose airport. He wrote down a number and dialed again. He waited for them to get to his call, in-the-order-received. He turned his back to Main.

Main looked around the office. The walls were covered with other pictures: Mannock ancestors, work crews, the house and outbuildings in various stages of completion. On the desk there was a recent color photo of Richard holding a baby. Main picked up the picture. He tried to remember her name. He realized he didn't know it.

Richard confirmed that the tickets were being held for him at the desk and hung up. He'd mentioned the flight number, no destination.

Main said, "She's pretty," turning the picture toward Richard. Richard went to him and snatched it out of his hand.

"You might get her killed doing this, Richard. Kidnappings are very delicate. Please let me help."

Richard hesitated, then shook his head as if he'd been in a momentary trance. "You know who's in charge of the case?" he asked. "Buns. The Mass."

Main didn't catch on.

"Buns. Vic Huerta."

"Vic Huerta!"

Richard nodded as if that would explain all his behavior. Main remembered that Huerta was a Lieutenant with the Sheriff's Department. He put it aside to take in later. "Give me five minutes," he said again. "You wouldn't be taking off for Mexico unless you had something to go on. What is it?"

Richard hesitated again — Main was his oldest audience and he was tempted.

"What is it? What do you know?" Main persisted.

Richard shook his head again and went to the wall behind the desk. There were two ancient Colt .45's on the wall pointing at each other. They had ivory handles. The cracks were black with the dirt of history. Richard reached up and took one down.

It would have been funny if it weren't so... unfunny. "Richard, you're kidding."

Richard threw it in the duffel bag and opened a desk drawer for a couple boxes of ammunition.

"It works?" Main asked, distracted from the line of his argument.

Richard said, "I'd love to stand here and chat but I've got a plane to catch." He picked up the duffel bag and headed for the door.

Main took a quick step to block it. "Goddammit, Richard! This is not the frontier, this is not a football game." Richard put out a hand to push him aside. Main pushed back. "This is real people. A real daughter and a real wife."

Richard narrowed his eyes. "I'll take care of my daughter, a lot better than Buns will. And I'm sure you'll take care of my wife. Right, old sport?"

"What's that supposed to mean?"

Richard punched him on the shoulder, playful, and hard enough to throw him off balance. He swung through the door, catching Main with the duffel bag over his shoulder and knocking him back.

Main leaned against the door. Richard went down the stairs and out the front door, which he slammed, without a word to Carmen. This confrontation with Richard had ended the way all confrontations with Richard ended, only this time the stakes were higher.

He heard Richard start his car and gun the motor. He went over to the window and looked out.

Richard roared down the drive, his red Mercedes sportscar flashing stroboscopically between the evenly spaced palm trees, and was gone. As always, when Richard was gone, the silence was almost palpable.

Richard had always straddled the line dividing the sublime from the ridiculous but with age he was falling onto the wrong side of the line. Still, no matter what they'd all said behind his back, they'd never thought he was stupid.

This time, Main thought, Richard was doing something very stupid.

FOURTEEN

Carmen was waiting for him at the foot of the stairs. She must have heard the last bit, when they were shouting at each other, and she'd seen Richard leave, without a word to her.

They stood at the foot of the stairs for a moment, awkwardly, and he shrugged at her. She seemed almost dazed. If it had been any other woman, someone he hardly knew, he could have put his hand on her shoulder, taken her by the elbow, but this was Carmen

"Let's sit down," he said.

She nodded and he followed her into the living room. He took an armchair on one side of the coffee table; she sat on the couch on the other side.

"Crisis control center," she said, gesturing at the array of things on the coffee table: phone, a legal pad covered with notes and doodles, a pencil, a pack of Winstons, matches, a glass and a bottle of Richard's George Dickel sour mash. "I'm supposed to be waiting for a ransom phone call." She suddenly stood up again. "Just a sec."

She left the room and came back with two fresh glasses and an ice bucket. She filled the glasses with ice and whiskey, gave a glass to Main and held up hers as if she was going to make a toast. Then she took a sip and said, "Don't worry. I've only been an alcoholic for thirty-two hours now."

Main looked at his watch. It was five-thirty. He should have done something about his court appearance that day, or skipped it.

He looked out the window. It was a large picture window that was new since the last time he'd been there. It opened the view all the way to the dunes. The barn, the irrigation pipes and farm machinery, the rust-colored workers' cabins were all gone.

Carmen picked up the pack of Winstons and knocked one out of the pack. She offered it to Main.

He said, "I quit."

"Oh, me too," she said and put it in her mouth. She lit a match. Her hand was shaking and she bent her head to the flame rather than bringing the match to the cigarette. She inhaled and exhaled noisily and looked at the cigarette in her hand as if she didn't quite know how it got there.

There was a silence, then Main said, "The barn is gone. There are new buildings over by the dunes."

"Condominiums," she said. "Part of Mannock Enterprises. We don't farm anymore. Now we're really rich." She didn't seem very impressed.

"You still teach?" Main asked.

"Oh, yes."

There was another silence. Small talk didn't sound right and he wasn't quite ready to get down to business. He looked around the familiar room. The heavy old Mannock pieces were still there, mixed in with the Spanish Colonial pieces Richard had started collecting when he'd married Carmen. Richard had begun collecting them — Main had always supposed — to show her how open he was to her culture, as if East Salinas grocers' daughters grew up surrounded by carved Spanish coffers, Peruvian paintings, Bolivian candlesticks. He took a slug of his whiskey. Richard had overachieved even in his cultural sensitivity. It *had* been a grand gesture though. The stern Mannocks had been outraged at the mésalliance.

Main looked back to Carmen and said, "Hell." He reached over to the pack of cigarettes and took one out. "You're a bad influence on me, Carmen."

He'd said it without thinking but when she smiled he remembered it was a joke from their affair. She answered as she always had, "That's why I'm good for you."

"Yeah, right."

She'd been good for him up until she'd decided they couldn't go on and broke it off, promising she wouldn't call him, as if he'd asked her not to. She'd kept the promise for five years.

"It's going to make you dizzy," she said as he took a drag on the cigarette.

He concentrated on smoking. It tasted awful like they always said it did when you went back and it did start to make him dizzy but all the gestures — hand to mouth, suck, the rigmarole of inhale/exhale — all that seemed entirely natural, the reflexes of a former, truer Calvin Main. He stubbed it out about half finished.

"Strange, isn't it?" Carmen put out her cigarette, smoked down to the filter, and another silence descended. After a minute she said vigorously, "So. To bring us up to date. My baby has been kidnapped and my husband just walked out."

He still wasn't ready. "There's something I have to ask you first," he said. "The things Richard said to me upstairs... he knows, doesn't he?... about us?"

She smiled as he stumbled to the end of his question. "No." She finished her whiskey and the ice cubes clinked against her teeth as she got the last drops out. She put the glass on the table and looked at him. "No, he doesn't know we had an affair. But Richard and I have had our problems, to put it mildly, and Richard has developed a sort of problem with jealousy. Richard's not the type to age gracefully, know what I mean?"

"No, he's not."

"He kind of thinks I've had an affair with everyone." She smiled uncertainly and then with sudden bitterness added: "Which is an exaggeration. Somewhat."

He looked away, uncomfortable: She'd answered his question in more detail than he was ready for.

"I'm sorry, Cal," she said. He looked back to her. After a pause she said, "You know, our affair seems like the Age of Innocence to me now. The first affair is a little bit like losing your virginity again. After the first one it just gets raunchy." She stopped, embarrassed by what she was saying. "God! Listen to me! I'm drunk."

"Ingrid and I have had trouble too," he said and looked away quickly. He wanted her to know he understood but the last thing he wanted to do was get into Ingrid.

She understood. She rubbed her eyes and forehead with her hand and said, "Anyway, the baby was supposed to save our marriage. And it was sort of working... it was sort of working..." She sat absolutely still, looking past his shoulder, and tears spilled over her cheeks in a shiny path. She went on: "You couldn't exactly say Josefina brought us together again but she shifted our focus and we sure..." She broke off and closed her eyes. Tears squeezed out, got stuck in the wet lashes.

Main knew he should go over to her and he knew he shouldn't.

She opened her eyes and blinked quickly a couple of times. She held out her hand to keep him in his seat as if he'd made a move to get up, which he hadn't. She took a deep breath and said, "If there's one thing I hate it's a weepy woman."

"Well, under the circumstances, Carmen..." Under the circumstances you had to be a little flexible about principles. He reached for the cigarettes.

"I think I need a couple minutes, Cal." She got up and went to the picture window.

She stood with her hands on her hips. She took a deep breath and her breasts rose. The sun was low enough now to pour through the window. It outlined her hair in copper and her breasts were visible through thin white cotton. He looked with the familiar pang. The undercurve of her breast was fuller. She was older.

The pang started to become desire and he looked out the window again. He smoked and ran through the memories he'd rehearsed and polished for seventeen or eighteen years.

The Meeting: She'd answered an ad he'd put on a bulletin board looking for a Spanish tutor. She'd called and they'd arranged to meet at the Cafe Espresso in Berkeley on the northside of campus. He'd spotted her from his table in the rear as soon as she'd entered, pausing to survey the cafe with a kind of superb disdain. He looked back to Carmen now, at the window. She was perhaps more beautiful now at thirty-six than she'd been then at eighteen. Age had softened her features; then they'd been sharpened by her anger: Berkeley was teaching the scholarship student from East Salinas how oppressed she was and she was exhilarated and focused by the knowledge.

He'd raised his hand in the back of the cafe to get her attention. She saw him and nodded as if to say he was exactly what she'd expected and walked briskly to his table. She shook hands with him and told him what her fees were. She'd used that word, fees, and it had seemed odd to him. He agreed and she asked him if he was flunking Spanish. He said he was getting A's but wanted to work on his accent. His sincere interest in learning Spanish had softened her for a moment, until she heard his accent. She told him it was awful.

On the back wall of the cafe there was, at that time, a large canvas with a García Lorca poem painted in an elaborate calligraphy. His first lesson, and the warm-up exercise for every other lesson, had been to repeat the poem after her, phrase by phrase, then line by line. He would watch her from the side as she read each line, studying her profile: slightly curved nose, well-defined lips, high cheekbones, slightly tilted eyes. And repeat after her.

He leaned his head back against the armchair and blew smoke straight up into a shaft of sunlight that lit up the smoke. The poem was *La Guitarra*. He could still remember a few lines, though he didn't know if he was remembering them correctly. It was about the sound of the guitar, the wail or moan of the guitar. There was something about the cups of dawn breaking. And the Southern sands begging camellias. The monotonous wail, unstoppable, unconsolable. He was sure he remembered the last lines exactly:

> Oh guitarra!
> Corazón malherido
> por cinco espadas.

O guitar... heart fatally wounded... by five swords. The first time Carmen had asked him if he understood. He hadn't even been trying to understand, he was just trying to say it the way she was, in her grave poetry-reading voice. She'd explained that the five swords were the five fingers playing the guitar, wounding it like a heart. Less poetically, as if she couldn't count on him to understand even the explanation, she'd added: "You know, like the fingers are making holes in the heart."

He told her he understood, and that was how he'd fallen in love: watching her from the side, reciting that poem. As simply and foolishly as that.

The Romance: They'd begun dating. She'd let down her guard, though she'd hardly needed one with someone as hopelessly in love as Main. They'd spent weeks holding hands and having inarticulate conversations at a time — pre-AIDS — when people had just flopped into bed. Main, now, could hardly recognize the twenty-year-old he'd been. Finally they slept together, exactly twice.

The Tragedy: Richard came from Stanford to spend the weekend with him and she was swept away by his grand manner. It must have been a relief to her after Main's tongue-tied sensitivity. He realized she hadn't really loved him. She'd been disarmed by the intensity of his love for her and too young — it had been too flattering — to reject it.

The Aftermath: A year later she had married Richard. A year after that everything had been forgiven, at least officially, and he was their best friend.

The Affair: After Carmen and Richard had been married seven or eight years, he'd had an affair with Carmen which lasted three months. Three months of weekly meetings, usually in motels in San Jose, midway between him and her. Once they had made love in the bed upstairs with the salmon cover. In between meetings there had been six days of tormented desire.

It had been the most perfect time of his life, the time that no other time could match. Then Carmen had broken off the affair. Ingrid had never known about the affair but that was the one that had ruined the marriage because that was the one Ingrid could never match.

These were the memories that he thought of as painful but that wasn't really true. He had arranged them and worked them over through the years until he had them just right, until the painful memories were better, and more satisfying, than real life.

He studied Carmen again. Richard was gone, Ingrid was gone. Did he want to start again?

Carmen had to know he was staring but she didn't flinch or acknowledge him. Did she know her hair was fire-tipped in the sun? Did she know her breasts showed through the thin cotton? She wasn't wearing a bra. How much was accident and how much was design?

He stubbed out his cigarette. "Carmen?" he said softly.

She looked at him and nodded. She came back to the couch and sat across from him.

FIFTEEN

"Carmen," he said, "I don't think I'm the right investigator for this case."

"We're not a case, Cal."

"That's what I mean."

"It has to be you, Cal." She looked away sadly. It made him want to help her. Design or accident?

"I can't be objective," he said. "I know some good people, one of them near here in Monterey."

She looked back to him. "It has to be you." She took a deep breath and held it, raising her breasts against the white cotton. He kept his eyes fixed on hers. She said, "I never called you in five years. I wanted to lots of times but I didn't. I called this time because it *has* to be you and not someone else."

He leaned back in the armchair. It was no use pretending he wasn't going to end up doing what she wanted. "Why?"

"There are things I can only tell you," she said, still thinking she had to convince him.

"Okay." He held up his hand. "Okay, okay."

"I'm not playing a game," she said with a flash of anger. "It has to be you because there are things I can only tell you — that I couldn't trust another investigator with. That's all I meant."

"Okay. Sorry. Let's do business. Start with the secret, the thing you can only tell me."

She leaned forward on the couch and clasped her hands together. She started to say something, then reached for the cigarettes and lit one.

She said, "Our adoption isn't legal. She drew on her cigarette nervously and then held it off to the side of her head. Her hand shook. "I guess it's not legal, I don't know."

He looked out the window, away from that hand, to give himself a minute with the implications. Then he said, "Jesus," objectively, and looked back to her.

"I couldn't tell anyone else that. If they found Josefina, then took her away from us because of the adoption...." She shuddered and her hand fluttered to her mouth again. She watched him over the tip of the cigarette, then took it out of her mouth. "We only had her for six weeks and now I can't imagine living without her." She laughed bitterly and hugged herself. "And I thought I didn't even want children...."

He got up and went to the couch and sat a couple of feet away from her. "Tell me about it."

She told him about the stranger who had visited, about the Mexican birth certificate he had shown them, the way he'd asked for money, then seemed to lose interest.

"Would you have paid him?"

"Of course. Richard's line afterwards was that we'd held firm and scared him away, but if he'd pushed a little we would have paid up. I wouldn't have left it up to Richard."

"Did he contact you again after the visit?"

She shook her head. "Two weeks after he was here, Josefina was kidnapped."

"You haven't heard anything since the kidnapping?"

She laughed bitterly, and pointed at the pad of paper next to the phone. "I'm supposed to sit here and wait for the message. But I think Richard knows more than me."

"Why?"

"You know how Richard can't tell a lie. It's obvious — to me anyway — he's been lying to Huerta when Huerta asks him if he's heard anything."

Main said, "I think you're right. Richard wouldn't leave for Mexico if he didn't know something."

"We were fighting about that when you got here this afternoon."

"Does Huerta know Richard is lying to him?"

"You can't tell with him. He doesn't show anything."

That was true. Main reached for his drink and sat back for a moment. Then he said, "So how does Huerta strike you?"

"Big! He's so big."

"Yeah, well, how *else* does he strike you?"

"Richard says he's not too bright."

"I wouldn't count on that," Main said with exasperation. "Richard's slant on things is, uh, subjective. Huerta just *seems* a little slow." He finished the last half inch of watery whiskey and put the glass down. "What did Richard do today? Tell me everything you can remember."

"We were awakened at seven this morning, by Huerta. Richard talked to him in his office for fifteen minutes, Huerta left. Richard said it was just routine questions. We had breakfast. We argued about whether to call you, again. We'd already argued about it last night and I'd already called you, so I thought I'd better try to bring Richard around to the idea..."

"You didn't succeed."

"I didn't succeed." She paused to remember the rest of the day. "Richard went out after breakfast and came back a couple hours later. We didn't do anything, then we had lunch, then Richard went for a walk, then he came storming back into the house and said he was going to Mexico. We argued. You rang the doorbell. That's my day."

He didn't say anything.

"Can you help?" she asked simply.

He knew he would have to give her a more realistic slant on things. He moved closer to her on the couch and reached over to take her hands. "Carmen, first... first I have to tell you Huerta will most likely find out all about the adoption, whether you — we — lie or not." The way she looked at him he knew she already knew that at some level. He squeezed her hands. "But that doesn't mean there's no hope. Maybe the adoption can be done again, properly, uh, legally. There's no way to know until we find out what it's all about."

He relaxed the pressure on her hands and started to let go but she grabbed his hands tightly. "Why will he find out?"

"As far as Huerta knows there's been no ransom request. So the likeliest suspects are the real mother and father. Huerta will figure they might have changed their minds about the adoption and check them, and the adoption, carefully."

"I consider myself the real mother," Carmen said, picking up on the wrong piece of information. "The woman who carried her is the *biological* mother." She smiled at herself. "But I can't expect you to know the fine points."

"Sorry. But the point is Huerta will be looking at the

adoption."

"But *you* won't tell him, will you?" She squeezed his hands again and looked at him.

"We'll talk about that later. First I have to know more."

She started to protest then said, "Fair enough." She could extract promises from him later. "What do you need to know?"

"Everything. From the time you first decided to adopt."

She began slowly but picked up as if she felt she was doing something, talking. He asked her questions from time to time. She lit another cigarette at one point and he got his hands back. She had been talking about fifteen minutes when the doorbell rang.

They looked at the door in surprise and then back to each other almost guiltily. A reflex reaction. She got up and put her finger across her lips. That, he supposed, meant he was sworn to silence. She mouthed, "Huerta."

When she went to the door he got up and went back to his armchair.

The man he caught a glimpse of in the door wasn't Huerta.

SIXTEEN

"John," she said. Her voice was flat and the two of them stood there in the doorway for a moment.

The man, John, was lean and handsome, in his vigorous mid-forties. His close-cut gray hair emphasized his tan and his blue eyes. He noticed Main watching him and looked back to Carmen. He had a brown sack in one hand.

Suddenly Carmen reached out to him and took his hand, drawing him into the room. She hugged him the way she had hugged Main earlier.

She said, "John," again and he said, "Carmen." His voice was heavy with concern.

She stepped back from him, keeping a hand on his elbow. "You do know then?" she said. "I wasn't sure. You didn't call."

He nodded that he knew.

"Why *didn't* you call?"

"I was in San Francisco this week but Alison told me this morning when I called her. I guess I didn't know what to say on the phone."

"You could have said the same things as everyone else."

"I'm sorry. I should have."

"The phone's tapped," Carmen said.

"Well, that's not why I didn't call." He laughed and then looked uneasy as if he wasn't sure you could laugh about a kidnapping.

"It's tapped for when the kidnappers call with a ransom demand."

"Have they called?" he asked quickly.

She shook her head and John looked at Main, acknowledging

him with a nod. Carmen remembered he was there and led John over to him.

"I'm sorry, Cal. This is John Newkirk."

Newkirk freed his arm from Carmen's hand and shook with Main. He told Main he was glad to meet him, polite and stiff.

"Cal is our oldest friend," Carmen said. Newkirk looked at him for a second longer before letting go of his hand. Main smiled.

Newkirk was polite but edgy. Main supposed it was just the oddness of the situation, and his concern for Carmen, that made him uncomfortable. Or was he nervous because Main was there? How close were Carmen and Newkirk? It didn't matter, he warned himself. He was just going to be the best friend and work on the case. But being around Carmen made him think that way.

Carmen said, "I was just telling you about John and Alison, remember, Cal?"

She'd covered so much ground. He tried to remember. "Oh, yes." He looked at Newkirk. "You had something to do with the adoption. Wasn't that it?"

"You make me feel responsible," Newkirk said, smiling without warmth.

"I don't think that's what he means," Carmen said. She pointed at the heavy brown bag in Newkirk's hand. There was a circle of oil where something on the inside pressed against the paper. "What's that?"

Newkirk looked at the bag, remembering it with surprise. "Burritos," he said uncomfortably. "I was going by Hector's and I know you like them, and... I feel foolish now."

"It is hard to know what to bring to a kidnapping," Carmen said sharply and then regretting it, "I'm sorry, John." She put her hand on his elbow and took the bag from his hand. She led him to the couch. "You can stay for a minute, can't you?" She put the bag on the coffee table. "Please."

"Alison's expecting me for dinner."

"Just a quick drink. Alison will understand. Not only has Josefina been kidnapped, Richard has just walked out on me."

"What!" He sat down carefully.

Carmen left the room and Main took his seat in the armchair again. Newkirk looked at him for some explanation.

"Richard has left for Mexico. He's in the air by now."

Newkirk swallowed hard. "Why Mexico?"

"Richard's not saying. He seems to think the kidnapping has a

Mexico angle. Do you have any ideas?"

Newkirk was surprised. "How could I possibly?"

"Well, do you know if the agency you recommended handles Mexican adoptions?"

He considered. "Well, Jaime Sanchez is Mexican-American, but, I'm not sure, but I think Mexican adoptions are rather unusual. The girl we adopted through them was from Colombia... Colombia, Guatemala, I think that's more common." He stopped, realizing he was rambling. "But wait a minute" — he shook his head — "Josefina was born in California. It wasn't a foreign adoption."

"Oh, that's right."

They didn't have anything more to say. In another moment Carmen returned with a glass for Newkirk and poured the last of the George Dickel into his glass. She was about to go get another bottle when Main told her he didn't want any more himself. She sat on the couch near Newkirk.

Carmen said, "Cal is a private investigator."

Newkirk looked at him again. His face showed polite interest as he took in the new information: oldest friend *and* private investigator. "Are you going to help?"

"I'll try."

Newkirk turned on the couch to face Carmen. "What happened exactly, Carmen? Alison didn't have too many details."

Carmen swallowed. "Really? It was on TV." She looked at Main. "I didn't explain, did I? That grotesque interview was Richard's idea. He wanted to get out the reward idea."

Newkirk said, "Alison did say Josefina was taken from her daycare by two men wearing masks...."

"A man and a woman," Carmen corrected.

"Oh... well... what else do you know?"

"Almost nothing. We... I ... keep waiting for a ransom message, but...."

"Do the police have any ideas?"

"I don't know. No one tells *me*. I sit by the phone while all the men run around, fly to Mexico. Who knows?"

"Well, they must know something," Newkirk persisted. "I mean, were the men, I mean the man and the woman, black, or white...."

"Hispanic."

"You're sure?"

"They spoke Spanish."

"Oh."

"But that doesn't help much. There are a lot of people who speak Spanish around here."

"Yes. Did they have any distinguishing marks?"

"I don't know. Like what? They were wearing a pig and a duck mask. Is that a distinguishing mark?" She looked at Main. "John seems to be more of a sleuth than you, Cal."

Newkirk waved aside the idea. "No, I just mean...."

Main got up. "On that note I think I'd better get to work."

He went to the telephone on the table in the hallway. He got out the phone book and began looking for the number of the Monterey County Sheriff's Department. When he found the number he held his finger under it and looked back into the living room. Newkirk and Carmen were watching him. They looked away. From where he was standing he saw the back of Carmen's head and Newkirk's face. They sat stiffly without saying anything.

He dialed the number. When he got through he asked to speak with Lieutenant Huerta. Carmen turned to look at him when she heard Huerta's name. Main turned to face away from them.

The deputy on the line told him that Huerta was "in the field" and asked if he could "inquire as to what matter it pertained." Main said it pertained to the Mannock kidnapping and asked if he could have Huerta's home number. He was asked to wait just a moment and put on hold.

He looked over his shoulder. Carmen was pointing at the legal pad on the coffee table and mouthing that she had the number. He nodded and turned to the wall again.

He waited a minute or so and looked over his shoulder. They'd stopped watching him. They still sat stiffly without speaking. Carmen seemed to be studying her knees and Newkirk was watching her. His face showed more than concern. His eyes were hazy with love. Main jumped when a Lieutenant Gottschalk came on the line.

Main asked for Huerta's home number and wrote it down. He told Gottschalk he'd be at the Sheriff's Department at seven the following morning to talk to Huerta unless he heard otherwise before then. He told Gottschalk he didn't have anything to talk about until he saw Huerta. He gave Gottschalk Carmen's number.

He hung up and phoned Huerta's house. he spoke to a young woman who would be Huerta's daughter. She said her father wasn't home and they didn't expect him until late. He gave her the same message he'd given Gottschalk.

He hung up and looked up Newkirk in the phone book. There were two John Newkirks in the book, one in Seaside and one in Pebble Beach. He was sure the man with the silly look on his face in the other room was the Pebble Beach Newkirk

He went back to his armchair in the living room.

His presence had a sobering effect on Newkirk, whose eyes came back into focus. Newkirk told Carmen if there was anything he could do to help, anything at all.... He got up. He told Main what a pleasure it had been to meet him. Main stood up again and said something similar. Carmen showed Newkirk to the door but didn't follow him out.

When she came back she said, "Huerta?"

"Huerta."

"There's nothing else you can do?"

"Carmen, I've got to find out what he said to Richard this morning. And I've got to see what else he knows. He's been on this from the beginning, I just got here."

"You're not going to tell him about the adoption?" Her eyes were wide and worried.

"I think that would be best. I think we should try to get Josefina back and then worry about the adoption."

"No, please!"

"That is my professional advice."

"And if I ask you not to?"

"Carmen, you have to understand, you can't expect miracles from me. I know less than everyone else. And even if I can find out what happened, I can't make things go back to the way they were before. We have to be realistic."

"I understand." She gave him a look. It depressed him to know she could turn it on and off like that. "But please don't tell Huerta."

He shrugged but it was as good as a solemn vow. He wondered if he looked as foolish as Newkirk.

He said, "Who else knows about the adoption being, uh, irregular?"

"No one besides you. And Richard and me."

"Not even Newkirk?"

"Why would he know?"

"I just had the impression he was someone you would, uh, confide in. Share things with."

"Sure, I — " She stopped as she realized what he was implying. "What are you getting at?"

"Isn't it obvious?"

"No, what do you mean?"

"Oh, knock it off, Carmen. I just hope you're a little more subtle around Richard."

He stopped and reached for the cigarettes to have something to play around with for a minute. Why was he talking like that? Was it strictly necessary to make a fool of himself?

Carmen said, "I don't see what possible bearing that could have on anything." She sounded legalistic.

He smiled and, hearing herself, she did too.

"God, I'm sorry, Carmen." He got up again.

"What are you doing?" she asked anxiously.

"I'm going to find a place to stay."

"You're staying here."

"I'd rather not. I'll call you when I've got a number I can be reached at. Huerta might call here."

She got up and went to him. "Cal, please. Don't leave me. I feel like... like I'm spinning... and little bits of my life are flying away from me." She started to put her arms up to him, then dropped them. Her eyes filled with tears again. She looked at the floor and mumbled, "A weepy woman." She looked up at him. "I'm sorry. I'm not *trying* to use all the tricks but... under the circumstances."

He nodded.

"You'll stay here?"

"Yes, Carmen, yes."

"The guest room is made up, or the old study."

"The old study."

"Shall we eat those?" She pointed doubtfully at the greasy bag.

"Go ahead, I'm still going to go out for awhile."

She started to take a step toward him but he held up his hand. "You'll be fine," he said.

"I know, but...."

"Go to bed."

She looked at her watch. "At seven thirty?"

"Did you sleep last night?"

She shook her head.

"Go to bed, Carmen. This could go on for days."

SEVENTEEN

Twenty minutes later Main paid six-fifty to get into Pebble Beach like a tourist. The road wound down toward the water through dark stands of Monterey Pine. Some turns gave a glimpse of the rocky shoreline and the ocean. The ocean was dark and, where it caught the setting sun, gold. The last golfers in sherbet-colored clothes were finishing up in the sunset. Every so often a deer looked up and watched him pass.

At the bottom of the hill he followed the road for about a mile along the coast. When he found the address he turned in through two open wrought-iron gates and into a long semicircular drive. He drove past pink rhododendrons the size of small trees to a house that was an even paler shade of pink. It was a Mediterranean villa with a terracotta tile roof. At each end of the long façade a shorter wing reached toward the ocean, which could be seen beyond outcroppings of rock and stands of pine. When Main got out of his car he could smell the kelp and water.

He went to the front door and knocked a brass dolphin's nose against a brass stud. A soft-looking teenager with a moon face opened the door and solemnly examined Main with his small eyes. Main realized he had Down's Syndrome. A woman about forty appeared next to the boy. Mrs. Newkirk.

Main introduced himself as a friend of Richard and Carmen's. She opened the door for him and asked how they were doing in a hushed voice. He said Carmen was doing as well as could be expected but it was difficult under the circumstances. He didn't mention Richard and wasn't sure if her husband had told her Richard had left.

The woman listened with concern.

She was a thin elegant woman with blond hair shot with gray. She was wearing shorts and a blouse. She had small white teeth and a pearl in each ear. The pearls matched the teeth.

"Do you think I could talk to your husband for a minute, Mrs. Newkirk?"

"Of course. He just got home and he's having supper in the kitchen. Follow me."

He followed her through a long room filled with antiques — French Provincial, he guessed unconfidently — and into a formal dining room with a crystal chandelier, that certainly wasn't provincial. She opened a door at the end of the dining room and stood aside for Main to enter a kitchen that was larger than all the rooms of his apartment put together. The boy with Down's Syndrome crowded through the door with him.

Newkirk looked up in surprise from a table in the corner of the kitchen. Main just nodded at him and tried to take it in: light, air, gleaming appliances. The busy diamond pattern of the black and white tiles helped fill the space, as did tile counters, and an enormous work table in the center with brilliant copper pans hanging above it. There was a stove with eight burners and a wall oven, there were mixers, strainers, juicers.... Main gave up, he didn't know what a lot of the things even were.

Newkirk put down his glass of wine next to a bottle of Haut-Médoc and when Main had finished his examination of the kitchen, said, "I cook." So, evidently, did the cook who was transferring something from a high-tech frying pan to a plate.

Newkirk stood. "Alison," he said to his wife, "this is Mr. Main, the private investigator I was just telling you about."

"I'm sorry to bother you."

"That's all right." Newkirk put the white cloth napkin he was holding on the table.

"No, no," Main said. "Please have your dinner. If there is someplace I could wait."

"No...."

"Really, please."

Newkirk clearly wanted to talk to him right away, and get rid of him but Main politely continued to insist he have his dinner.

Newkirk bowed in defeat and said, "Billy, would you like to show Mr. Main to my office?"

The boy, who had been watching Main with frank interest, took him by the arm as if it was a special treat and led him toward a door on the opposite side of the kitchen. Main said, "Thanks" over his shoulder. Newkirk nodded and picked up his napkin again, watching Main and Billy leave the room.

Billy led him down a long hallway. One of the rooms was open and a girl, about eight, with dark skin and great brown eyes, looked up at him with surprise from her doll. The Colombian daughter.

They made a right turn into another shorter hallway at the end of which Billy opened a door for him. "Daddy's office." They went in.

There was a large desk in the middle, with a computer, modem, fax machine, printer, piles of manila folders. On one wall were two weavings, rotted away in spots, protectively sandwiched between panes of glass. A glass case against another wall held Pre-Columbian artifacts and statues. The wall behind the desk was covered with photographs.

Billy led Main to the photographs. They showed Newkirk meeting various people, including George Bush, playing golf with Clint Eastwood, riding a polo pony, being honored at some kind of dinner. One picture showed Newkirk smiling over his shoulder as he went up the steps to a cream and blue private jet. Another showed a grim young lieutenant in the jungle.

Billy pointed to each picture and looked at Main, who smiled at each one. They were both impressed with John Newkirk. Billy was proud but Main was annoyed with himself for being impressed.

The people he'd always thought of as rich before — like Richard and Carmen — didn't seem rich anymore. Not rich like Newkirk. He'd have to find another word for Richard and Carmen. He'd never met anyone who actually played polo, let alone played golf with Clint Eastwood or shook hands with a President.

Billy said, "Daddy's flowers." He pointed at the french doors at the end of the office and led Main by the hand into a small patio.

It was very simple: a bench faced two rows of magnificent begonias in Mexican pots. They were in full bloom, about two feet tall on thick furry stems. They were shaded by a tall tree that looked like black lace in the final light of dusk.

He sat on the bench with Billy. Main tried to convince himself there was a crime behind every great fortune, just to get himself in the right frame of mind but it would have worked better if Newkirk didn't also grow begonias, adopt children, have a son with Down's Syndrome. It wasn't his fault if he was filthy rich.

And if he was a... close friend of Carmen's, Main couldn't exactly take the high moral ground there either.

He talked with Billy about how to take care of begonias. Neither of them liked the way fish emulsion smells.

Main heard Newkirk enter the office and turned to him.

Newkirk was in the french doors. "Sorry you had to wait," he said.

"I've enjoyed talking to Billy."

"You know, Billy," Newkirk said, "I think your sister's about ready for that game of Clue if you are."

Billy politely said goodbye to Main and hurried off to play his game.

Main got up and followed Newkirk back into the office. Newkirk sat behind the big desk. "How can I help you?" he asked professionally, more at ease than he had been at Carmen's.

"Billy's a nice boy," Main said.

"Thank you. He is."

"The girl I saw is your adopted child?"

"Actually, Billy and Paloma are both adopted."

"Oh." It didn't help to learn that Newkirk had adopted a handicapped boy as well as a Colombian girl. He'd have to stop looking for valid reasons to dislike Newkirk and just go ahead and dislike him for ignoble reasons.

"What was it you wanted to talk to me about, Mr. Main?" Newkirk lay his hands flat on the desk and waited.

Main didn't say anything for a moment. He did have a question he wanted to ask Newkirk, but it was probably just a pretext. Wasn't he really there just to take another look at the man, to play with his own obsession?

"I wanted to talk to you about the adoption agency. Carmen is so upset. I thought maybe you could tell me something about how adoptions work. Tell me about Jaime Sanchez."

"Well...." He clearly didn't see the point to it. "If you think it would help, I'll tell you what I can."

Newkirk began a masterful exposition of the process, giving a lot of attention to the details: the role of an agency, the forms and questionnaires, the home study, the fees.

"Are you a lawyer?" Main interrupted.

"It shows." Newkirk smiled.

"What do you know about Jaime Sanchez?"

"Alison and I have known him for about ten years, not really personally, but fairly well. We have a great deal of respect for him."

He explained that Alison had first met him in connection with some refugee charity work she'd been doing in the eighties. Sanchez was an idealistic young lawyer who'd just gotten his state license to operate an agency. They'd been wanting to adopt a second child and had talked to Sanchez about it.

Newkirk began to go into the details of their adoption of Paloma: the orphanage in Bogota, their trip down there....

Main interrupted him again: "But he doesn't handle adoptions from Mexico as far as you know."

"Not as far as I know. You asked me that at Carmen's." He waited for Main to say something, then said, "What are you really getting at, Mr. Main? I don't see how the agency could have anything to do with the kidnapping."

"I think it may." He got up and went to study the pre-Colombian artifacts in the glass case. He turned to Newkirk. "You're having an affair with Carmen, aren't you?"

Newkirk was absolutely still, then opened his mouth to say something and closed it again. Perhaps he was going to tell Main to leave, or say, like Carmen, he didn't see what possible bearing it could have. The corners of his mouth tightened, probably just with distaste.

Main said, "I'm sorry, but it does have some bearing." He thought he sounded fairly professional. "You see, I want to talk to you about something I told Carmen I wouldn't talk about with anyone, but I think she wouldn't mind if I told you, if you're in her complete confidence."

"Maybe you should let Carmen decide what to tell me," he said very correctly and precisely.

Main went back to his seat. "Maybe."

Main didn't say anything else and neither did Newkirk but he had to be interested: there was a sheen of perspiration on his forehead. Finally Newkirk said, "Alison and I are friends of Carmen's. That is enough to ensure trust. You don't have to dig any deeper than that."

"I guess not."

Main told him about the man in black who had visited Carmen and Richard and shown them the Mexican birth certificate. He asked Newkirk if he knew anything that might help.

Newkirk shook his head slowly. His eyes were wide with dismay. His forehead was glossy with sweat and a vein throbbed at each temple.

Main said, "The man said Josefina was born in Mexico and her birth was registered in San Bernardino. It makes me want to know more about the agency but Carmen doesn't want me to talk to the authorities about it. I guess I'm just fishing but...." He looked at Newkirk.

"All I know is what I told you: what the standard procedures are."

"The man who tried to blackmail them is obviously our suspect," Main said.

"Yes."

"If I just knew where to start looking."

Newkirk shook his head, looking both tired and upset.

Main got up and Newkirk did too. "Maybe I shouldn't leave Carmen alone too long," Main said, "now that Richard's left."

"That's probably a good idea," Newkirk said neutrally.

As soon as Main had left Newkirk slowly let out his breath. He felt sick. Fausto Sanchez. He sat down again.

There was a picture of his wife on his desk, the same one he had in his office. He turned it toward him. His wife faced him with a confident smile, small white teeth bright between her lips, points of blond curl tucked under her chin, sharp blue eyes, little pearl earrings. He remembered Fausto Sanchez's knife on the glass of the picture, squeaking over his wife's features.

He'd done what he had to: gotten Fausto's friend Dedo out on parole. He'd shaken the hand with the missing finger — the distinguishing mark he'd stupidly been asking about. The memory made him want to wash his hands. He took out his handkerchief.

It had to be Fausto, who'd said he was Jaime's cousin. It was too much for coincidence, much too much.

He rubbed the back of his neck with his handkerchief. The heat felt tropical. He felt like he was in one of his greenhouses.

His wife smiled at him from the picture frame. He remembered the look on Carmen's face too.

There had to be something he could *do*. He'd always been able to *do* things.

"What are you doing?" He spun in his seat. His wife stood in the door, smiling. He tried to smile back and wiped his forehead

again. His wife said, "What did he want?"
   "I don't know, really."

EIGHTEEN

He opened the door quietly and walked softly toward the stairs so he wouldn't wake Carmen if she'd taken his advice and gone to bed.

She hadn't. She called his name from the kitchen. He set down the bag he'd brought in from his car at the foot of the stairs and went to the kitchen.

She was sitting behind a mug of tea, calm and composed. Her eyes were bloodshot though and he knew she'd cried her way to that composure.

He sat across the table from her. Above her head was a poster: The Fish of the Pacific. On another wall was Fromages de France. Their kitchen seemed humble after Newkirk's. Someday he'd tell her she wasn't rich anymore.

"How are you feeling?" he said.

"Fine. Where did you go?" She tried to make the question sound like small talk.

"To Newkirk's."

"I *am* having an affair with him."

"I know."

"Did he tell you?"

"No. He was a gentleman."

"Good." She drank some tea and shrugged unhappily. "Why pretend? Under the circumstances."

"Under the circumstances."

"Want some?" She held up the mug.

"No."

"I guess I'm very wicked." She didn't sound convinced.

"Yes. You know, Ingrid left me too."

"She did?"

He nodded.

"Why?"

"I was wicked." He smiled at her. "Why pretend, under the circumstances."

"We're so... so, I don't know... how did we get so crummy?"

She smiled dismally and got up from the table. "You eat?" He shook his head and she went to the refrigerator and got out the same brown bag with the grease on the side.

"I'm not hungry, Carmen."

She ignored him, unwrapped a fat burrito and put it in the microwave. She pushed some buttons and watched the timer count down with her back to him. When it was done she put it on a plate, got a napkin and fork and put the whole thing in front of him. "Eat. It's good for you."

"Then it would be good for you too."

"Should I divorce Richard?" she asked. She sounded as if she was really asking for his advice.

"God, Carmen, you know I can't get involved in that one."

She looked at him, almost smiling. "Why did you go over to John's?"

"I don't know."

"Just to check him out?" She seemed to mean the question seriously.

"No, I wanted to see if he knew anything about Sanchez or the agency that would help. He didn't." He opened up the burrito and played with the chile verde with his fork. He put the fork down.

"Thanks for coming, Cal. I mean it." Her eyes seemed to widen and she held him with a long look. He looked away.

"Have you got those cigarettes?"

She got up to go get them and he read: perch, halibut, cabezon, ling cod....

When she got back he played with the cigarettes, got one lit, etc.

He told her how he'd go visit Sanchez tomorrow after he talked to Huerta. They talked about what he could say. He finished the cigarette.

He said, "I think I'll go up. Are there blankets in the old study?"

She nodded. "You have a choice, Cal."

"I think I'd rather be in the old study than the guest room."

She gave him the same look, the one he could swim in. "That's not what I meant."

"What?" He laughed uncertainly. "What!"

"Why pretend, under the circumstances." She relaxed and laughed then went serious again. "Really, Cal. I'm scared."

"No."

"You're not playing hard to get, are you? After all these years."

"That would be a change. I'm just afraid I can't handle another emotion today, this week, this month."

"This life," she said.

He set down his bag and turned off the light in the room they called the old study, because it had been Richard's grandfather's. He went to the window. He could just make out where the sky ended and the dunes started. He looked for the straighter lines of the condos further to the north. There was just enough moonlight to make them out.

He remembered the room as it had been twenty-some years before. Richard's grandfather had already died. He and Richard used to hide out there, sometimes with whiskey they had stolen from Richard's father, or vodka Main had stolen from his. Main had cigarettes from a machine. Richard didn't smoke because he was always in training for some sport. They had been fourteen or fifteen.

Richard would sit at his grandfather's old oak desk; Main would sit in the old armchair and they would talk. Or Richard would talk, usually about a conquest, made or about to be made. Main would disbelieve and pretend he didn't care. Or they would talk about serious things, the way you stopped talking about things when you got older. They would plan out their lives and have big thoughts.

Richard, the ridiculous friend he'd always love. And his wife he'd always loved.

The room had been redone years ago but in the dark he could remember the exact look of the room twenty-plus years ago: old wallpaper (faded pink camelias) curling away from the walls in the corners. The smell of a lifetime of pipe and cigar smoke. The room had been old and they were young.

NINETEEN

Main got to the Sheriff's Department a couple minutes before seven. The building was new, buff, bunkerish. On the eastern side of the Salinas Valley the Gabilan mountains were old and scorched gray at the end of the summer.

He'd expected some runaround but was immediately taken up to the second floor by a deputy. When they got out of the elevator, the deputy led him down to an open door.

Huerta was bent over a folder, a square hand on each side of the folder. His head was down and his massive shoulders hunched. It looked like he was applying tremendous force to the few pieces of paper.

Main tapped on the door frame and Huerta looked up. His look of concentration softened slightly in recognition. Main hadn't seen him in about twenty years but he was unmistakably Victoriano Huerta: the broad mask of a face with serious, gloomy eyes and thick curly hair.

Huerta said, "Calvin," got up and went around the desk with his hand extended. He was wearing a mustard-colored shirt with the short sleeves starched so stiff they stood out in sharp creases from his biceps. He was wearing a maroon tie.

Main put out his hand, tensing it so it wouldn't get accidentally crushed. "It's good to see you, Vic." Huerta's grip was surprisingly delicate.

Huerta nodded and went over to the coffeemaker. He poured a cup for Main and went back to his desk and his own cup.

Main took a seat across the desk from Huerta.

"Well," Huerta said.

"You look great," Main said.

"You too. Are you married?"

"Yes," Main simplified.

"Children?"

"No. You?"

"Two girls. Nineteen, seventeen."

"That's great."

Huerta nodded, finished with the long-time-no-see. He said, "What can you tell me about the kidnapping?"

"Nothing, Vic. I just got here last night. I was hoping you could catch me up."

"Why did Richard and Carmen call you?"

"As an old friend more than anything, I think."

Huerta picked up a pencil and gripped each end with a thumb and a forefinger. A whole set of muscles popped out in his forearms. "And so you could do a little investigating?"

"Well... that's not the main thing really."

"We're on it, Cal."

"I know you are." He put down his coffee. "Look Vic, that's what I told Carmen. I know I'm too far behind on this to really catch up and I know this kind of case needs the resources you have. It's not a one-man kind of case. But I think it makes her feel better to think everything is being done. It's not that she doesn't trust you."

Huerta began tapping the eraser end of the pencil slowly on the desk. "I think there's more to it than that."

"What do you mean?"

Huerta kept tapping. "Another reason for calling a private investigator, especially a trusted friend, is if there's something you want to hide."

"I don't understand."

"Really? Richard's been lying to me from the beginning and I'd like to know what he isn't telling me."

"I don't know, Vic. I really don't." He hoped he sounded convincing.

"That's hard to believe. Richard showed up at the daycare only moments after the kidnapping, only no one had been able to notify him. He said it was coincidence, which I doubt. And he's been lying, very poorly, ever since." He had stopped tapping and held the pencil upright on the desk.

"Maybe the reason I don't know what you're talking about is that I hardly talked to Richard. He was storming off to the airport yesterday just as I arrived."

Huerta's face showed nothing. He picked up the pencil and held it by the ends again. He stared over Main's shoulder for a long moment, then snapped the pencil in two. The sound seemed to bring him back and he looked at the two pieces.

"Where'd he go?" he asked softly.

"I don't know. The flight left from San Jose. Mexicana. Richard called to confirm the flight about five-thirty. I heard the flight number but I don't remember it."

Huerta set the two halves of the pencil neatly side by side on his desk. He set his hands down and slowly curled them into fists and then slowly uncurled them. He got up and went to the window that took up most of a wall and looked out at the Gabilan mountains. The window was tinted. The tint took the color out of the morning sky and the dun mountains looked even deader. He stood with his legs apart. He did and undid his fists once more and then stood perfectly still for what seemed like a long time.

He looked over his shoulder at Main once and then gloomily swung his head back toward the mountains.

He stood there another minute or so and then returned to his seat. Main understood that he had witnessed what was, for Huerta, a tremendous display of emotion.

"It will be Mazatlán," he said and picked up his phone. He told a deputy what he needed to track down Richard's flight.

"I'll assume you're telling me the truth," he said to Main. "And I apologize if I was rude a minute ago."

Main shook his head.

"You know how it is with a case," he said. "You get involved. At first, I admit, I got involved because it was Richard Mannock and he was lying to me, but as we learned more there were other reasons to get involved."

Main waited for him to say more in his own good time.

"It's hard to let go when you get involved and you see a case getting out of your range. Mazatlán's way out of my range."

Main guessed where he was going but didn't say it. He said, "What's going on, Vic?"

"I guess I have to tell you. I can't see another way." He got up and went to the coffee machine for a refill, then topped off Main's cup, which was still nearly full.

He sat down and said, "We think we've got a lot of the pieces: I'm pretty sure about the who, and the why has to be money. We're getting bits of the how — only bits though. And now you've confirmed our suspicions about the where, if it turns out Richard's gone to Mazatlán."

Huerta stopped again, as if reconsidering whether he really wanted to talk to Main. Then with sudden force he said, "Smuggling *babies!* How could I not get involved?"

Main nodded. Out of loyalty to Carmen's version of things he said, "But Josefina is from San Bernardino."

Huerta picked up another pencil, slowly turning it between his fingers and examining each of the six facets. Main remembered that it had always taken Huerta an age to tell a story and how maddening it was. Still studying the pencil, Huerta said, "Of course we did talk to the woman in San Bernardino, the so-called real mother...."

"Biological mother," Main corrected him.

Huerta ignored the distinction. "We contacted the San Bernardino police and they sent a detective over to talk to the mother. The baby was — supposedly — born at home and registered with the county offices about a month later." He stopped and looked up from the pencil. "How many poor unwed Mexican girls have home births, do you think?"

"I have no idea."

"Me neither." Huerta stopped again to consider the question more thoroughly than Main would have. "Alternative birthing is more a middle class thing, I think. A poor Mexican girl would be glad to have a hospital, wouldn't she?"

Main shrugged and waited.

"Anyway, it struck the detective odd and she didn't seem to have any very clear explanation. He began to ask her routine questions about the adoption. Why she'd decided to adopt, how she'd found out about an agency at the other end of California, if there had been any financial settlement with the Mannocks. That sort of thing. The girl didn't seem to know what was going on. When he pressed her she said a friend had told her about the agency and they had handled the paperwork. The detective got the friend's name, politely thanked the girl and left.

"He went to his car, called in to have the girl's name and her friend's name run through the computers and went for coffee." Huerta stopped and looked at his mug. He decided to fill it up and looked at Main, who put his hand over the top of his mug. Huerta went to the machine and came back.

"It turned out the friend was an ex-con, loser named Chato, and the girl ran with a gang and had been picked up a couple times for prostitution and once for drugs. The detective went back to see her. He wasn't as polite this time and convinced her he could make life very uncomfortable for her friend on parole and for her: if the police really decided to take a look at her it would take about fifteen minutes to find some reason to take her in. He asked her what really happened." He gave a sigh that was almost a groan, sick to death of the police world he was summarizing for Main.

"She talked. The baby wasn't hers. A man named Leopoldo Sanchez had brought the baby to her, paid her a thousand dollars to register the baby as a home birth, put her in touch with the agency and come to pick the baby up again when everything was ready. Leopoldo Sanchez is the father of Jaime Sanchez, who runs the agency Carmen and Richard adopted through."

He sat back as if talked out.

That was that for Carmen's version of the adoption and Main didn't look forward to telling her.

He said, "Sounds like a pretty flimsy scheme if they hadn't even coached the girl about what to say if she was questioned."

Huerta shrugged. "I spent yesterday in San Francisco with people from the SFPD and the FBI going over Jaime Sanchez's records. The agency insists everything is legal but the books are fascinating. In the last year they've handled six adoptions just like Josefina's — home births, registered late — and another five from an orphanage in Mazatlán, which is apparently unusual. Most Latin American adoptions seem to come from Central America or Colombia, for some reason."

Main nodded. "Why are they doing it? Just to increase the supply of babies for adoption, or are they taking big fees under the table?"

"Or maybe blackmail."

Main didn't say anything. No, Huerta wasn't that stupid.

Huerta said, "Today people will be talking to the other adopting couples all around Northern California and someone will talk."

"You think Josefina's in Mexico? And somehow Richard found out?"

Huerta shrugged. "I don't know."

"You want me to go to Mexico? That's what we're talking about, isn't it?"

"Yes, but not until we know more, after we've talked to the other adopting parents."

"Have Jaime and Leopoldo been arrested?"

The muscles in Huerta's neck flexed, straining his collar. "No. I'm out on a limb there, but I'm sure they're not really behind it. Jaime's a pillar of the Hispanic community and Polo, Leopoldo, hasn't got the brains for it."

"Jaime couldn't just accidentally be putting these babies up for adoption."

"Of course not. There's a lot I haven't got figured out yet but I'm sure the brain behind this is Fausto Sanchez, who is Polo's nephew, Jaime's cousin. It's another long story...." He didn't seem to like the idea of telling Main another long story, but he'd have to. The phone rang and saved him from it.

Huerta picked up the phone, listened and wrote some notes on a pad. He hung up and looked at Main. "Richard took the seven o'clock Mexicana flight to Mazatlán last night."

Main nodded again.

"We've held off making any arrests," Huerta backtracked, "while we try to find Fausto. Though I doubt we will."

Main waited for him to explain and when he didn't, prompted: "Why?"

"As you said, the scheme is flimsy. As soon as we take a look it falls apart. He wouldn't risk a kidnapping which would bring the whole scheme down around him if he planned to be here when it came down."

"Is he smart enough to think it through?"

Huerta nodded gloomily. "This Fausto's a long story...."

The phone rang again. Huerta reached for it and listened for a minute without saying anything. He closed his eyes as he listened and tapped his heart four times with a thick forefinger. The gesture was familiar to Main and he tried to call it up. He remembered — Huerta had made the sign of the cross.

Huerta said, "Where?" and wrote something on the pad, finally putting his pencil to use.

He hung up and looked at Main, then slowly rolled his chair back from the desk and swiveled to face the window and the dead mountains. After a long minute, still facing the mountains, he said, "Do PI's handle homicide?"

TWENTY

Huerta drove fast but carefully, hunched over the wheel. His shoulders were so broad he had to point his arms inward to grab the steering wheel, which half disappeared in his grip. His eyes were fixed on the road and his jaw muscles popped out every few seconds.

Main had already asked him once what had happened, as they walked to the car, but Huerta had just kept walking. Main turned to look at him as he drove but Huerta still didn't seem very conversational.

Main watched the road again. They were on 101 and headed south. They would be out of Salinas in a couple minutes, which would explain why the call had gone to the Sheriff's Department.

Huerta mumbled something and Main looked at him. He doubted Huerta had said what he thought he'd heard. "What?"

"I said it's my fault," Huerta said without taking his eyes off the road. He was holding the wheel a lot tighter than he'd been holding the pencil. Main waited for him to say more.

"What do you mean?" he asked.

Huerta shook his head.

"Do you know who it is?"

"The deputy hasn't made an I.D. But I know."

"Who?"

"Not Richard."

Main looked at Huerta, who was driving as if it took every last bit of attention. It had never occurred to him that it might be Richard, who was in Mexico.

Huerta pulled into a left turn lane, braked and waited. When there was a hole in the oncoming traffic, he shot through it then braked hard again to stop in the mouth of a dirt road on the other side of the freeway.

The dirt road ran straight ahead about a quarter mile and stopped. It divided two fields that were plowed under. A eucalyptus windbreak grew along one side of the road. About two-thirds of the way down the road there was a green and white Sheriff's Department car and just in front of it a big blue van. A deputy got out of the Department car and stood next to the door waiting.

Huerta didn't budge and the cloud of dust he'd raised braking began to settle over them. He pointed a thick finger down the road. "I wish he hadn't driven up the road. Of course he didn't know."

Main nodded but he didn't really have the thread.

Huerta shrugged, still without letting go of the wheel. "But when was the last time a real murder was solved by footprints or tire tracks?"

Main shook his head. He had the thread now: if there was a body up the road, someone had had to walk or drive away from the scene of the murder. He looked out his window at the ground. He doubted the parched dirt, almost like dust, would have held a print.

He didn't tell Huerta that the PI from the big city had never investigated a murder. A guy had killed his wife once but there hadn't been anything to investigate. Huerta finally let go of the wheel and got out. Main followed him down the edge of the dirt road, which Huerta examined carefully as they went. Just being thorough, Main supposed.

When they got to the deputy he saluted Huerta and said, "Sir."

Main could see a dead-looking arm hanging out of the driver's window of the van — a big Silverado — in front of them.

"Deputy Clare," Huerta said in brief greeting. "How did you find him?"

Main, who would have gone to look in the Silverado, waited patiently. The Deputy explained that he'd first noticed the truck when he'd been on his way south at six a.m. When it was still parked there at seven-thirty when he'd gone by again going north, he'd decided to check it out.

Huerta nodded. "No signs of other vehicles?"

"No sir."

"Struggle?"

"Yes, sir." He pointed at an area of vague marks in the dust that could have been due to a struggle. Between the marks and the Silverado there was a smoothed out swath where, no doubt, a body had been dragged.

Huerta stepped carefully to the edge of the marks. Main looked at the arm in the window but Huerta called him over to show him some brown spots where blood had dried the dust into crusty little circles. Main nodded — it hardly seemed necessary to start with drops of blood — and looked back to the Silverado: from where they were standing now they could see a form slumped over the steering wheel of the truck. Huerta looked briefly at the truck then back to the marks in the dust. Main waited for Huerta to finish.

"You've called the Techs?" Huerta asked the deputy.

"Yes, sir."

"Thank you, Deputy Clare. You can back up now and park so the mouth of the road is completely blocked. Stay there and make sure the Tech guys park out there."

Huerta looked back to the Silverado and the arm hanging out and said, "Okay," as if they were going to look at it just to humor Main. They went over to the door.

Main stood behind Huerta, looking over his shoulder. A man slumped over the steering wheel. A crease in his skull ran from his left eye to just over his ear. It was clearly visible through short straight hair, which was matted down with blood on either side of the crease. The force of the blow had popped the left eye from its socket. It looked permanently startled. Main swallowed and pulled his own eyes away from that eye. The hilt of a cheap switchblade stuck out between two vertebrae at the base of the neck. It held in place a piece of paper that said "Puto" in crude lettering.

There was a statue of the Virgin of Guadalupe on the dashboard and a holy card of the Sacred Heart of Jesus taped onto the vinyl above the rear view mirror. Jesus pointed at his wound. There was a tire iron on the front passenger seat.

Huerta took a step back from the door and crouched laboriously to look at the arm hanging out the window. Main bent down over his shoulder. The back of the hand was raw and dirty, as if it had been stomped on. Two of the fingers stuck out at unnatural, broken, angles. Huerta took a pen out of his pocket and gently moved the fingers with it. They were starting to get stiff but they moved. He raised himself up again and bent to reach into the cab. He took a handful of the short hair and slowly lifted the head up off the steering wheel. The eye changed its position on the cheek. The lower lip was burst and the teeth were broken. There were marks on his cheek and his forehead. Huerta slowly lowered the head again to its resting place on the wheel.

He put his hands on the small of his back and straightened all the way up. He said, "Leopoldo Sanchez," without looking at Main. He looked off at the field for a long moment and Main wondered if he was still thinking it was his fault.

Huerta shook his head slowly and turned to look at Main. "There's some rigor mortis but not much," he said, focusing on his job, "so — we'll see what the pathologist says — but I'd guess late last night, very early this morning. Which lets Richard off."

"Richard?"

"I have to be thorough." Huerta pressed his lips together, grimly. "I told Richard about Leopoldo and Fausto yesterday morning. I was trying to impress him with how much I already knew so he'd stop hiding whatever it was he was hiding. So if he didn't know who Sanchez was before, he did after I talked to him. But he was in the air by the time Sanchez was murdered."

"Who's next on your list?" Main asked.

"Oh, Fausto did it," Huerta said. A cloud passed over his features after he said it: his fault.

"Why?"

"Sanchez knew too much."

"But if Fausto was planning on being gone by the time the investigation led to him...."

"Leopoldo would know where he was, in Mexico."

"But why would he do it like that?" Main pointed at the battered body in the cab.

"Fausto's sick."

"But his own uncle?"

Huerta gave Main a look he might have used on rookies. "Fausto once killed a man by ripping his heart out while he was alive in a fake Aztec sacrifice. I don't think we can count on normal... restraint."

"What's he doing out on the streets?"

"No proof. But he did it." Huerta bent to look in the window again and then straightened up. "There's no blood around the knife wound. I bet he was already dead and the knife is just to hold the piece of paper. You know what that means?" He pointed at the paper with the word "Puto."

Main nodded. Male whore, but the scorn it conveyed in Spanish was lost in translation.

"The Fausto signature," Huerta said with disgust. "He likes to leave a Mexican touch: tear out a heart, stick a Mexican curse on the dead man's neck. Some ethnic pride. Probably hire a mariachi band for his next murder."

Main looked at Huerta, who usually didn't give much commentary on things. "Leopoldo must have crossed him."

"I guess so but it's hard to see how." Huerta took one last look in the cab and walked slowly down the road to talk to Deputy Clare.

Main looked in the cab once more, then went around the front of the truck and stood between two eucalyptus trees. He wasn't going to learn any more watching the eyeball dangle.

He picked up a clod of dirt and threw it at a flock of red-winged blackbirds. The flock rose at the same instant, banked in a flash of red and swooped back down about fifty yards further on. He felt strangely empty and supposed it was some kind of reaction to the murder.

He heard an airplane surprisingly close and looked off to his left. A couple hundred yards away a sleek Lear jet was taking off and he realized they were across from one of the runways of the Salinas airport. He remembered the photo of Newkirk in front of the cream and blue private jet.

He realized what a favor he'd be doing Newkirk by going to Mexico and leaving the coast clear, giving him a clear shot at Carmen. None of his business, he sternly reminded himself, but before he realized what he was thinking his mind filled with the image of Newkirk on top of Carmen, his ass bobbing and writhing between her legs. What was happening to him? He shook his head and started to go back to the truck — the eyeball was better than Newkirk on Carmen — when he saw Huerta coming back down the road. He waited for him.

"What are you thinking?" Huerta asked.

"Nothing very constructive," Main said.

"There's not much to do until the Techs and the Coroner get here." Huerta stood with his legs apart and his hands clasped behind his back, at ease. "Though I don't know what they can tell us. If the Techs find Fausto's fingerprints all over the truck, on the tire iron, so what? They would be. He used the truck, he *lived* with Leopoldo and his wife."

"You said Fausto's a long story. What is it?"

"Why do you think he picked this spot?" Huerta asked, ignoring his question.

Main shrugged.

"I was thinking," Huerta said reflectively, "if Fausto and Leopoldo were in the Silverado together, Fausto would want to find a spot secluded enough to rough him up and kill him, but close enough to civilization to be able to walk out." He pointed at the convenience outpost a couple hundred yards away across the plowed field: gas station, Denny's, motel, each with a forty foot sign facing the freeway. "We'll check. Maybe someone saw him."

"Does Fausto fly?" Main asked, pointing at a small plane approaching the runway to land.

"I don't know, but...." he nodded appreciatively. "Two heads *are* better than one." He nodded and stared out at the empty field.

Main looked out at the field but didn't let himself drift. He didn't want to snap to again and find himself thinking of Newkirk and Carmen. He tried to figure out practical little things, like how he could get Huerta to tell him what he needed to know to go to Mexico, how long it would take him to get to San Francisco, get his passport, throw some things in a bag — he remembered Richard throwing things, including a Colt .45, into the duffel bag — and get to S.F. International. Could he make an afternoon or an evening flight?

He looked at Huerta, who had as much expression as a statue. He certainly wasn't imagining anyone in bed with anyone. Main would have to wait for him to come back.

In a couple more minutes, without looking at Main, Huerta said, "It's my fault."

Main waited some more; maybe he'd get the explanation this time.

"I don't think that I've ever been responsible for someone's death."

Main looked at him.

"I knew Fausto was involved," Huerta said in answer to the unspoken question, "and I didn't try to protect Polo. Didn't even talk to Polo because I didn't want Fausto to know we were that close to him."

"You couldn't know he'd kill his uncle."

"It didn't even occur to me." Huerta slowly looked from the field to Main, as if he'd just admitted something shameful and wanted to see what the reaction would be. "That's the worst part. I should at least have thought of it. After all, I've always wondered if Fausto didn't kill his own mother." He looked away again.

Main realized Huerta's man-of-few-words style hid a dramatic flair. He hid his frustration. "Tell me about Fausto, Vic."

"I've known guys like Leopoldo Sanchez all my life," Huerta said, refusing to follow Main's lead, staring at the plowed field.

"My *father* was like Leopoldo Sanchez. Sanchez is a simple man. *Was.* Worked like a dog. He was probably a little crooked, he was a labor contractor and they're usually a little crooked, but not *bad*. The kind of guy who probably gets drunk on Saturday night but not *bad*. Not in the same league with someone like Fausto." Huerta looked at Main again. "Virgin of Guadalupe on the dashboard."

Main nodded. He realized Huerta's eulogy for Sanchez was also a description of his dead father and his irritation was gone. Huerta had never, ever talked about his family. None of them had seen Huerta's home when they were in high school.

"Tell me more about Fausto," Main tried again. "This..." he pointed over his shoulder at the truck, "has convinced me how dangerous he is, and I want to get going to Mexico. I don't trust Richard...." He didn't finish his sentence: He didn't trust Richard not to get himself killed.

Huerta looked out at the field again and grunted. "Wait until we know more. There's no point to rushing off and then spinning your wheels when you get there."

"We have the name of the orphanage, or rather you do. I could talk to them and do routine things like check hotels."

"You can talk to the people at the orphanage better if you wait until we have an idea what happened. They're not just going to spill the beans. If there are any."

"I'll phone you from Mazatlan and find out what you've found out."

"I want to give you some pictures."

"Fax them."

Huerta turned to face him. "No one asked Richard to leave. He has criminally withheld information from us. I don't think he's in any immediate danger — he's got enough of a head start on Fausto, but if he is, that's not my fault. What I want is to find out about the babies. That, not Richard, is my main concern."

Main took a deep breath, slowly. He fought down the urge to point out to Huerta that none of that explained why they couldn't use the phone or a fax machine. He suspected Huerta was holding off, trying to see if there was some way he could go himself. He was having trouble letting go.

"Tell me about Fausto, you said it was a long story."

Huerta nodded. He seemed to be getting ready to tell the story but just then the Tech van pulled into the dirt road. Huerta hurried ponderously down the road, staying on the edge again, and in a few minutes returned, helping two men carry their cases of equipment. He told them what to fume and photograph. Main went to the Silverado and watched them for a few minutes and then went back to the edge of the field. Time seemed to go slower looking out at nothing so he went back and watched the Techs again.

Fifteen minutes later another vehicle arrived with the Coroner and his assistant. They went to join Huerta and the Techs at the Silverado. The Techs got out of the way for the official identification. The Coroner opened the door, reached behind Sanchez to dig his wallet out of his back pocket, opened it, looked at the driver's license. "The dead man seems to be one Leopoldo Sanchez."

"How long would you say he's been dead?" Huerta asked.

The Coroner took a close look at Sanchez, probed a bit and said, "A guesstimate? Eight to twelve hours."

Main looked at his watch. It was ten o'clock.

The Coroner and his assistant were busy for another ten minutes, then the assistant went back to their van and wheeled a gurney down the dirt road. Huerta helped them lift Sanchez out and lay him on the gurney. He looked even deader there, resting stiffly on his side in more or less the same position he'd been in for the last eight to twelve hours in the cab of the Silverado: legs up, torso forward, head bent over, knife and message still there. Bloody line on the side of the head. Eye on cheek. Absolutely dead.

TWENTY-ONE

Driving north, to talk to Sanchez's widow, Huerta was hunched over the wheel again, squeezing it. He said, "This part is murder."

Main looked at him. He didn't seem to intend any irony, and since he didn't joke about anything else, he would hardly joke about this. At any rate, Mrs. Sanchez would already know when they got there. Huerta had called in to have a woman deputy sent over with the news.

"Tell me about Fausto," Main said again.

"Yes," Huerta said quickly, perhaps glad to have something to do besides think of Mrs. Sanchez. But after agreeing he just squeezed the wheel tighter and drove for another couple of minutes.

Then he said, "Fausto has a fully documented life. We have files and reports from the police, from social workers and psychologists and teachers. But I don't know if any of those reports explains the dead man on the steering wheel."

He paused again, then began to speak slowly, with pauses, as if synthesizing all those reports:

The record began with the murder of Fausto's mother when Fausto was thirteen. He was living alone with his mother, in L.A. There had never been a father. His mother had done what she could to raise the boy, including some fairly casual prostitution. One night Fausto heard screams coming from his mother's bedroom and arrived just in time to see a man finish stabbing his mother to death. Of course he didn't know who the man was, there were often men in the house.

He looked at Main. "That's the official version and I really have no reason to doubt it, but at some point it occurred to me there is no proof Fausto didn't kill his own mother." He looked back to the road and concentrated on it even harder.

"There *was* a man there, a neighbor saw him running down the street, but they never found him. There is no reason Fausto couldn't have driven the man away with the knife and then killed his mother. At the time no one would think of that: Fausto was only thirteen and hadn't been in any trouble yet. Who would think a kid would kill his mother? But looking back it's at least possible.... You can imagine a thirteen year old, at the beginning of puberty, cracking, hearing his mother in the next room with a different man every night." He shrugged and drove in silence for a minute."That's just speculation," Huerta said, as if he'd been guilty of weakness. "After the murder he moved to Salinas to live with his aunt and his uncle. Leopoldo Sanchez. The dead guy."

Huerta went back to his flat summarizing voice: In Salinas Fausto had gone into a deep depression for several months and the state had provided psychological counseling to the boy. The counseling had generated another pile of reports on Fausto. The reports described him in a variety of terms, often contradictory, but one piece of hard data stood out among all the psychological adjectives: He had an exceptional IQ.

In Salinas Fausto had also gone back to school and lasted about two years, until he was fifteen, when he ran away, back to L.A. They found him a couple of months later, or, more exactly, he was arrested a couple of months later for breaking into a house and trying to steal a television, and from that time on he hadn't been out of trouble.

The police discovered that he had been sleeping in a friend's garage. The friend was named Alfonso and Alfonso's parents, feeling sorry for the boy, offered to be his foster parents, an act of kindness they would regret. Fausto moved in with them, went back to high school and attended often enough to recruit members for a gang he was forming. His first recruit was Alfonso, who would later earn the nickname Dedo when he lost a finger to a rival gang.

Huerta took his eyes off the road. "They took off his middle finger with a pair of pruning shears and mailed it to him in a frozen pie. Gang humor, get it?"

Main nodded. "Keep your fingers out of other people's pies." He wanted Huerta to get on with the story. Even private investigators who just handled cheating husbands knew all about horror. They had TV's and read newspapers.

Huerta looked back to the road.

The gang was called *Los Soles* — the Suns — and used a lot of Aztec mumbo-jumbo in their initiation rites and so on. The gang managed to attract attention — even the jaded LAPD gang unit took notice — by their practice of carving pictures of the sun into their chests.

Fausto did some time, inevitably and uselessly, in Juvenile Hall, which generated more files and corroborated the IQ tests done earlier.

An enterprising Outreach officer at UCLA heard about him and got him into UCLA in a special program and Fausto, at eighteen, began college as a film major. He'd lasted until the middle of his sophomore year.

Huerta decided the car could drive itself again and looked back to Main. "In February of his sophomore year a Sol, one of the gang members, was found in a house in East L.A. with his heart torn out of his chest, Aztec-style. A guy named Domingo Saavedra. The police questioned everyone and it turned out that Domingo had been having problems with Fausto, maybe challenging his leadership now that he was spending so much time in Westwood. It was never clear and Fausto never cracked under questioning. Nothing. There was never enough to indict him." Huerta suddenly looked back to the road. "But there's not much doubt in my mind."

They were pulling off the freeway in East Salinas and Huerta speeded up the last part of his summary: They hadn't been able to indict Fausto for Saavedra's murder but at about the same time the mother of a student in the campus video club asked the faculty sponsor of the club how her son could afford thousands of dollars of cameras and editing equipment. This time they were able to put it together and make it stick. Fausto had supplied the club members by a series of robberies in which the clerks were viciously beaten, whether necessary or not.

Fausto and the loyal Dedo had gone to Soledad. Fausto had gotten out about a year ago. Dedo, who'd had some trouble in prison, had gotten out ten days ago.

Main looked at Huerta. "So the timing of the kidnapping and the rest of it is not arbitrary."

"Right." They pulled to a curb behind another green and white Sheriff's Department car in front of a small house. "Do you know what one of the terms of Fausto's parole was?"

Main shook his head.

"He had to live with his aunt and uncle again. Help his uncle with his labor contracting business. Work hard, get back on the track. You get the idea."

Main nodded. "Tell me, what is this Fausto's IQ supposed to be?"

"164 the first time they tested him, 168 the second."

"That gives him a couple of points on me," Main said.

"And on me."

"And on Richard," Main said uneasily.

"More than a couple on Richard."

Main looked at him. That *was* humor. It had to be. But Huerta wasn't waiting for the reaction; he was staring at the little house.

It was the best house on a not-good block. A plaster burro stood in a front yard filled with crushed rock and surrounded by a waist-high cyclone fence. There was nothing growing anywhere: the labor contractor had left his work behind him in the fields. The rear end of a blue bus with a field toilet attached was visible in a dirt alley behind the house.

The little house made Sanchez seem real, like a guy who'd worked all his life and didn't have much, like the kind of guy Huerta said he'd known all his life. Before, with his head on the steering wheel and his eye on his cheek, he'd been a murder, a horror, not a real person.

"The only thing worse is telling parents their kid is dead," Huerta said.

They both thought of Josefina and Huerta let go of the steering wheel and opened the door with surprising determination.

TWENTY-TWO

The woman deputy opened the door and Huerta thanked her for coming, as if she'd been performing an act of charity rather than following an order.

They went into the room. A heavy woman in a print dress was lying on the couch. She was about sixty. Her face was strong with deep creases, which caught her tears in a glistening web. Her heavy breasts rose slowly and then collapsed in a series of sobs. She worked a dainty hankie with her fingers on her stomach.

Another woman about the same age sat on a stool she'd pulled up next to the couch. She was a friend who somehow had already been notified. She had her hand on Mrs. Sanchez's shoulder and was speaking to her in Spanish. She had looked up briefly when Huerta had entered, but only for a moment.

Huerta seemed to accept that he was outranked by Mrs. Sanchez's grief and stood still. They looked around the room, or rooms: The small living room was divided from the kitchen and dining nook by a low counter, which was covered with bright formica. The living room had a couch and two matching armchairs covered in shiny plastic. Mrs. Sanchez had evidently been vacuuming when the woman deputy had arrived with the news. The thick pile on the carpet was fluffed up and the vacuum sat in the corner. Their tracks in the pile were clear.

There were some shelves with knickknacks: little boxes, porcelain animals, some framed pictures. On the wall there were large photo-portraits of Leopoldo Sanchez and his wife. They were surprisingly large, almost two feet by eighteen inches. They were formal portraits in black and white. He was in a suit and she was in her best dress. They were very good, much better than most portraits of that type. The shadows in the creased skin gave the old man and woman weight and dignity. They captured character, or maybe used skill to create it. Main wondered if Fausto, the film major, had done them.

Huerta cleared his throat and went to the woman on the stool. He touched her shoulder and she looked up. With a look he asked her if he could have her place.

She got up and he carefully lowered himself, resting one haunch on the stool. The other leg had to bear part of his weight and the thigh muscle flexed through the fabric of his pants.

Mrs. Sanchez opened an eye and closed it again. Huerta began speaking to her very softly in Spanish and laid his hand lightly on her shoulder. Main could only catch a word here and there until Huerta raised his voice in conclusion and said, *"Era buen hombre."* He said it again in English, sadly: "He was a good man."

There was a moment's silence and Mrs. Sanchez whispered, "You knew him?"

"I met him once a few years ago, at a breakfast. *Era buen hombre.*"

She nodded and clenched her jaw to control herself.

Huerta gave her another moment and said, "I will have to ask you some questions, Señora."

She drew a deep breath which raised her bosom. She let out part of the breath, held the rest and played with the hankie. She let out the rest of her breath.

"When was the last time you saw your hus... saw Polo?"

"Late last night," she said weakly.

"Do you remember the time?"

She nodded and plucked at the hankie. "11:17. The phone rang and woke me up. I saw the numbers on the clock."

"Who was it?"

She shook her head. She didn't know.

Huerta leaned forward more and the muscle in his leg strained at the cloth. "It was Fausto, wasn't it?" He squeezed her shoulder slightly.

She sucked in a deep breath and held it but it escaped in a series of little sobs.

"It was Fausto," Huerta said gently.

"Polo didn't say who it was. He just left. I asked him, he didn't say anything." She plucked at the hankie almost angrily. "He never did."

She began to sob freely. Her friend hovered at Huerta's shoulder, waiting for her stool back. Huerta squeezed Señora Sanchez's shoulder again and got up, giving Main a look. It was a look of relief, that said, there, I did it.

Main thought he'd done it well. He followed Huerta into a carpeted — and vacuumed — hall. They looked in the first door on the left, the couple's bedroom. The bed was white with gold trim on the fancy headboard. There was a large framed picture of the Sacred Heart above the bed — the same image that was in the cab of the truck. The Jesus with the bland face and the finger at the lip of the wound.

The next door, on the right, was the bathroom and the next an office: a desk, absolutely bare except for a radio; a single shelf of black plastic binders, each one labeled with a year; a framed picture on the opposite wall.

They both went to the picture, a color eight by ten. It showed a proud Leopoldo Sanchez standing formally in front of his Silverado, with his hand on the hood ornament. He stood in a cobblestone street; behind him a high sidewalk rose almost to his knees. A low adobe building with a tile roof stood flush with the sidewalk. The adobe bricks were visible in places where the plaster had fallen off. There were two shuttered windows and an empty open door that looked like a black rectangle in the picture. In the corner of the photo there were two children watching Sanchez get photographed.

"Picturesque," Main said.

Huerta snorted and corrected him: "Poor." He pointed at the picture thoughtfully. "You know what this is?"

Main shook his head.

"My father had a picture of him sitting in his 1960 Chevrolet Impala parked in the dirt square of a village in Oaxaca. He went back to show everyone how far he'd gone, and to remind himself.

"You think this is where Sanchez is from?"

"Sure could be."

Huerta went to the shelf and took down one of the binders. He began leafing through Sanchez's records of his activities as a labor contractor. He said, "We'll have to go through these," and put the binder back in the shelves.

He took one more look at the picture on the wall and left the office for the room just across the hall, another bedroom almost as ascetic as the office: a single bed, tightly made with a checkered spread; an absolutely bare desk and a wooden chair; a dresser. Main went to the desk. There were names carved in the surface.

"This is a student desk," Main said.

"Fausto's," Huerta said. "Or maybe it dates all the way back to Jaime."

Main wondered if the Señora had tried to recreate the old room when she learned her nephew was getting out of prison. Or maybe she had always kept the room the way it had been when Fausto lived there as a high school student. Main looked around the room again. It looked like any boy's room, minus the mess and the pictures on the walls. It didn't look like it belonged to someone who ripped people's hearts out or beat his uncle to death.

Huerta went and opened the closet. "Looks like these got left behind." Main went over and looked in. There were a pair of neatly polished docksiders and a couple of ironed teeshirts on hangers. They made the closet seem more cleaned out than if it had been absolutely empty.

Huerta said, "Let's go," and Main followed him back to the living room, where nothing had changed. Mrs. Sanchez was on her back on the couch, her friend was on the stool, the woman deputy standing in a corner.

Huerta went over to the woman on the stool and touched her shoulder again. She got up without a word and Huerta took his uncomfortable seat again. "I'm sorry," he said. "It won't be long. Just a few more questions."

Mrs. Sanchez nodded. She'd stopped worrying the hankie. It lay on her stomach and her hands were clasped just above it. She stared at the ceiling.

"Mrs. Sanchez. That picture of Polo in the study, is that where he was from?"

She nodded.

"Where's that?"

"Little town near Mazatlán."

Huerta gave Main a look. "What's it called?"

"San Ildefonso."

"Are you from there too?"

She shook her head and looked from the ceiling to Huerta. "Why?"

Huerta shook his head: It didn't matter, he was just making conversation. "Polo go back often?"

"He travels a lot. I'm not always sure where he goes." Her

voice caught. "Went."

"Business, I guess."

She nodded. She'd given up trying to figure out where he went years ago.

"Do you know when he got that picture?"

"A few months ago."

"Did Fausto go with him to Mexico?"

"I don't know." She concentrated. "No, I don't think he could. He was on... on parole."

"Oh, yes. I wonder who took that picture."

She shook her head and looked back to the ceiling, losing interest.

"I guess Fausto lives with you, doesn't he? As one of the terms of his parole."

"Yes," she said quickly.

"When's the last time you saw him?"

She hesitated. She'd had experience not trusting anyone in law enforcement who asked about Fausto. "Few days ago."

"Where has he been?"

"Often he doesn't stay here. He has a *novia*, so...."

"Who's the girl?"

"I don't know. He never brought her here."

"Mrs. Sanchez, when did Fausto pack his things?"

"He has a girlfriend. I guess he wanted to live with her. I...."

"When, Mrs. Sanchez? This week?"

She nodded but the answer didn't mean much. She'd say he'd only been away for a couple of days so he wouldn't be in violation of parole, even if she hadn't seen him for weeks.

"Can you tell me how to get in touch with him?"

She shook her head and started to cry again.

Huerta said, "I'm sorry." He leaned closer to her again and began speaking in Spanish. Main couldn't make it out. Mrs. Sanchez nodded as he spoke and crossed herself. Huerta crossed himself openly and got up. The friend took her station on the stool again.

Huerta was more relaxed as they drove back to the Sheriff's Department but a deeper gloom had replaced the tension. Eventually he said, "I wonder if Josefina is from San Ildefonso. And if she is, I wonder if Richard could know that. I don't see how."

Main didn't say anything. He wondered if the Mexican birth certificate Fausto had tried to blackmail Richard with could have said San Ildefonso.

When they stopped in the parking lot, Huerta said, "You be at Carmen's until I can get back to you?"

Main nodded. "How long?"

"As soon as possible. I promise. But it may take awhile to get all the information."

"Look, Vic...."

Huerta stopped him before he could make his case again: "An hour ago we didn't know about San Ildefonso. In a few more hours, we'll know more. Wait for me, don't take off. I want to send you with as much information as I can."

"You're not *sending* me, Vic," he said sharply. Reminding himself he did need Huerta's help, he said, "But I'll wait." He got out and leaned back in the window. "It's been kind of an odd reunion, Vic, but it was nice to see you."

TWENTY-THREE

The next part would be murder too, he reflected as he drove back to the coast wondering how to tell Carmen that Huerta already knew all about the adoption. No doubt it was better this way — she'd been clutching at straws before — but it wasn't going to be easy.

And he would have to tell her about the Sanchez murder, and she would realize that everything had become even more serious, and Richard was in danger....

And yet as he drove down the palm-lined drive to the old house he knew he was also looking forward to seeing her. He imagined her sitting at the coffee table, nervously drinking coffee and smoking.

But when he went in the house she wasn't there.

He packed his bag, made an airline reservation, ate a sandwich and made a pot of coffee. He sipped the coffee and wondered again where Carmen was. Wasn't she supposed to be manning the phone — womaning it, personing it? The whole line of thought — Carmen — led to motel rooms and Newkirk. Maybe his jealousy had some psychological curiosity but it was a hard way to fill up an afternoon.

He got up without finishing his coffee. He went for a walk along the dunes, up and down the dunes, to tire himself and then went back to the house. He checked the answering machine, which was blank, and phoned Huerta, who was in the field, as the deputy who answered — a different one — again put it. It seemed to be the standard answer at the Sheriff's Department and suggested tremendous activity, which only made Main's enforced inactivity more frustrating. He phoned the Monterey Public Library and asked the reference librarian if they had any books that dealt with international adoptions. They did and he drove to Monterey and back — in the field.

He tried Huerta again, tried the answering machine again, and heated up the pot of coffee again. He put the three books he'd got in a neat pile in front of him on the coffee table. He went to the rack that held Richard's CD's — he was doing a good job of recreating his fine collection of jazz LP's on CD — and loaded five into the player.

Cannonball Adderly began and he began his first book, or the chapter that dealt with international adoptions. He had to read each page a couple of times and realized why people relied on agencies and lawyers. Of course the music didn't help and he should turn it off but the sax, as much as it was distracting him, was the only thing keeping him awake.

He got through the relevant portion of the next book, two more cups of coffee and the first two cuts on the Thelonious Monk disk. He got up, tried Huerta and went back to the couch.

He lay down with the third book. After a few more pages on visa forms for foreign adopted babies, the book sank onto his chest. He raised it again but didn't fight back when it sank a second time. He hadn't slept well the night before and sleeping was as good a way to fill time as there was. The coffee hadn't kept him awake but it gave sharp edges to the images that filled his mind: Newkirk on Carmen again, but he was awake enough still to will it away.... Vic, his hand on the grieving woman's shoulder... those same heavy hands on the steering wheel, driving... Sanchez slumped over *his* steering wheel... the eye on the cheek, weeping itself... he was floating on liquid and sleep was coming, rocking him, and his eyes were straining under his lids... REMs....

...he listed, something brushed his face... he opened his eyes....

Carmen was sitting on the edge of the couch next to his hips. Her hair was wet and he thought his cheek was damp, he wasn't sure. Had she kissed him?

"I fell asleep," he said.

"I see." She was wearing a blouse with parrots on it and old jeans. Her unbrushed hair stuck in wet points on her neck.

"Your hair's wet."

"I took a shower."

"How long have I been asleep?" He realized the piece of music playing was Sonny Rollins, so he'd slept through a whole Coltrane disk. He struggled to get up, get in the field....

"Working hard?" she teased and put her hand on his chest. Her touch felt like a ton of feathers and he subsided into the couch again. The brief touch — the skin memory of the five fingers — started the whole hydraulics of desire. And the squeezing at the heart.

He tried to sit up again and she lay the ton of feathers on his chest again. She didn't remove her hand. He went back under a new kind of gravity. His blood seemed to be building up with the drums behind Sonny Rollins. He looked at Carmen. She still had the dark wedges under her eyes and the lines biting into her features. He lowered his eyes briefly — her nipples poked against the sheer synthetic parrots on her blouse — and looked back to her face.

Her hand was still on his chest.

"Is this what I think it is?" he said.

"Yes. Last night I gave you a choice and you made the wrong one, so this time, no choice. Why fight it?"

Why indeed? He never had before. His refusal the night before had been an aberration.

"Where did you go?" he asked, deferring the decision, or pretending he was.

"Out. I thought I'd go crazy if I spent another day here with the phone." She opened and closed her fingers on his chest. He'd forgotten what it felt like.

"One afternoon here and I know what you mean," he said.

"I went food shopping, I went out to lunch, I even went by the college to talk to the woman who is taking my classes for me."

He laughed and closed his eyes. He felt like he was going to suffocate or explode, whichever came first, and she was talking about shopping, about teaching. He supposed she'd changed her teaching methodology since his lessons in the Cafe Espresso: *corazón malherido!* He smiled again and opened his eyes.

"I thought," she went on, still explaining, "that if I started doing normal things I might start feeling normal."

"Did it work?"

She shook her head sadly and lowered her hand to his stomach.

He said, "Carmen, we have to talk. I talked to Huerta today."

She nodded as if she knew all about it already. "I have to say something first." She opened and closed her fingers on his stomach. "I've missed you. Ever since we... broke off."

He almost said something about Newkirk, it almost came out before he realized what it was. Instead he said, "We do have to talk, Carmen."

"We will, in five minutes." She took her hand off his stomach and undid the top button of her blouse. She undid the other buttons and the parrots slithered off her breasts. "I need you, Cal. You really don't know how I feel."

Sonny Rollins had built up to a driving rhythm and the saxophone seemed to be his own blood beating in his ears but instead of pulling her down on him he said, before he could stop himself this time, "Don't overdo it."

She only smiled very slightly, took his hand and placed it over her breast. He looked at her face: lips, slightly arched nose, sharp cheekbones, black, black eyes, tilted up a bit.

She said, "I love you, Cal."

He did a sit-up and buried his head in the wet hair on her neck, smelling the perfume, fresh for the seduction. He pulled back and bent to kiss her breasts. "Don't overdo it," his demon made him say again.

"Shhhhh." She leaned forward so he couldn't say any more, with her breast in his mouth.

He pulled back and began working on his shirt buttons as fast as he could.

She stood up quickly, shrugged the parrot blouse off, popped the buttons on her blue jeans and worked them off. She was barefoot.

As Main was bent over his shoes — undressing, the comic relief of lovemaking — she bent to the jeans and got a condom out of the pocket, to prepare for modern love. He stood up to get his pants off and took a step to embrace her. She kissed him and squeezed him to her, then broke out of his clasp and put her hand on his chest again, this time as if to stop him. She pushed back gently but he didn't understand.

She looked at the couch and said, "I have never technically, literally, seduced a man. Let me finish."

"I think the job is done," he said, but took another step back and sat on the couch. He stretched out again under the slight pressure of her hand and she took her hand off him to work on the foil of the condom.

"Male fantasy," he said, as Sonny Rollins built up to a crescendo.

"Female too." She rolled the condom, a party raspberry color, onto him. She leaned to kiss his chest, his neck, his throat, then straightened and tried to straddle him on the narrow couch. He moved until he was half off the couch and she was able to lower herself onto him; they both drew a sharp breath and closed their eyes. Then he opened his and watched her move slowly on him, her forehead and eyes squeezed tight with concentration.

For a moment, in an act of will, he lay absolutely still and listened to the bleating saxophone. Then he began to follow her lead, clumsily on the edge of the couch. They moved very slowly until on a hidden cue they lost control and half slid, half tumbled to the floor, where they made love in a wild burst, rolling over once, and then again. She shouted something and he thought he did too and they were finished — before Sonny Rollins, whose horn was making gasping sounds but still building.

She'd finished where she'd started, on top, and pitched forward as she came. He held her tight against him as they tried to catch their breaths, feeling their hearts banging together. He pushed her back to kiss her throat, her jaw, behind the ear, tasting the sweat in the perfume, as much in love as he'd ever been.

Sonny Rollins went on and on; the sax screeched and raced around the ceiling.

Then the crescendo burst into lyrical little fragments.

Main rolled them onto their sides, careful not to spill out of her, and continued the same careful motion until he was on top of her. He raised his torso and bent to kiss as much of her as he could reach, lightly, as the music spilled down on them and the congested feeling returned.

She pressed tight against him as he began to fill her again. "I love you, Cal."

They made love again, more slowly, finishing just seconds before Sonny Rollins finished, finally.

When he caught his breath he said, "I guess we have our song."

She squeezed him and ran her hands into his hair.

The fourth CD began, an early Miles Davis. "Oh no," he laughed. "I can't take any more. I've got to turn it off." He slowly pulled himself out of Carmen and looked down.

He gave up: "I love you," and bent low to kiss her. She moaned

and closed her legs over his ears. The pressure of her thighs on his
ears increased and decreased in a slow, slow rhythm and he was
lost....

Suddenly she threw her legs open and scrambled back from
him. He tried to understand: she was getting up quickly, there was
a new sound mixed in with the trumpet. Another instrument?
Carmen was gathering her clothes and pointing urgently at the
door. She gave him a look of mock horror and ran for the stairs
clutching her clothes.

The new sound was the doorbell. He staggered to his feet and
started putting on his clothes. He kicked his underwear under the
couch and got his slacks on over his raspberry penis. He got his
shirt on and stuffed the tails in his pants. Put his socks neatly in
his shoes and left them next to the couch. He ran his fingers
through his hair as he went to the door.

TWENTY-FOUR

He opened the door and involuntarily took a step back from Huerta, who filled the frame and must have been standing with his nose practically touching the door.

"Vic."

Huerta looked tired. The mustard shirt was full of sharply starched creases. Just as Main was about to ask him if he'd had a hard day, Huerta beat him, saying, "Hard day?"

Main knew he must not look too crisp. "Fell asleep. Guess I slept too long. A little groggy."

"Slept with that on?" Huerta gestured to the CD player. Miles Davis was punching holes in the atmosphere with his trumpet.

"I guess so." Main shook his head at the improbability of that and ran his hand over his face like a man having a hard time waking up. He smelled Carmen on his hand and shoved it in his pocket.

He gestured Huerta into the room and hurried over to turn off Miles Davis. The silence was a relief and he let out a sigh. "Have a seat, Vic. I'll be right back."

He went to the bathroom to give himself a couple minutes to make the transition. He splashed water on his face and looked at himself in the mirror. His normally uneventful face looked as if *something* had happened. He started to laugh and caught himself. He thought: Murder, Kidnapping, Richard. The post-love giddiness was gone and his face began to look about right.

He ran the comb through his hair, then went to the toilet to get the condom off. The giddiness almost came back: nothing looked as pathetic, as used up, as a used condom, especially one that's pale raspberry. He washed his hands and returned to the living room.

Huerta was on the couch and had a very official-looking attaché case open on the coffee table. Main took the armchair across from the couch, hoping he wasn't giving off a cloud of Carmen's perfumes.

"I got here as soon as I could," Huerta said to dispose of the subject before Main decided to make it an issue. "And I think things are a little clearer than they were this morning."

Main nodded, giving Huerta that point. He felt clear now. "Good."

"We know *how* it worked." Huerta may have wanted to gloat but was too tired to pull it off.

"How?" Main said.

"Fausto visited each of the adopting couples night before last and blackmailed them. He had Mexican birth certificates to convince them their papers were false and they would lose their babies if they didn't pay up."

"I see," Main said.

"And he had a cassette that he showed everyone. The cassette showed bits of the local news about Josefina's kidnapping and bits of Dedo tearing the heart out of a chest."

"Good Lord."

"They all agreed to Fausto's terms."

"So that's why Josefina was kidnapped — to make a videotape?"

Huerta rubbed his eyes, tired. "I don't know. I have a hunch Fausto may have tried to blackmail Richard and when it didn't work decided to kidnap Josefina to teach him a lesson, which he could use on others. That would explain what Richard was lying about."

"Maybe," Main said skeptically but secretly impressed that Huerta had guessed himself to the right answer. He wanted to get off the topic of Richard's lying and said, "So you have proof Fausto did that Aztec-sacrifice murder, like you thought."

Huerta nodded. "The fact that he let us have that just proves he's not planning on coming back."

"He didn't make enough to retire on, did he?"

"No, but he made enough to set himself up in the drug business, which is all that is going on in Sinaloa, in Mazatlán and to the north."

"I see."

Huerta popped open the top of the attaché case. "There's been another development today. Jaime Sanchez has flown to Mexico."

Main whistled softly. "Did he talk before he left?"

"Nothing."

"And you still think he's not really involved?"

Huerta shrugged, took an envelope from the attaché case and handed it to Main. Main opened the envelope and took out four pictures. He set them on the coffee table and looked to Huerta, who pointed to them individually and said, "Leopoldo, Fausto, Dedo, Jaime."

Leopoldo didn't look as distinguished as he did in the portrait in his living room. His face seemed empty and he just looked like an older man. Dedo's was a mugshot; Fausto sneered; Jaime exuded concern. Huerta was right, he didn't seem to fit in.

When Main was finished looking at the pictures Huerta handed him a folder. The first sheet inside had a man's name and a woman's name, an address and phone number: the adopting couple. Then it said Kevin Schmidt / Jose Guadalupe Merilla: the two names of the adopted baby.

"Keep going," Huerta said and Main looked at the next sheet. It was the Mexican birth certificate Fausto had used to blackmail the couple.

He looked quickly through the rest of the file. There were nine more sheets with names and addresses, a photocopy of a Mexican birth certificate with each one. On each certificate there was a black bar about half an inch wide and two inches long.

Main held one up and pointed at the black bar.

"He cut out the line that tells where the certificate was issued and the hole came out black when he photocopied them," Huerta explained.

"San Ildefonso?"

Huerta shrugged and handed Main another envelope. He opened it and took out several baby pictures. Each one looked about the same to him, like a baby. He turned one over and saw the name written on the back. He counted ten pictures.

Huerta handed him another envelope and said, "That's a letter for the American consul in Mazatlán. I've spoken with him and he will introduce you to the nun who runs the orphanage."

Main smiled and nodded. Huerta wasn't leaving much up to chance.

Huerta handed him a map of Sinaloa. The town of San

Ildefonso was circled in red ink.

Main laughed. "This is a regular detective kit. Everything but a magnifying glass."

Huerta seemed to think the humor was inappropriate and handed him another photo. It was a scene-of-the-crime photo of a man taped to a table. His head hung off one end so only his chin was visible from the angle the picture was taken. There was a gaping hole in the chest and a brown lump on the stomach: the dead man's heart. Main nodded, studying the picture, and wondering how to react to Huerta's dramatics.

He looked up and nodded. "What is this for?"

"To convince you not to try to be a hero," Huerta said undramatically. Main didn't say anything and Huerta explained himself: "This morning I think I let my feelings cloud my judgment. I said I was interested in the babies and Richard wasn't my concern." He paused and Main nodded to show he remembered. "Well, I think you'd better try to get Richard out. Bring him back."

"That's why you've given me all this information about the babies?"

Huerta shrugged. "It's a question of priorities. Find Richard; if you happen to find out about the babies too...."

"Yeah, I get the idea." Huerta's interests hadn't changed but his conscience had been bothering him. Main smiled. "Just bring Richard back?"

Huerta nodded.

Main laughed. "Have you ever tried to get Richard to *just* do something he didn't want to do. *That* is being heroic."

Huerta didn't think it was funny. He got up and wished him luck, like a commanding officer to his commando. Main didn't say anything clever. Huerta was too obviously sincere.

When Huerta left Main hesitated for a moment before going up to talk to Carmen. His gears were going to be stripped if he had to keep shifting them so often. It was hard to believe it had only been fifteen minutes or so since his senses, his feelings, had been pitched to Sonny Rollins' horn. And now... and now he had to go up and talk to Carmen about real things like kidnapping, baby smuggling, murder, Mexico. Talk straight and keep his pants on.

He looked at his watch. It would be impossible to catch the flight from San Francisco that evening. He'd have to catch the earliest flight in the morning... go home tonight, get ready, sleep in his own bed. That wasn't very inspiring. He headed up the stairs.

She was in the bed he'd been in once before, lying flat with the salmon comforter pulled up to her chin, almost protectively. She looked worried because she knew what was coming. "Is it really bad, what you have to tell me?" Suddenly she sat up in the bed, pulling the comforter with her. "No. Wait. Five minutes can't make any difference. I want to finish the other thing, make a transition."

"After fifteen minutes with Vic I'm afraid I've already made the transition," he said unromantically, but he did sit on the edge of the bed.

She pinned the comforter to her chest with her chin and reached to her night table for the cigarettes and an ashtray. She got two going and gave one to Main. She looked uncertain and said, "It would be like it never happened if we just started right in talking about the... kidnapping."

"It didn't exactly just *happen*, Carmen."

"You're glad though, aren't you?"

He nodded. He supposed so. He didn't know. He didn't know what to say. He loved her and at the same time it was just another episode in the saga of his emotional entanglement with Carmen. The giddiness was gone.

"Was I especially marvelous?"

He smiled.

She dropped the bantering tone. "Do you love me?"

"I have always loved you." He sounded tired, matter of fact, back to taking it for granted he was in love with Carmen.

"I think I've always loved you too," she said.

He looked skeptical. "Well...."

"What does that mean?"

"It took you eighteen years to finally decide?"

She puffed almost angrily on her cigarette. "I loved you but I just couldn't see."

"Ah," he laughed.

"I mean it. People make mistakes."

He nodded. That didn't require an answer.

"Marrying Richard was a mistake," she said. "He was so rich and beautiful and sure of himself, he didn't look like he could make a mistake. I figured if he wanted me — the grocer's daughter! — it must be because he knew something I didn't know." She sounded wistful as she remembered being dazzled by Richard. "But it was a mistake. I've missed you the last five years."

"I've missed you too." His voice was still matter of fact.

"That lacks passion, Cal."

"What do you want me to say? Fall on my knee, declare myself. Haven't I done all that a couple times?"

"How do you feel now that Ingrid's left you?"

He looked at her in surprise. The truth was he didn't think Ingrid had entered his mind all day. He wasn't having an angry day, or a guilty day. Just a day of tagging along on a murder and being in love with Carmen. He held his hands out helplessly.

"Relief? Do you feel relieved?"

"Maybe you could call it that. If I've already failed I don't have to feel I *am* failing. You could call that relief."

"So you're a free man now."

"Free for what?"

"For me."

"I guess so."

"That still lacks passion."

"I'm having trouble following this conversation, Carmen, finding the right tone."

"It's simple, I'm trying to get you to tell me you love me."

"I did."

She leaned back and worked on her cigarette.

He found the ashtray and stubbed out his. "Okay. How's this? Will you marry me?"

The question seemed to surprise both of them. Carmen didn't say anything. He explained, "Divorce Richard and marry me. Or if this is a game, stop playing it."

"He's, he's...." she laughed nervously. "He's my husband."

"Of course he is, otherwise you couldn't divorce him!"

They both laughed and he wasn't even sure he'd been serious.

She leaned forward and took his hand, letting the comforter fall to the bed. "Be my lover again, Cal." She got on her knees to kiss him. "It's much better than being married to me."

"No, marry me." He wasn't sure if his obstinacy was humorous or serious.

"I can't."

"Why not?"

"Richard needs me. Richard's the kind of man that falls apart in middle age." She squeezed his hand. "I'm not faithful but I'm responsible."

He laughed: the whole conversation was humorous, not serious. "That's a hell of a distinction."

"I'm serious. Be my lover."

"You already have a lover, remember? Newkirk."

She flinched but didn't let go of his hand. "Why did you have to say that? The whole thing was so perfect downstairs."

He nodded.

"Be my lover?" she said.

Her hand lay on top of his on the comforter. He took her hand and grasped it in a handshake. "Lovers."

"Don't be cynical."

He nodded without knowing what he really meant and then, realizing he was making a mess of the one thing he absolutely didn't want to make a mess of, nodded again, meaning it.

She was kneeling over him with her legs slightly spread. She smiled and raised her breasts with a deep breath. She pulled his hand, which she still held in a handshake, toward her and placed his fingers between her legs. She left her hand over his.

"What are you doing?" he said.

"I don't want you to forget me."

He laughed. "I haven't forgotten you in the last eighteen years...." He twisted to get on his knees and kiss her, mumbling, *"Corazón malherido."*

She heard him and smiled. She pressed his fingers hard against her, shuddered and said, *"Por cinco espadas."* She let go of his fingers to put both arms around his shoulders and put her head against his neck. She squeezed him tight for a long moment, then abruptly pulled back. She got up and put on a robe.

He told her all the things Huerta had told him.

TWENTY-FIVE

It wasn't quite noon when Main stepped out of the plane but it was the end of August and the air was already steam. For a moment it didn't feel like he was really breathing. He was wet by the time he cleared customs.

He had the taxi driver take him to the Hotel Freeman, where he and Richard had spent most of a summer nineteen years ago. The chance that Richard had picked the same hotel for old time's sake was almost nonexistent but the Freeman was close to the consulate and it would give him a place to park his bags.

He registered under a large dusty sailfish that had been frozen in the same leap for at least nineteen years. He decided it wouldn't hurt to try and showed the desk clerk a picture of Richard. He shook his head and left Main to get his own bags up to the room.

He opened the door, took one look at the room — a bed that sank in the middle, a table and chair that didn't match, a sink, a rusted air conditioner sticking out of the wall. He set his bags on the floor, locked the door and left.

He crossed the broad street in front of the hotel to the Malecon, the tiled sidewalk along the seawall. The old green light poles were still there, topped by iron dragons with streetlights between their spread wings. He'd always wondered who'd dreamt them up. He leaned on the seawall and looked at the beach he'd swum in every day that summer, the last pre-Carmen summer of his life. Now the beach was empty and treacherous with broken glass. The tourists had moved north with the nice hotels and left this part of town behind.

He turned his back to the seawall and looked at the old hotels across from him. He decided to show Richard's picture to the clerks on his way to the consulate and crossed over to the first one. The hotel was almost empty and the clerks were barely polite. There wasn't any need to be with the tourists gone. They hadn't seen Richard and neither had the clerks at the other two hotels on his way.

He walked a couple of blocks away from the water until he found the consulate, which hadn't withstood the general decline of the old part of town much better than the hotels. It was a fifties modern box, worn and streaked with moisture. There was an enamel plaque over the door. The eagle was chipped and pocked with rust.

Inside it was different. The air was an icy shock and he stopped for a second to let his metabolism adjust. A pretty Mexican receptionist looked up crisply. The air, the receptionist: he was in an oasis of can-do. No decline here.

When he asked her if the consul was in he was led in immediately. She didn't even pick up the phone on her desk to announce his arrival.

Main found himself shaking hands with a burly man in his mid-fifties, Hiram Ballard. A Mr. Coffee was brewing patriotically in the corner and Mr. Ballard told him it was almost ready.

Ballard got him seated and said, "I talked to Lieutenant Huerta again this morning and he told me you were coming. I decided to wait a little longer before going to lunch."

"Thank you. I forgot all about lunch with this heat."

"It'll cool off in a couple of weeks."

Main nodded and the consul looked to see if the coffee was ready. He was wearing a tie and a short-sleeved white shirt. He was probably one of the only people in Mazatlán wearing a tie but it was obviously just a concession to duty. His powerful arms were burned dark and the brown hair on them had been bleached blond. On the wall behind him were a series of pictures of him standing next to huge fish hanging by their tails. Each picture had a date and a weight written on it. There was a picture of Bill Clinton on the wall too.

"It's a bad business," the consul said, shaking his head sadly. He seemed like a normally cheerful person who wasn't used to bad business.

"It's a mess all right," Main said and handed the consul the letter of introduction from Huerta, which hardly seemed necessary.

The consul glanced at it and handed it back. "I take a personal interest in this matter."

"You do?"

"Yes. The consulate is involved in the adoption of foreign babies. We issue the I-600 visa and see a lot of the other paperwork. More than that, I know both Sister Remedios at the orphanage and Jaime Sanchez. Fairly well." Remembering them seemed to upset him. "We did more than just paperwork, we tried to facilitate these adoptions. It seemed to me we were doing a good thing."

Main didn't know what to say.

"I love this country," the consul said, "and it is falling apart."

"Sorry?"

The consul smiled. "I guess I sound a little odd. What I mean is, all we seem to do any more is work on the drug problem. The consulate is practically a branch office of the DEA. So when the chance came along to find good homes for orphans, I jumped at it. It's hard to find an opportunity to do the right thing." He smiled at his foolishness and held his hands palm up.

Main sensed they could get to work. "Would something like a hundred thousand dollars be enough to set up in the drug business?" he asked, thinking of Fausto.

"Sure, if you had contacts. Otherwise it would be a good way to get killed. You don't just hang up a shingle."

"What is Jaime Sanchez like?"

"Fine young man. I thought he was a fine young man. No, I take that back. I still do." He looked at Main as if waiting to be challenged.

"When is the last time you saw him?"

"This morning."

"This morning!"

The consul looked at him for a moment before answering. "Jaime is trying to do the same thing as you, Mr. Main, the same thing as Lieutenant Huerta. He's trying to find out what has happened with the adoptions."

"I don't think the police were done talking to him yet."

The consul shrugged. "Jaime said it would look bad, but he's not hiding out."

"Where is he?"

"At the Camino Real."

"What did he want to talk to you about?"

"He wanted me to help him find his cousin, Fausto Sanchez."

"Do you know him?"

"Never heard of him."

"Did Jaime tell you where to look? What Fausto is up to?"

"He doesn't know."

Main doubted Jaime could put through an impossible string of home-birth adoptions without knowing what Fausto was up to, but he wasn't going to argue the point with the consul, who obviously wasn't going to change his mind about Jaime. As for himself, he wondered if Jaime was looking for Fausto to kill him. He asked, "What did Jaime say about his father's murder?"

A look of pain crossed the consul's face. "He didn't know about it. I had to tell him."

"You're sure he didn't know?

"Positive. I saw his reaction."

"Do you think he's gone home now that he knows?"

"His first reaction was shock but then he sort of dug in his heels, seemed even more determined to find this Fausto."

"Could you call the Camino Real for me and tell Jaime I'd like to talk to him?"

The consul nodded and picked up his phone, relaying the message to his receptionist. He hung up and in the moment's silence remembered the coffee he'd promised but never poured. He got Main a cup and the receptionist called back to say that Jaime was not in his room but had not checked out of the hotel.

Main thanked him and took out the envelope with the pictures of Jaime, Fausto, Dedo and Leopoldo. "Do you recognize any of these people, besides Jaime, in connection with the adoptions?"

He looked at them and shook his head. "I've never seen them but Jaime gave me a picture of Fausto, which I've already sent out to have copies made."

"What will you do with them?"

"Give them to the police and some of our people."

"DEA?"

The consul shrugged. "You know, I can't pull anyone off what they are working on, but if someone came across something...."

"And the local police, or federal police, or whatever they are?"

He held his hands open again. "They will politely tell me they will do everything they can, but...."

"Yes, I see. Have you talked to Sister Remedios about all this yet?"

"Of course. She is as flabbergasted as I am. Everything seems perfectly in order as far as we can see. Frankly, we are hoping to learn from you, Mr. Main."

"I can tell you part of it but that's all I know. Is the orphanage far?"

"Walking distance. But I'd better warn you, these nuns are a pretty unlikely bunch of evildoers."

Main smiled and got up. He looked at the pictures on the wall as he waited for the consul to get ready. "You're quite a fisherman," he said.

The consul gave a rich laugh, giving a glimpse of the happy man underneath the unhappy situation. "You fish?" he asked hopefully.

"No."

He wondered what anyone would want two thousand pounds of marlin for.

TWENTY-SIX

Orfanatorio La Sagrada Familia was an old two-story building with a sober facade that took up most of a block. On the street level there were large shuttered windows behind iron grilles and on the second story another series of smaller windows. There was a large entrance portal and inside a courtyard filled with potted plants. Large old doors gave into rooms off the courtyard and an arched gallery, supported by columns, ran around the second-story rooms.

Main and the consul stood in the entranceway for a moment, waiting to be noticed. Two girls about ten or twelve swept the already clean courtyard and younger boys carried plates and cutlery from one room to another. It was quiet.

One of the girls saw them, set her broom aside and hurried into a room, returning with a nun. The nun exchanged courtesies with the consul, who introduced Main and asked if they could talk to Sister Remedios.

They were led through two rooms to a third. The door was open and an older nun, hearing them approach, looked up. She got up and went around to the front of her desk, smiling at the consul, whom she greeted formally but with warmth. They made small talk. The second nun went to stand in a corner.

The room was austere but attractive. It was pleasantly dim, lit only by a bar of light where the jalousie shutters stood ajar. The old walls were thick and the room relatively cool.

A grisly crucifix dominated the room. The body was laced with blood and the torn knees exposed muscles and tendons rendered in careful detail. It was a religion that worshipped a man being tortured to death.

The consul turned to him and praised the nun's good works with obvious sincerity. She shook his hand and bowed her head slightly at the praise. The consul didn't describe who Main was or what he did but the nun seemed to know.

The consul said, "Perhaps Mr. Main can explain these problems with the adoptions."

"I hope that yes," the nun said, speaking English very slowly and precisely, translating word by word from the Spanish.

She went back to her seat behind the desk and Main and the consul took the wooden chairs across from her. She watched Main, waiting for him to clear things up. Her face was calm and resourceful. Her tinted glasses sat slightly awry on her strong nose and her hair was pulled back in a stern bun. She wore a navy blue dress buttoned to the throat.

"I will tell you what I know, Sister, but I think I should tell you there is a lot we don't understand yet. Maybe you can help me understand those things."

"I will try." She gave a very brief nod and waited.

He unzipped his plastic case and found the envelope with the pictures. "But first, Sister, can I ask you if you have seen this man? I'm trying to find him." He set in front of the nun the picture Carmen had given him of Richard holding Josefina.

She looked at the picture and her jaw set more firmly. She nodded. "He was here this morning."

"This morning?"

She nodded. "This morning." She spoke very carefully, perhaps thinking Main hadn't understood her because of her pronunciation.

He didn't say anything, wondering what Richard had been up to for the last thirty-six hours if he'd just been by the orphanage that morning.

"He think we have his baby." The nun pointed at Josefina in Richard's arms in the picture. "She was never here, that baby, and I never see her." She looked at Main for explanation, then grimly added: "Your friend, he comport himself very badly. He is, he is a" — she paused to search for a word — "he is a wrathful man."

"He is, Sister." The nun's Biblical diction was perfect for Richard. "But he has suffered much recently." He would talk the same way. "His baby has been kidnapped. He thought you might have seen her."

"But why?" the nun asked steadily.

"It's complicated," he said, putting off answering her question. "Did Mr. Mannock, my friend, tell you where he is staying in Mazatlán?"

She shook her head. That would have been too easy.

"Did he say what he's been doing since he got to Mazatlán?"

She shook her head again.

"Did he mention a town called San Ildefonso?"

"No."

"Do you know the town?"

"Not personally. Is a small town of mining, not far."

"Have any of the babies at the orphanage come from San Ildefonso?"

"Yes." She looked at him levelly through the crooked green glasses. "They come from all parts."

He thought she had hesitated but decided not to push it. "So, you were not able to help my friend?" he summarized.

"No. His baby is not here. Was never here. Never one of ours. And no one of ours is ever return." There was a note of hurt professional pride.

"Of course not."

"Now please, Mr. Main, you will explain me what is the problem with adoptions."

She clasped her fingers together and waited. He realized his turn to ask the questions was over and said, "Of course."

He began to explain the problem of the home births and how the parents had been blackmailed with Mexican birth certificates. He used Spanish at points and the consul helped him out.

When he finished she was sitting in exactly the same position, still watching him. After a moment she said, "I never believe Jaime do that." She waited for him to challenge her, then said, "Anyway, you talk of home birth and home birth have nothing to do with us." She was still speaking English.

"No, Sister, but, you see, the parents who adopted through your orphanage have been blackmailed in exactly the same way, and by the same person, as the people who adopted the home-birth babies. So there has to be a connection." He waited for it to sink in.

"What you want to say, Mr. Main?" she said, starting to get angry.

The consul spoke in Spanish: "He doesn't mean... he isn't accusing you... the orphanage..." He looked to Main for help.

"No one is accusing the orphanage. But I wonder if someone

used the orphanage."

"Jaime use us?" She looked at the consul again in disbelief.

Main wanted to avoid the topic of Jaime, who seemed to be beyond suspicion. "Maybe not Jaime."

"Who?"

He made a vague gesture, not wanting to get into that yet. "When did you first place a baby through Jaime Sanchez's agency?"

"Four years ago."

"How many have you placed with him so far?"

"Eight."

"How many in the last year."

She looked to the consul and back. "Five."

"That is a lot for one year." The year that Fausto had been out of prison.

"We work hard for augment number," the nun said with conviction. "We are very happy we find Jaime. Americans are so rich" — she seemed dissatisfied with the word — "so generous. And the babies need homes."

Main nodded sympathetically. He found the sheet of paper with the names of the adopting parents. He had already starred the five couples who had adopted through the orphanage. "Do you know these people?"

She glanced. "Of course. We don't give babies to strangers."

The consul explained: "A couple planning to adopt would fly down, see the baby, begin the paperwork and return home to wait for the Mexican end of the adoption to be completed. They would meet Sister Remedios, naturally."

"I see. Sister, how does a baby... uh, how does the orphanage find the orphans?"

"Maybe someone bring them. A relative, a neighbor, a auxiliary social."

"A social worker," the consul quickly translated.

"And if no one brings them how do you get them?"

"Many are abandoned. Maybe the poor mother — she cannot feed another baby — she leave her baby in a church or here, in front of the orphanage."

"Really?"

"There are too many children and we can help only a few."

"I understand." He pushed the paper with the names on it a little closer to the nun. "Could you tell me, Sister, exactly where the babies these people adopted came from?" He pointed at the five starred names again.

She didn't have to study the names. She'd been expecting the question. "Three we find abandonated. Two come from clinic of government." She set her chin and waited.

The three abandoned children were a dead end. "Where is the clinic?" he asked.

"Is an IMSS clinic."

The consul explained: "Kind of a Social Security clinic."

"Yes, but where is it?"

She swallowed. "San Ildefonso." She waited. She knew there was something significant about San Ildefonso because he'd asked about it earlier.

He wished he could question nuns all the time. They didn't lie. "Did you go to the clinic to get the babies?"

"No, they brought them here."

"Was it a young man who brought them?"

She shook her head.

"A man my age? Older than me?"

"Older. His name is Porfirio Santos."

Main looked in his plastic case again for the envelope with the pictures. He took out the picture of Leopoldo Sanchez and set it in front of the nun. She studied it carefully and said, "No."

He didn't say anything but there was something in the way she answered and he was no longer certain nuns didn't lie. Had she looked at the picture too carefully, answered too firmly? Had something changed in her expression? He didn't know but he thought she'd recognized Leopoldo Sanchez.

She said, "We have all the papers."

He didn't doubt that. He got the picture of Fausto out of the envelope and put it in front of her. She said, "No," without hesitation. He put the picture of Dedo on the table and she just shook her head.

He put his finger on the picture of Fausto. "This man beat this man" — he moved his finger to the picture of Leopoldo — "to death."

Nothing crossed her features. If he'd seen anything earlier it was hidden now. She wasn't scared. "I never see them."

Main glanced at the crucifix and then looked at the other nun still standing quietly in the corner. "Sister, have you seen any of these men?"

She came to the desk and looked at the pictures carefully. She shook her head and went back to her corner.

"Thank you very much, Sister Remedios," he said. "I'm sorry I had to ask you these painful questions."

"We are not finish," she said, catching his tone. "You no explain how someone use our orphanage."

He pointed at the picture of Fausto again. "This man blackmailed all the parents who adopted the home-birth babies and the ones from your orphanage. He worked with this man." He pointed at Leopoldo again. "They were smuggling babies, both by themselves, and through this orphanage." Her face began to tighten with anger again and he quickly added, "Though the orphanage didn't know what they were doing."

"I do not understand." Her jaw set more firmly.

"I mean they may have brought these babies to the orphanage as a way to legally smuggle them into the States. They may have placed those abandoned children wherever you found them. And the clinic...." He shrugged.

"Those babies are orphans!" the nun said with surprising vehemence. She seemed surprised at her own outburst and stood up to hide her confusion.

TWENTY-SEVEN

The consul insisted they have lunch and took Main to a place called Ostioneria El Puerto. The restaurant looked cool — there were banks of crushed ice covered with oysters, clams and shrimp — but it wasn't. Electric fans on long cords batted at the sluggish air without making any difference. Main stared at the banks of ice.

A waitress in a fresh white apron appeared and the consul ordered oyster cocktails for both of them. He told Main that was the thing to eat there. He ordered a couple beers.

They waited in silence for the waitress to return with the beers. The bottles still had bits of crushed ice stuck on them and Main picked up his and rolled it across his forehead.

They were settled in, they'd ordered, they had their beers. The consul went right to his question: "So what did you think?"

"I think five adoptions in one year strain belief when they had been averaging one a year for the previous three years."

"Well, as Sister Remedios said, they had decided to try to increase the number of adoptions. To help the children."

"It's not encouraging that three of the babies were abandoned, just conveniently turned up, and the other two are from San Ildefonso, which is where we already suspected these babies might be coming from."

He explained that San Ildefonso was Leopoldo Sanchez's home town and the consul listened with a pained expression. When Main finished he made a simple rebuttal: "Nuns don't do things like that. Sister Remedios is not a baby merchant."

Main drank some beer and then rolled the bottle across the back of his neck to get the last coolness. "She may not know what's going on."

"*May* not? Take my word for it, if anything's wrong it's got nothing to do with Sister Remedios."

Main hesitated, sensing he was using up the last of the consul's considerable good will. "I think she was lying to me when she said she didn't recognize Leopoldo Sanchez."

The consul slowly shook his head in disbelief. "That's not possible." He took a slug of beer and shook his head again. He looked at Main warily. "Why do you think she's lying?"

"Just a feeling."

He visibly relaxed. "A feeling is not much to go on."

Main agreed it wasn't. The oysters arrived in tall parfait glasses and the consul looked at them with relief. He began dousing his with salsa. He picked up his spoon and said, "You have to admit it sounds a little unlikely, a bunch of nuns in a baby racket. What would they do with the money?"

"Maybe it's not for money."

"What then?"

"I don't know. Maybe they think it's a way to help the babies."

It was vague and unconvincing. The consul shook his head once more, happy that Main wasn't able to seriously disturb the order of things, and put the first oyster in his mouth with a look of concentration and pleasure. After savoring the first one he went to work on the rest with more energy.

The oysters were too mushy for Main. He ate a couple and watched the consul.

The consul came up for air and said, "Not hungry?"

"The heat."

"It'll be cooler in a couple weeks," he said almost defensively and went back to his oysters.

When he was finished Main offered him his parfait glass. The consul declined regretfully and patted his belly in explanation. He looked around the restaurant for the waitress and aimed a "Pssst" at her back.

She turned and nodded.

"I never got comfortable doing that," Main said.

"Hissing?" The consul shrugged. "That's how they do it here." The waitress came over and the consul ordered two coffees.

The consul's expression became serious again, the interlude of pleasure finished. "What's next, Mr. Main? Are you going to San Ildefonso?"

Main hesitated, realizing that's what he wanted to do. He shook his head. "I think the first thing is to try and find Richard. This Fausto's awfully dangerous."

"Do you think Mr. Mannock really knows where to look for Josefina?"

"I guess not, if he was at the orphanage this morning looking for her."

The consul shook his head skeptically. "Finding a Mexican baby in Mexico... needle in a haystack."

"Maybe I'll be able to talk to Jaime Sanchez sometime today since I'll be trying all the hotels."

"The Camino Real is the northernmost hotel so you could start there — see if Jaime's there — and work your way south," the consul said helpfully.

Main nodded and the consul picked up the small leather portfolio he had with him and opened it, taking out an envelope which he handed to Main.

"Another envelope," Main joked.

"I don't know if it will help."

The envelope had the official seal of the United States on it. He took out a piece of paper with the same seal and read. It said, in elaborate Spanish, that the consul of the United States of America would be most grateful to anyone who might be able to help Calvin Main in his investigation of a point of some urgency to the American Consulate in Mazatlán. It stopped short of saying Main had any legal status — he didn't — but implied he was plugged into Power. The fierce eagle with arrows in his talons looked convincing

"Thank you. It might be very helpful."

"There is a different attitude to authority here," the consul said and shrugged. "A piece of paper might help."

Main looked at the glare of heat in the open doorway of the restaurant and told himself to get going.

Before he could move the consul said, "Where are you staying?"

"I've got my bags at the Freeman but I'm going to go get them and start looking for Richard. If I find him I'll stay where he is; if not, I don't know."

"Will you please call me when you have a hotel?"

"Of course."

"And will you let me know when — if — you go to San Ildefonso and call again when you get back?"

"Why?"

"It's dangerous out there, an American wandering around in the mountains asking questions... with the drug business we were talking about earlier."

"I will keep in touch." Main got up and felt almost dizzy for a second. He shook hands with the consul and thanked him for all his help.

On his way out the restaurant he grabbed a handful of crushed ice and rubbed it on his face and neck.

At the Hotel Freeman he took a lukewarm shower — even the cold water was warmed up — and put on fresh clothes. He repacked his bags and slung his camera bag, which contained his automatic, over his shoulder.

He paid and checked out under the gaze of an indifferent clerk.

He caught a cab and haggled half-heartedly over the fare to the Camino Real. He melted into the back seat as the driver drove north past several generations of luxury hotels. It was like an archeology of tourism: as one bunch of luxury hotels began to age a new bunch would spring up a bit further north and the older ones would lose a star or two.

At the Camino Real he told the driver to wait for him.

TWENTY-EIGHT

At the desk the consul's letter produced such a reaction that Main decided not to dilute it by showing his investigator's license. The clerk who had read the letter went off to find the manager while a second clerk stood smiling hospitably at him.

When the manager arrived, also smiling, he barely glanced at the letter. He was in the tourist business: American Consulate was all he needed to know.

Main asked if Richard Mannock was staying there and the manager checked on the computer, shaking his head. Main showed him Richard's picture, which he studied carefully before shaking his head regretfully. The manager showed it to the two clerks, who hadn't seen him either, and asked Main's permission to send one of the clerks to ask the other help — in the bars, by the pool, in the restaurants, on the beach. Main thanked him and the clerk with the smile hurried off looking important.

Main asked the manager if Jaime Sanchez was staying there. The manager, who obviously knew who Sanchez was, raised his eyes in surprise and said he was. He called Sanchez's room for Main but there was no answer. He told Main that Sanchez was traveling with a lady friend who had another room and tried that room as well. He gave Main another regretful smile and at Main's request wrote the room numbers on a slip of paper.

The manager's desire to please was making Main uncomfortable. He told the manager he thought he'd look at the grounds if he didn't mind and went out the glass doors opposite the desk.The grounds were a riot of hibiscus, jacaranda, bougainvillea. There was a pool, then tennis courts, then stairs down to a cabana restaurant and bar overlooking the beach. It was hard to imagine Richard anywhere out there, spread out under a cabana on the beach or bobbing around in the pool in an inflatable chair with a coco loco in his lap.

He took the pictures out of one of the envelopes in his camera bag and put in forty dollars. When the clerk who had been showing Richard's picture hurried up the steps shaking his head Main thanked him and went back in to the desk with him. He thanked the manager profusely for his help. He explained he didn't have a hotel yet himself so couldn't leave a number where he could be reached but would call back. Perhaps the manager would be kind enough to tell him if Jaime Sanchez had returned. And perhaps he wouldn't tell Señor Sanchez that he'd been asking about him.

The manager would be only too happy to do anything he could. Main shook his hand and gave him the envelope.

When he left the lobby the hot air closed in again. By the time he was back in the cab his shirt stuck to him as if he'd been vacuum packed.

He told the driver to drive south and stop at the first hotel. He went in, showed his letter and his picture again and came out. He told the driver to try the next hotel, and the next, and the next. The driver tried to recommend a hotel to be helpful but smiled when Main explained he was looking for a friend. The driver would be very happy to keep the meter running.

Coming out of the fifth hotel he noticed a dusty black Buick Riviera that he thought he'd already seen at the third hotel. There was a man with very short hair and dark glasses behind the wheel.

He told his driver to go to the next hotel and turned in his seat to see the Riviera pull out in the traffic a few cars behind them.

He turned around and quickly went through the possibilities. If he had been followed from the Camino Real — though he really didn't know that he hadn't been followed earlier — then the most likely people to suspect were the manager, and the consul, who knew he was going there. It was also quite possible the consul had talked to Sister Remedios, to compare notes on the interview, and told her where Main was going. Or it was possible either of them had talked to Jaime Sanchez, wherever he was. There were plenty of possibilities.

He went into the next hotel, did his routine and came out. The Riviera was parked on the street about fifty yards up from the hotel.

He signaled to his driver to wait for him and started walking toward the Riviera. He put his hand in the camera bag and put his fingers around the grip of the automatic. The man behind the wheel saw him coming but didn't make a move. Main didn't recognize him. None of his pictures showed someone in dark glasses with very short hair.

He got to the driver's door and looked in. The hand on the steering wheel was missing a finger. "Dedo," he said.

"Main man," Dedo said sleepily.

They looked at each other for a moment. Main wondered how Dedo knew who he was.

"Who told you to follow me?" Main asked without expecting an answer.

He got a slow smile instead of an answer.

"We've got your scam pretty well figured out, Dedo."

Dedo's smile didn't change. Huerta was right: They didn't care if the trail led to them as long as they were safe in Mexico.

He tried one more question: "Have you seen Richard?"

"Look, man, I'm just following you. I'm not looking for a conversation. Why don't you just get back to work?"

"You can save me a lot of hot work if you tell me where Richard is."

"I don't know nothin' 'bout nothin', mon."

Main went back to his cab and got in. Maybe they really didn't know where Richard was, which would be good, all he could hope for really. He told the driver to try the next hotel.

He was glad to have Dedo behind him. It showed something was happening even if he didn't know exactly what. If he could find Richard he could perhaps work as an honest broker between Richard and Fausto: keep Richard from getting killed, arrange a pay-off, get Josefina back. He could see things happening.

His enthusiasm didn't hold up long in the heat as he tried several more hotels. The consul's letter continued to work but it was slow. His picture showed Richard in a business suit and the clerks had to mentally re-dress him in shorts, sportshirt, sunglasses, hat. When they did he seemed to resemble a lot of other men with paunches vacationing in Mazatlán. The clerks had to consult and wonder if it could be the man in room number....

There were two false alarms. On the first the clerk helped him find an enormously fat man spilled over a bar stool. Richard was losing his quarterback shape but he was still nothing like the man on the stool.

The second false alarm was more difficult. The clerk was less helpful. He said Richard looked like one of their guests, who turned out not to be in his room, and suggested Main look on the beach, where this man spent most of his time. Main again doubted Richard would be out sunbathing but he trudged fifty yards up the beach and then fifty yards down, looking for someone who looked like Richard. He found no one and decided that he would have to keep the hotel on his list and check it out again.

When he got back to the cab he was almost sick with the heat.

They tried two more hotels and then at the third the clerk said yes without the slightest hesitation. Main groggily assumed the clerk had misunderstood him and explained again what he wanted. The clerk was positive Richard was the Mr. Johnson in room 422. Absolutely positive: He himself had checked him in that morning.

Mr. Johnson was out.

He went back to the cab and went into three more hotels, checking to be sure Dedo was still behind them. In each of the hotels he sat in the lobby for a moment cooling off without showing his picture to anyone. When he came out of the third hotel he told the driver he had found his friend and paid the enormous fee on the meter. He added a good tip and shook hands with the driver, insisting on carrying his own bags into the hotel.

When he got in the lobby he walked right past the registration desk and kept going through the open arches into the gardens that led to the beach. He hurried down the path to the beach and onto the sand. He went down to where the sand was wet and firm and began walking doubletime, sweat pouring off of him in the sun. When he got to the next hotel up the beach he did the same thing in reverse: crossed the sand to the gardens of the new hotel, hurried through the gardens, through the lobby to the taxi stand in front of the hotel.

He collapsed in the back of a new cab and told the driver to go north. He slipped low in the back seat so no one could see him, and to recover from his exertions. He let the driver go farther than necessary and then sat up, keeping an eye out the rear window to see if the Riviera was behind him. When he was sure he had lost Dedo he told the driver to double back to the Hotel Los Sabalos, the hotel where the clerk was sure Richard was staying

He took his bags in and registered. He got a room on the same floor as Richard, who still hadn't returned. He went up to his room, peeled off his wet clothes and took a cold shower. The hotel was new and luxurious and the water was even cold.

He got a beer from the hotel refrigerator, put on a pair of shorts and went to the phone. He considered calling the consul but only for a moment: for all he knew it was the consul who had had Dedo follow him. He called Carmen instead and left a message on her answering machine, saying he thought he'd found Richard's hotel but Richard wasn't there. He said he'd call again when he'd talked to Richard and left the name of the hotel, the number and his room.

He got another beer and tried the Camino Real to see if Jaime Sanchez was back. He wasn't.

He got out his phone book and phoned every car rental agency listed. Stretching things, he said he was phoning from the American Consulate and trying to find an American citizen on a personal emergency. He gave Richard's real name, assuming he'd have to show a license and a credit card or travelers' checks to rent a car, and when that didn't work tried the Mr. Johnson alias as well. There were naturally two Mr. Johnsons and he had to spend some time determining that neither was Richard.

He tried the front desk to see if they'd rented a car for Mr. Johnson. It seemed that no one had. He hung up and then phoned down again and arranged for them to rent a car for him. He was finishing his beer when they called back to say a convertible Caribe — a Mexican Rabbit — would be delivered to the hotel and he would be able to get the keys at the desk. Mr. Johnson still hadn't returned.

He put on a shirt and went out into the hallway. He walked the halls until he found a boy with a room service trolley. He waited while the boy made a delivery and then gave him his letter with twenty dollars folded in it and asked him to open Richard's door for him — he wanted to surprise his friend. The boy didn't even consider the flimsy pretext. Either the letter or the money had been unnecessary.

The boy led him down a hall and opened the door to room 422.

Richard had thrown his bag onto the middle of the bed without opening it. It was the same duffel bag Main had watched him angrily stuffing in his bedroom before he left for the airport. He opened the bag. Everything he could think of to look for was there — many of the clothes soiled — except the huge Colt .45. Nothing in the room had been used as far as he could tell.

He was close but he'd feel a lot better if he actually had Richard with him. As it was Richard was running around with the Colt, being wrathful, as Sister Remedios put it.

He sat on the edge of the bed. He had a choice: sit and wait or race off to San Ildefonso. Running off would make him feel like he was doing something but it actually wouldn't make much sense. Richard had undoubtedly already been to San Ildefonso if he was going to go there. He must have been doing something in the day and a half before he showed up at the orphanage and checked into this hotel.

No, the sensible thing was to wait. Richard had checked into the hotel that morning. He was planning to sleep there. The duffel bag was there; Richard would be.

If Richard had already been in Mazatlán for that long without getting himself killed, Main would have to count on him to get back to the hotel in one piece.

In the meantime what made sense was a drink: relax and figure out how he was going to get Richard to go along with him when he showed up. He would need the inspiration of a drink to figure that one out.

He put some ice in a glass and took one of the mini-bottles of Herradura tequila from the refrigerator and went out onto the balcony. He was tired, the chair was comfortable, the breeze was delightful after the day's heat. He relaxed with the drink, convincing himself Richard would be all right.

He finished the drink, went in to try the Camino Real again — still no Jaime — and got two more of the little bottles. He might need a lot of inspiration to convince Richard.

He went back to the balcony. In forty-five minutes he was watching a sunset like he hadn't seen for nineteen years. It looked like a child's watercolor of a sunset. A screeching sunset. A Sonny Rollins' sunset.

A drunk sunset.

He thought of Carmen.

Corazón malherido. Fingers stabbing at the heart. White camellias. He recited the bits he could remember at the delirious sunset, where some of the reds were darkening into purples.

He got up and tidily collected the empty little bottles. He went to the phone and called room service to bring up huge quantities of food. He tried the Camino Real. No Jaime, so he could eat.

He ate, wishing Richard would get back to his room, and watched the purples turn to black.

At eight thirty he called and was told Jaime had just returned.

TWENTY-NINE

At the Camino Real the manager, still there after a long day, greeted him happily, glad to be able to tell him Jaime was still in his room. He doubted that the manager had been the one to put Dedo on him, but maybe the man was a bit too helpful to be true....

On the third floor he came to Jaime's "lady friend's" door first. It was ajar and he pushed it open a few inches more. The room was empty. Jaime's room was two doors down from hers. His door was also ajar and he could hear low voices. He supposed the lady friend was making a quick visit to Jaime.

He listened but the voices were too low for him to make out.

He opened Jaime's door a few inches wider. Jaime and the woman were seated on the edge of the bed, facing the open door to the balcony, their backs to Main. Jaime was wearing pants but no shirt. He was very thin and sat in a dejected slump. The woman was saying something to reassure him. She sat straight and had her arm across his shoulders, barely touching them, as if the extra weight might be too much.

Main cleared his throat and knocked lightly on the door frame. The woman jerked her head around and looked at Main. Jaime didn't budge. She had long red hair and watery but determined blue eyes. Her face was burned a bright red but her shoulders, exposed beneath a sleeveless white blouse, were the color of skim milk. She got up, carefully taking her hand off Jaime's shoulders, and took a step towards Main, running interference for Jaime, who still hadn't turned to look.

"Who are you?" she said.

"Calvin Main."

The name didn't seem to mean anything to her. She said, "Do

you know Mr. Sanchez?" She looked at Jaime on the bed but the sloped shoulders gave no clue.

"No, but I would like to talk to Mr. Sanchez about the adoptions done through his agency."

Jaime still didn't move but an extra weight seemed to settle on the thin shoulders.

"Mr. Sanchez isn't answering any questions," the woman said, sounding like a press agent.

"Jaime," Main said softly, "I was with the police when they found your father. We want to find his murderer."

The weight pressed on the shoulders, then Jaime turned slowly to face him. Main pointed to the armchair across from the bed. "Can I talk to you for a minute? It's very important."

Jaime didn't say anything and Main went to the chair.

"Jaime," the young woman protested.

Jaime ignored her and watched Main, waiting for him to speak.

Jaime Sanchez was in his late twenties but looked younger. He had a brown beard that was soft and sparse; his rosy skin showed through in places. Main had to remind himself that Jaime must be tougher than he seemed or he wouldn't have gotten himself into such a mess. But he didn't seem to have much in common with the dead old man, slumped over the steering wheel, let alone with his psychotic cousin.

When Jaime spoke it took Main by surprise, though he spoke very softly. He said, "Everything is ruined."

"What do you mean, Jaime?" Jaime just stared at his hands on his knees and Main decided to start again more simply. "When did you get here?"

"This morning."

"You didn't know about your father yet when you got here?"

Jaime winced and shook his head slowly. "Hi told me."

It took Main a second to realize that Hi was his buddy the consul, Hiram Ballard. "But your father was found yesterday morning."

Jaime sighed. "I was... out of touch." He pointed at the red-haired woman. "I was staying at Deirdre's. Hiding out I guess you could say." He shook his head at the sound of the words. "I didn't think they'd let me leave San Francisco."

"Why did you? Why did you come here?"

Jaime didn't answer and as he waited Main found himself

thinking like the consul and the nun: Jaime *couldn't* be involved in this.

"Jaime?" he tried. "Why did you come here?"

"To find Fausto. To find out what happened."

"Did you find Fausto today?"

"No."

"You do know he's the one who killed your father?"

Jaime looked as if he'd been slapped and then shook his head. He didn't look surprised exactly. He looked as if he'd been told what he'd been hoping against the odds he wouldn't be told. He said, "Fausto is... Fausto... needs help."

That stopped Main. Wanting to help Fausto was an idea he wasn't ready to consider. He tried another small question: "Who did you see today?"

"Hi Ballard. Sister Remedios."

"That's all? You've been out all day."

Jaime shrugged and Deirdre nodded with more conviction.

"You went to San Ildefonso?"

He didn't get any special reaction from either of them.

He said, less gently, *"Did* you find out what happened?"

Eventually Jaime said, "I guess everything was working okay... except Fausto backslid."

"Okay? Backslid!" Main dropped the last of his calm therapeutic manner.

"Something like that," Jaime said.

"Can you tell me what is *okay* about all this?"

"Don't talk to him," Deirdre said. Jaime might say anything in his shock and depression.

Jaime spoke to Main: "It's all over, isn't it?"

Main nodded. "Yes. We know the adoptions are illegal. We just don't really know why you did it."

"Don't talk to him," Deirdre said more urgently.

"Don't you see, Dee?" He spoke forcefully for the first time, almost sharply. He lowered his voice apologetically and said, "Don't you see, Dee? What we did is not nearly as bad as what they think we did. They think we're selling babies or something like that."

Main nodded and looked at Deirdre. "You can stonewall, but the questions and the problems aren't going to go away. We know the adoptions are illegal and we'll trace them to San Ildefonso."

Her pale blue eyes flashed with anger and she shook her head at Main's ignorance. "We never took a penny," she said defiantly.

"Maybe not, but Fausto took ten thousand dollars from each adopting couple. He showed them the adoptions were illegal — he had the real Mexican birth certificates to prove it — and told them to pay up, or else lose their babies. He made some vivid threats too."

"We had nothing to do with that! That was Fausto!" She had her hands on her hips and was standing over Main in his chair. Jaime had drifted off again to his own thoughts. "He must have had some fake papers made up. Those babies aren't from San Ildefonso." She laughed at his theories. "They aren't even Mexican."

When it seemed she was going to leave him hanging, he said, "Go on."

She looked to Jaime. He nodded. She said, with pride, "Those babies are Guatemalan war orphans. Fausto has taken advantage of the situation in the most unbelievable way."

Main didn't say anything. He had to think: Even his most farfetched calculations didn't include war orphans.

"Let me see if I understand this," he said. "You are running some kind of underground railroad through Mexico for these babies?"

She nodded, with pride.

"You get them to the orphanage, or to San Ildefonso, then north for adoption? The orphanage and San Ildefonso are like train stations on this underground railroad?"

"Yes, that's it."

That explained what Sister Remedios was doing involved in all this, what Jaime was doing, but there sure were a lot of things it didn't explain.

He looked at Jaime. "You're right. This sounds better than what people are suspecting. But it's going to take a lot more explanation."

Jaime nodded gloomily at the floor but Deirdre took him up on it: "We're a faith community." She stopped to see if Main understood and he nodded. "Our goal is to re-make ourselves, and our world, in God's image." She stopped for him to protest. He nodded. "Our sword is love, the militant caritas of the faith community. The struggle is the sign that God is breaking into history."

She paused again but he didn't nod any more encouragement.

He looked to Jaime. "Can you explain it on a more practical level?"

"We belong to an organization at our Church called Christian Action. We are involved with the refugee problem."

He nodded that he understood the translation. "How does it work?"

"You may know that for years and years the Guatemalan military has been trying to get rid of the guerrilla insurgency in the Guatemalan highlands by the simple expedient of getting rid of the people who live there — the Indians."

"I know."

"Thousands and thousands of Indians have fled across the border into Mexico, into Chiapas. The media have lost what little interest they had but the camps are still there. Conditions being what they are, there are plenty of orphans."

Deirdre broke in: "They are afraid to go back to Guatemala, even with the 'civilian' government there now. In Guatemala the difference between a military government and a civilian one...." She made an angry dismissive gesture.

"Anyway," Jaime resumed, "one of the priests whose ministry is in the camps is trying to get at least the orphans out. We are trying to help."

"The ends justify the means," Main said moralistically, though he was sure they often did in the real world.

"There are three million abandoned children in Latin America!" Deirdre said.

"This priest somehow gets the babies as far as Mazatlán and you take over here," Main said.

"That's right," Jaime said softly.

"You either get them to the orphanage or bring them north yourselves and register them as home births in California."

"Yes."

"How do they get to Mazatlán?"

"I don't know exactly," Jaime said. "Through the priest's organization."

"What is the priest's name?"

"Padre Tomas."

"That's all?"

"That's all the name priests have," Deirdre explained.

"Nonsense," Main said bluntly. "Have you been to the camps?"

Jaime shook his head and Deirdre said, "No, but we've seen videotapes. The conditions are unbelievable."

"How do you communicate with Padre Tomas?"

"We wait for him to communicate with us. It's practically impossible to get a letter or call through to the camps."

"How did you meet him?"

There was a pause and Main looked back and forth between them. Deirdre said, "He approached me, in connection with my work."

"In San Francisco?" Main asked skeptically.

"Yes."

"So, in a sense," Main said uncomfortably, "you are taking this Father Tomas on faith."

"Exactly," she said. Jaime watched him for a sign of what he was thinking.

"Jaime, exactly how did Fausto and your father get involved in all this? We know they were coming down here and I suppose they were doing some of the actual... smuggling."

"Transportation," Deirdre said.

"I told them about it. We had started working with Padre Tomas but we were having this problem of having more babies than we could place through the orphanage. Then we had the idea to bring them directly north and register them as home births."

"Fausto had the idea, you mean," Main said.

Jaime shrugged, as if it was a meaningless detail.

Main paused. He had the feeling that Jaime was what he seemed to be — a genuinely good person — and he felt the same uncomfortable mixture of distress and admiration he always felt in the presence of good people.

"Jaime," he said, "why in the world would you want to talk about something like this with Fausto of all people? Didn't you wonder why he'd want to get involved in charity work?"

Jaime closed his eyes at his terrible error and said, "Fausto had found God in prison."

"Found God!" Main exclaimed before he could stop himself. He saw it all and felt almost sick.

"I know it sounds funny now," Jaime said, "in the light of... of everything. But I believed it. My father is very religious... was.... I am a religious man, so I hoped...."

"A lot of people find religion in prison," Deirdre interrupted. "A lot. The greater the pain, the greater the chance you will find God. It makes perfect sense to think Fausto would find God."

Main sat back in his chair for the first time since he'd sat down. His temples throbbed from the mini-Tequilas and he wished he had one of Carmen's cigarettes. It was impossible to imagine Fausto finding religion — except maybe Aztec sacrifice. He wasn't going to enjoy being the one to enlighten Jaime.

He took a deep breath. "Fausto didn't by any chance introduce you to Father Tomas, did he?"

Jaime shook his head and asked suspiciously, "What do you mean?"

"Is Padre Tomas missing a finger?"

Jaime shook his head and Main realized it was impossible: Dedo was still in prison when "Padre Tomas" was setting things up.

"What are you getting at?" Deirdre said sharply.

"Look, I'm sorry," Main said, "but... Fausto never found God. Fausto is a killer, a psychopath."

"I know it looks funny now," Jaime said without much conviction.

"He didn't backslide," Main pressed on. "He set you up, Jaime."

Jaime didn't say anything and Deirdre looked back and forth between them.

Main said, "That's why you're looking for Fausto, isn't it? To ask him if he set you up? To find out if those babies are orphans?"

"I don't understand," Deirdre said accusingly.

"Deirdre," Main said, "Fausto invented Padre Tomas. Fausto got the supply of babies started. He stepped in more directly when he needed to get more babies to the States more quickly. He pretended to find God so you'd lower your guard."

"But Padre Tomas -"

"There *is* no Padre Tomas, there's just some friend of Fausto's dressed up in a black suit."

"Jeans."

"Jeans then. Look, Deirdre, this is something Fausto cooked up in prison. He knew Jaime had a perfectly respected adoption agency, and a good heart. If he could just think of some way to turn that to advantage. He hit on the political angle as the one you'd be most sympathetic to. He put this "Padre Tomas" in touch with you. All that was left to do was to start supplying the babies, who don't come from Guatemala. They are Mexican and those birth certificates may be the only thing in the whole scheme that *aren't* fake."

Jaime got up — finally moving — and went to stand out on the balcony. From behind, Main and Deirdre watched him take a couple of deep breaths. He turned and came back into the room and said, "You realize this is all conjecture, nothing but conjecture."

Main nodded. "It's all conjecture. But the only alternative is to believe Fausto found God in prison. I don't believe it."

"Maybe," Jaime said uncertainly, "maybe you're right."

"No," Deirdre said.

"Maybe," Jaime muttered again.

Main stood up. "Do you have any idea where Richard Mannock is?"

"I didn't know he was here."

Back at the hotel Main went straight up to Richard's room and checked the door: The tiny piece of paper he'd slipped between the lock and the jamb was still there. He didn't think Richard had returned.

He pushed the door open. The room hadn't changed since he'd left.

He spent a nearly sleepless night waiting for dawn.

His faith that Richard could keep himself alive didn't make it through the long night.

THIRTY

The mountains around San Ildefonso blocked the arrival of direct sunlight. At seven o'clock when Main arrived the light was still gray-blue and the town seemed deserted. There was a light on at one corner of the zócalo and he parked just down from it.

He got out of his Caribe, set his camera bag on the hood, opened it and took out the automatic. He put it in his belt under his loose shirt. He didn't care if anyone saw him; it might be better if they knew he was armed. No matter what he wasn't going to pass unnoticed in this town and he wanted to be able to get at his gun if he needed to.

He looked around the zócalo. It was small and poorly tended but there were benches around the sides, big trees and a fairly elaborate gazebo. There was a church on one side and on the other three the buildings were uniform: low, adobe and picturesque, like the building behind Leopoldo Sanchez in the picture of him and his Silverado. He remembered Huerta's correction: they were not picturesque, just poor.

The thick-walled church listed noticeably and was shored up on one side by heavy tree trunks angled against the wall. It looked like it could date back to the colonial period and perhaps it did. Sister Remedios had said San Ildefonso was a mining town and the Spaniards had been very interested in mining.

He still didn't see any people but the animals seemed to know it was daytime. Chickens walked around on the paths of the zócalo. A donkey was tethered at a rail. A dog chased a family of pigs into the church, stopping at the threshold to bark at them, observing the rule of sanctuary.

Main walked toward the light on the corner. As he

approached he could read the hand-painted sign above the door: Conasupo, Tienda Rural. A government store. He wondered where the government clinic was, or if such a thing existed. A young boy — his first human being in San Ildefonso — left the store carrying a bag and was practically on Main before he looked up and saw him. He jumped a foot and hurried past, looking over his shoulder twice. No, he wouldn't pass unnoticed in this town.

He decided to walk around the town for a few minutes before going into the store, which would stay put. The streets were steep and irregular. They were mostly dirt, though every here and there islands of cobblestones stuck out between ruts. At one time the whole town had probably been cobblestoned. The sidewalks were so high in some places that steps led from the sidewalk down to the road. He supposed the streets flooded every year in the rainy season as the water rushed down from the surrounding mountains.

The town was tiny. Walking in more or less a straight line out from the zócalo, he reached the last houses in a few minutes. He walked the whole perimeter in less than fifteen. Everything he saw looked the same: old and adobe, picturesque or poor. He didn't find a government clinic or the one palatial residence he expected to find in an old mining town. He didn't see any place that Fausto was likely to be holding Richard prisoner.

If he had Richard. Main had to remind himself there were other reasons Richard might not have returned to his hotel room.

But in the gray-blue ghost town he had trouble believing in those other reasons.

It wasn't quite a ghost town anymore. In his walk around the perimeter he'd surprised a young boy and girl who had hurried off and then returned to follow him at a safe distance. By the time he got back to the store they'd picked up another kid somewhere.

They stayed outside when he went into the store, where an old woman stood behind an ancient cash register on a high wooden counter. She looked him over quickly and then stared past his shoulder. Had word already gotten around about the mysterious stranger or was this how all strangers were received in San Ildefonso? The store was gloomy, lit only by the gray-blue light coming in through the door and two high windows.

"*Buenos días,*" Main said.

She nodded at the empty space behind his left shoulder.

He looked around the store without moving. There were a few staples — masa, beans, rice — in bins on the floor. The shelves held a sparse, dusty assortment of canned foods. On a shelf behind the woman was a row of empty bottles indicating the store's collection of refrescos.

He smiled and pointed. *"Un Esquirt, por favor."*

The woman bent to slide back the cover of an old Pepsi ice box and took out a Squirt. Without straightening up she turned to the side of the ice box and fit the bottle into the cap remover. She put a little weight on the bottle, popping off the cap, and painfully straightened up to hand him the bottle.

He took a couple of gulps and smiled as if complimenting her on her soft drinks. As he drank the store perceptibly filled with light. The miraculous light didn't have any effect on the woman but Main went to the door. The gray-blue was gone and the zócalo was filling with light. He looked up to where the sun was just clearing a peak in the Sierra Madre to the east.

He went back in the store and said it looked like it was going to be a nice day. The woman just glanced at the door. Every day was the same in August.

He told her he was American, which was obvious, but she examined him a second time, more carefully, and looked off past his shoulder again. He said he had friends from San Ildefonso. She nodded politely but showed no interest, as if people were always dropping in from the States.

He said, "I'm a friend of Fausto Sanchez." There was no reaction so he said, "And Jaime Sanchez and Leopoldo Sanchez." Still no reaction.

He got out his pictures of Fausto and Jaime and Leopoldo. She glanced at them and shook her head. He put his picture of Richard and Josefina on the counter in front of her. She glanced at it and shook her head again.

"You don't know any of them?"

She shook her head.

"Not even the baby? I'm sure she's from here."

She shook her head again.

He went to the doorway to finish his Squirt. Everyone in town would know Leopoldo Sanchez, the hometown boy who'd made good and came back in a Silverado. If the old woman was denying knowing him she was indirectly telling him San Ildefonso had something to hide. But that didn't tell him anything he wasn't already sure of.

He looked at the group of kids hanging back. There were five of them now. An old man had taken a seat on a bench on the sidewalk and a woman was walking along the other side of the zócalo. The town was coming to life with the sunlight.

He watched the woman who was only in her thirties but already slack and used up from hard work and childbearing. He realized he hadn't seen an able-bodied man yet: They would be working all over North America, coming home just often enough to account for all the kids around.

He went back into the store, paid for the soft drink and thanked the old woman.

He went out and tried his bit about having friends from San Ildefonso on the old man and showed him his pictures. He seemed willing to talk but didn't have any teeth and Main couldn't understand him. He got the idea though. He didn't know his friends.

There were six kids in the group now and they were closer than they had been when he first went into the store. He crossed over to a bench in the zócalo and the children followed in a minute, as he knew they would. They formed a group again, closer yet. They all had teeshirts of some kind, all but the youngest had pants, only three had shoes. They were good-looking kids.

"*Cómo se llaman?*" he asked.

A couple of them were overcome with shyness and looked down. The others smiled and one intrepid one answered his question: "Jose."

He asked the rest of them one by one and they answered, nudging each other and laughing. The intrepid one asked him what his name was. They all laughed and tried to say it. It came out Call-bean.

They had been inching closer. He took out his pictures of Fausto and Leopoldo and Jaime and held them out so the children could see them. Conversationally he said, "*Mis amigos.*"

Curiosity got the better of them and they took the last few steps to get a better look.

Main said, "Do you know them?"

They conferred and the spokesboy said, "Sure. They're gringos."

Main smiled. It was a nice twist, these kids thinking of Fausto and the others as gringos. They were, though, driving around in a Silverado. Trying not to show too much interest he said, "They here now?"

The boy shrugged.

"When was the last time you saw them?"

They didn't know.

He took out his picture of Richard and Josefina and told them he had another friend. They nodded.

"Do you know him?"

They nodded confidently.

"When was he here?"

That was a harder question, but after comparing impressions they decided it was yesterday.

"What did he do while he was here?"

That question was much too hard.

He took out his wallet and opened it. There was a picture of Ingrid behind a plastic window. It was already a bit of a shock to see her staring out at him; it seemed like months ago she'd walked out. He took the picture out and passed it to the ringleader. He thought he recognized this friend too and passed it around to the other kids, who were pretty sure....

He reached out for the picture, wishing he hadn't introduced a control into his experiment. The kids were saying they recognized Ingrid just to be helpful, but he had the impression they really had recognized the others. The recognition had been quicker, more certain. Why had he confused the issue, and himself?

"Where is the clinic?" he asked.

They all looked at each other. It wasn't a yes/no question so it was tougher. The boy made a vague gesture over his shoulder.

"Are you sure there is a clinic here?"

The boy nodded and then punched the boy next to him, changing the topic very effectively. As the boys were clowning around two older girls hurried into the zócalo and approached the children purposefully. They had obviously been sent and began rounding up the children.

Main tried to get them to look at his pictures but they wouldn't. They wouldn't look at him directly either and he felt he had the evil eye. He tried one more question before they got away: "Señoritas, where is the clinic, please?"

Without looking at him one of the girls said distinctly, "No hay," as she herded the younger ones away.

There was no clinic. That was easy enough to believe. Fausto could have found someone to forge the clinic papers, especially because Sister Remedios didn't really care, thinking the babies were all refugee orphans anyway.

Just to make sure he went back to the store and asked the old woman several times about the clinic until she finally answered him to get rid of him. There was no clinic.

He left the store and crossed aimlessly over to the church, to think, to get away from the eyes he imagined behind the chinks in the shutters.

The church was cool and very dark. The only windows were high and tiny, set in three-foot-thick walls, which confirmed that the church probably was colonial. As his eyes adjusted he could make out tattered oil paintings along the walls, the Stations of the Cross. The paintings themselves could have been a hundred years old.

There was a small chapel with a crucifix that made the one in the orphanage seem repressed. A thousand pinpricks of blood dotted the painted plaster; a real crown of thorns sat on the head; the hair was matted; the face was almost covered with blood; the knees were torn; lips of purple flesh curled away from the wound in the side.

On the other side there was a chapel to the Virgin. With the Christ on the crucifix as the alternative it was clear why Mexicans were drawn to the Virgin. This one was only about two feet high and was dressed in a fancy lace dress. She looked almost like a doll except for the suffering, understanding eyes. There were rows of votive lights in front of her, several of them lit ruby red. On the wall next to her were milagros attesting to her intercession: a couple of little silver arms, a leg, a curled old photo of a baby.

He stood in front of the candles. He was alone, so he could think, but what was there to think about? He had learned nothing, absolutely nothing, that would help him. San Ildefonso was his last lead, what was he going to do next? Light a candle to the Virgin and promise to put the picture of Richard and Josefina on the wall if She helped him find them?

He left the church. The sun outside was even brighter after the dark church. He squinted until his eyes readjusted and when they did he saw the town was deserted again. He'd turned it into a ghost town with his questions. He started slowly walking through the streets again. He wondered if the consul could have DEA agents come out to the town.... To do what exactly?

He wanted to talk to Fausto. Yesterday Dedo had been following him and now that he wanted to talk to them there was no one in sight. People fled from him.

He turned a corner and surprised a woman crossing the street. She doubled her pace to get away but he ran after her and took her by the elbow. She was terrified. He held her tight while he dug out the picture of Fausto one more time. "Where can I find Fausto?" The poor woman shook her head helplessly. "You sell him babies, don't you?" She shook her head weakly and he let go of her. She crossed herself quickly and hurried into a doorway, closing and bolting the door, trembling after her encounter with the Evil One.

He walked back to the Caribe and sat in the driver's seat to go through it one more time. Richard had been to San Ildefonso yesterday, if he was to believe the kids, and he did. He had never come back to the hotel.

He had disappeared, or *been* disappeared. And he didn't know what to do next.

He got out of the car, took his gun out of his belt and fired twice into the air. *"Busco a Fausto Sanchez,"* he shouted at the empty streets. "I'm looking for you Fausto!"

He fired again and shouted the name of his hotel twice: Hotel Los Sabalos.

He drove very slowly out of town, stopping once more to fire the gun and shout his message. Even the chickens disappeared. It was like a Western.

It was stupid. He wasn't in charge of anything. He drove slowly back to Mazatlán, giving the black Riviera plenty of time to catch up, but it never did.

THIRTY-ONE

Back at the hotel he checked with the desk to see if Richard had returned. He hadn't and there were no messages for him.

He went to a corner table in the lobby bar to wait and see if Fausto would take him up on his invitation. From his table, with his back to the wall, he could see the entrance to the hotel and most of the lobby.

He drank a couple of coffees very slowly and watched the entrance. That took about an hour. He abandoned his post long enough to buy a Cuban cigar in the lobby gift shop and returned to his table. He smoked a couple of inches of the cigar and put it out. When his watch had crept around to a quarter to twelve he asked the bar waiter to place an order for him in the restaurant. He asked for everything he could think of to make the meal last as long as possible: soup, ceviche, barbecued fish, coconut ice cream. He forced himself through the meal, trying to ignore the sick feeling that Richard really had disappeared and he didn't know where to look. What good had his dramatics in San Ildefonso done? If you thought about it, why should Fausto want to contact him? What was in it for him?

He went and checked the desk again for messages and went back to his table. He did what years of waiting for people had taught him to do: shut off and watch. No thoughts; let his mind be a screen and see if anyone walked onto it. The difference was this time he wasn't waiting for a faithless spouse to come out of a motel and his hand was on his camera bag because that's where his gun was, not so he could grab his camera and get the evidence.

Somehow he didn't see Dedo come through the entrance. He was already in the middle of the screen, the middle of the lobby,

when Main snapped to and glanced quickly at his watch. He had
been blank for exactly an hour and thirteen minutes.

Dedo was slouching toward his table, in dark glasses and a
Hawaiian shirt. When he finally got there, he dropped wearily
into the chair across from Main and said, "Main." He began waving
for the waiter with slow exasperation.

"Hiss," Main said, but Dedo kept waving, showing off his
mutilated hand.

"You got my message."

"Don' know nothi' 'bou no message."

When the waiter arrived Dedo ordered a Planter's Punch and
charged it to Main's room. Main nodded his okay to the waiter.

Dedo turned his chair away from the table, stretched his legs
out in front of him and slid low in the seat. He took a box of Clásico
matches and a pack of Delicados from his Hawaiian shirt and lit
one. He inhaled once and put his elbow on the table, supporting his
head in his hand; the cigarette in his hand seemed to stick right
out of his short thick hair. He held the box of matches in his other
hand, between the first and third fingers, in the hole where his
middle finger should have been, and idly shook it.

Main said, "To what do I owe the pleasure?"

Dedo looked at him with no expression. The dark glasses were
impenetrably black and slightly iridescent. The waiter arrived
with his drink. Dedo tasted it, made a face and poured three little
packets of sugar into it. He tasted the drink again and it seemed to
be all right.

"So," Main prompted.

Dedo shook the match box again, holding it up and looking at
it. "These boxes crack me up." He handed the box to Main, who
glanced at it. It showed a painting of a train passing through
maguey fields and said, Alfonso Muriera, 1834-1886. Dedo said,
"Who *are* all these fucking landscape painters? Every box is
different. *You* ever fucking see a landscape painter in Mexico?"

"No."

Dedo reached over for his box again, giving Main a good look
at the fresh needle marks on the inside of his arm. It hadn't taken
him long to find a hobby when he got out of prison.

"Where's Fausto?" Main said.

"He wanna talk wi' jou," Dedo said. He took off his dark
glasses. His pupils were pinpoints in the shaded bar.

"Here I am."

"He don' wanna come here. He's the discrete type."

"I don't want to go there. I'm the cautious type."

"Up to you." Dedo picked up his drink and downed most of the tall glass. "You da one been askin' questions."

Dedo got up with a show of fatigue — protesting the things life imposed on him — and began his slow walk to the door.

Main got up and followed — because they'd called his bluff, or because he didn't know what else to do, or because he'd slept with Carmen, or because he knew he wanted to again. He didn't know but he followed, thinking almost calmly that he was going to die for it.

They got in the dusty black Riviera and headed south through the various strata of tourist hotels. Main asked once, "Where's Richard?"

Dedo shrugged and they didn't talk any more.

When they stopped they were all the way downtown where the fishing boats were pulled up on the sand. The area was full of cheap restaurants, cheap bars, cheap hotels and no tourists. They were parked across the street from a hotel that said, "Hotel Viajero — Precios Económicos." Traveler's Hotel — Cheap: what kind of hotel was that? A tired-looking woman in a shiny miniskirt sat on the steps in front of the hotel making the answer pretty obvious.

"That's where Fausto is?"

Dedo laughed and opened the glove compartment, taking out a thick envelope. "Spend a couple years in prison you have a hard-on *all* the time."

He got out and floated between the cars stopped at a red light. By the time Main gave in to the game and got out the light had changed and he risked his life getting across.

When he went up the stairs to the hotel the woman in the mini-skirt gave him a tired look, thinking it was going to be one of those evenings that started in the middle of the afternoon. To her relief, he went on by her and into the hotel, into a lobby the size of a postage stamp, with four green chairs, one of which held a girl about fourteen and another a woman between thirty and forty.

Dedo was at the counter across from the chairs. There was a man behind the counter and another at the end, leaning against it. The man behind the counter was opening the envelope Dedo had given him and was looking in it. He reached under the counter and took out another envelope which he handed to Dedo. Dedo opened it, glanced in, closed it and put it in his front pocket.

"Aren't you going to count it?" the man behind the counter asked.

Dedo shook his head. "Mine's right so I *know* yours will be."

The man nodded.

Main felt almost disappointed: the terrible, brilliant Fausto was involved in entry level door-to-door pushing. He'd done all he'd done to be able to sell envelopes of heroin to whores at Traveler's Hotel — Cheap.

Dedo didn't seem to mind starting at the bottom. He turned away from the clerk and looked at the two women in the green chairs. He went over to the older one who was painting her nails. She studiously concentrated on her nails, hoping he'd go away. He said, *"Conchita, mi paloma."* He held out his hand.

Conchita, not looking anything like his dove, looked up resignedly. She held out the hand she hadn't been painting and he hoisted her onto her beaded high-heeled sandals and nodded at the clerk who tossed him a key.

Dedo pointed from the clerk to Main and the clerk threw Main another key, nodding in the direction of the barely teenage girl. Main threw the key back to him.

Dedo, the clerk and the man leaning against the counter all laughed. Dedo said, "You ought to do some time. Get it up for you."

The man leaning against the counter acted it out for him: he lifted his arms from his sides as if lifting a barbell and at the same time slowly curved his pelvis up, bit his lower lip and sucked in noisily. The other two laughed.

Main went up to Dedo and said, "You're absolutely sure I'm going to see Fausto when this show is over?"

Still laughing Dedo said, "Sure, man, sure." He still had Conchita by the hand.

Main grabbed him by the throat and threw him against the wall. Conchita let go of his hand with a little cry. Dedo, full of enough anesthesia to ignore the hand on his throat, was still smiling defiantly. Main squeezed tighter, cutting off his air, and Dedo began to pay attention. He kept the pressure on. Dedo tried to kick him between the legs but he twisted to the side. Dedo held still, his eyes growing wider. Squeezing just a bit tighter Main said, "I don't handle stress well and I want to see Fausto."

He let go and for a moment Dedo slumped back against the wall and caught his breath. He straightened up, rubbed his neck and twisted his head. Then without saying anything he gallantly held out his elbow to Conchita and said, "*Mi paloma?*" They started up the stairs, slowly. Conchita wobbled on her high heels, waving one hand to dry her nails.

Main left, ignoring the other two men in the lobby, and crossed the street to an open air restaurant on the beach, which consisted of a thatched roof supported by poles over a concrete slab. He had a coke. He could still feel the adrenaline. I don't handle stress well! Where was this coming from? Firing a gun in the empty streets, slamming a junkie against a whorehouse wall. He was losing control but it seemed almost funny to him, and there'd been a low pleasure in it, he couldn't deny that. It had something to do with the equation of his life these days: My life minus Ingrid plus Carmen minus Richard times Fausto equals Throw Dedo against a Wall. The adrenaline was calming down.

He watched the fishermen on the sand below the restaurant as they cleaned the last of the day's catch. Pelicans thronged around the boats, fighting for the guts and illustrating the survival of the greediest.

He finished his coke and went back to the hotel. Conchita was already back in her green chair in the lobby, working on her nails again. The teenage girl, to make the scene too perfect, was reading a romance comic called Devouring Love: *El Amor Devorador*. The clerk was working with a calculator and the other man was gone.

Main looked at Conchita questioningly. She pointed up the stairs with her whole hand, her fingers spread like a fan, and shrugged. He looked at the clerk, who told him the room number. No one seemed too concerned about saving Dedo.

He went up the stairs to the room and opened the door. Dedo was on the bed, naked, lost to the world. On the table next to the bed were a syringe, a rubber tube, a spoon, the box of matches he'd shown Main earlier, and a bunch of burnt matches. Main doubted he'd had any use for Conchita, prison term or not. He'd just wanted to shoot up. And he'd taken off his clothes to... for what? For some more comedy, for some more shit for Main to deal with. Another rush of anger was starting.

He went to the bed and roughly shook Dedo. He opened his eyes and then let them drift closed again. Main swore, grabbed his clothes off the floor, propped him into a sitting position, got his arm across his chest in a lifesaving grip and dragged him down the hall. Dedo opened his eyes once, looked around, alert enough to decide everything was okay, and closed them again. Main let his heels bounce on the stairs as he went down.

When he got to the lobby Main dropped Dedo on the floor and threw his clothes on top of him.

"*Hijo de la chingada,*" the clerk swore approvingly.

Conchita smiled and looked at the girl in the chair down from her. Even the woman in the mini-skirt came in from her post on the sidewalk. Main seemed to be winning over the whorehouse.

Dedo came to — Main doubted he'd ever really been out — and smiled vaguely.

"Somebody going to dress him or do I take him like this?" Main asked.

The clerk shook his head, smiling, and gestured to Conchita and the girl. They protested, then went to work on Dedo. As they were dragging his pants on, Main reached into the front pocket to get out his car keys. Main told them to skip the shirt and the shoes. He dragged Dedo to his feet and the girl gave him Dedo's Hawaiian shirt and the shoes. He slapped Dedo hard and handed him the clothes to carry. Dedo smiled dreamily. "Now walk," Main said and grabbed his arm above the elbow.

They crossed the street. Dedo was doing better. When they got to the Riviera Dedo leaned his elbows on the roof while Main opened the passenger door. He took Dedo by the arm again and jerked him from his resting position. He pushed him into his seat and bent over to get his legs in. Suddenly he felt a sharp point in the middle of his spine. It was very hard, very small and concentrated.

He was still bent over and a voice behind him said in Spanish, "Behave or you'll be in a wheelchair for the rest of your life."

"Fausto." Main straightened up very slowly.

THIRTY-TWO

Fausto slipped the camera bag off Main's shoulder and took his arm in a vise grip just above the elbow. He told Dedo to get in the driver's seat, and when Dedo climbed over the emergency brake, he seemed fairly revived. Fausto still had the point of the knife against Main's spine and while they waited for Dedo to change seats he kept whispering, "Paraplegic, paraplegic."

Fausto pushed Main to get in and Main saw him for the first time: hawk profile, hollow cheeks, sunglasses, long black hair combed straight back. Fausto leaned in and placed the point of the knife against his neck. With his free hand he checked him for a weapon. He was wearing a Philipe Patek watch with a gold band: Richard's watch. Main watched the hand with Richard's watch move over his chest, armpits, sides, the waistband of his pants, crotch, thighs, calves.

Fausto got in the back seat. Main heard him unzip the camera bag. "Bingo," Fausto said. "Real shutterbug."

Dedo laughed and Main felt his own automatic at the base of his neck. It felt blunt after the knife.

"You too fucked up to drive or what?" Fausto said to Dedo.

Dedo seemed focused enough to drive but he still wasn't going to pass any reflex test . He pulled into the traffic and made a U-turn. After a couple of blocks he turned right, away from the water.

Dedo turned to him. "Shouldna hurt me, fucker."

"He hurt you Dedo? That what you saying? He hurt you?" He poked the back of Main's neck with the gun as he spoke, his voice full of sickly concern.

He dropped a pair of sunglasses over Main's shoulder and told him to put them on. They were fisherman's sunglasses with contoured side panels to keep out the glare and an elastic athletic band between the two earpieces. He put them on and felt Fausto's fingers tightening the band. He waited for his eyes to adjust to the darkness, but they didn't.

The insides of the glasses were painted black. He felt a rush of panic as he realized this. He took a deep breath and — senselessly — closed his eyes for a moment. It made the darkness seem natural.

Main said, "You disappoint me." His voice sounded tinny and far away to him. It sounded like the voice of someone who was scared trying to pretend he wasn't. "Pushing dope in cheap whorehouses. That's the best you can do with all the money you made with the babies?"

Fausto just laughed through his nose.

"Where's Richard?" Main said.

"What is this shit, nervous chatter?" It was Fausto again, a voice coming out of the blackness.

Main gave up and sat wide-eyed in complete darkness. He knew they were going to kill him. They had no doubt already killed Richard. Or were they still holding Richard prisoner? Would he see him before they were both killed? He was going to be dead. That would give him plenty to think about without asking stupid questions in a tinny voice. He kept seeing Richard's gold watch as Fausto's hand patted him down. Sunlight flashing off the gold watch, his dead friend's watch.

In a few minutes they stopped and Main could hear the traffic whizzing by. They turned right and accelerated. Main knew they had turned onto the freeway, Nacional 15, and were heading south: the first leg of the jaunt to San Ildefonso. In about fifteen minutes they turned left, east: the second leg. In another fifteen minutes or so they turned left again, onto a dirt road to judge by the bumps. San Ildefonso was down a dirt road but one that was off to the right of the main road. So they were somewhere near San Ildefonso, but not at San Ildefonso itself.

A hundred or a hundred and fifty yards down the dirt road they stopped and Main felt the automatic nudging his neck again. "Leave the glasses on," Fausto said.

Fausto got out, opened Main's door and reached in to help him out. He held his elbow like they were going to the junior prom. They took a few steps and Dedo came up to his other side, grabbing that elbow. He walked between the two of them, tripping a couple of times on the uneven path.

Then suddenly he lost his footing completely and would have fallen if they hadn't had him by the elbows. After he'd tripped down three or four steps, Fausto said, "Steps."

They took a few more of the steps and stopped. Fausto let go of his arm and went off to the right. Main heard the sound of metal hinges opening and then the sound of metal on metal, like tools in a toolbox.

Dedo still had him by the other arm. The air had changed. It was wet and cool now, old and still.

Main shouted, "Richard!"

Fausto laughed. "Shout all you like. It's no good to bottle things up."

Richard's name echoed somewhere ahead of them.

Fausto came back to them and Main heard two clicks. He gave something to Dedo.

Main said, "Flashlights."

"Clever boy," Fausto said.

"This is a mine."

"This is not a fucking IQ test."

Fausto hit him on the shoulder with the flashlight, grabbed his arm above the elbow again and they started off with a jerk. The path became steeper and slipperier. A couple times Main stepped in puddles deeper than the tops of his shoes and the cool air was becoming almost cold. They were walking fast and Main stumbled between them. Suddenly he smacked his head against a low rock and shouted in surprise.

Dedo said, "Watch out."

Fausto laughed, "Duck."

They started again and Main walked stooped forward. Every reflex told him to go slow but he was propelled along at each elbow. After another ten or fifteen steps the hands suddenly let go and he walked into space, landing with a wrenching thud. Perhaps he'd only fallen two or three feet but he'd sprained his ankle. They laughed and jumped down beside him.

"Watch your step," Fausto said.

They took him by the elbows again and hauled him up. They took another twenty steps or so and let go of him again.

"Go on," Fausto said.

Main put his foot out and felt around. Fausto laughed and shoved him from behind. His shoulder hit a rock wall. "Sideways," Fausto said and pushed again. He turned sideways

and felt the rock wall at his back. He took a couple steps and felt a
rock wall against his chest too. He stopped in an attack of panic —
he was in the black, closed in, with two psychotics. Fausto pushed
again and he took another step, trying to make his chest small.

Fausto was right behind him, prodding with the flashlight.
He took one more step and was able to breathe more easily, another
and he didn't feel the wall at his back. He took two more steps and
was in some kind of chamber. Fausto squeezed in behind him, then
Dedo. Main took a couple more careful steps and bumped into a wall
again. It was a small chamber, then.

"At ease, soldier," Fausto said.

Dedo came up to him and took his hands, placing them behind
his back. He coiled a cord around his wrists three times, then knelt
behind him and rapped his twisted ankle with the flashlight
until Main placed his two feet together. Then Dedo wound the cord
around his ankles three times and stood up.

Suddenly, simultaneously, his wrists flew back and his lower
legs flew up, bending at the knees. He crashed onto the rock floor,
landing on his knees and pitching forward onto his chin. He could
feel blood run onto his neck and heard more laughter. It took him a
second to figure out what had happened: Dedo had yanked on the
piece of cord connecting his wrists and ankles, pulling his legs out
from under him.

Dedo knelt down next to him and pulled on the same piece of
cord until his wrists and ankles were practically touching behind
him and tied some kind of knot in the rope to hold him in that
position. He was arched back, trussed. The muscles in his thighs,
stomach and shoulders were all taut. The immobility brought
another rush of panic.

"Shouldna hurt me, fucker," Dedo said. Main felt an explosion
of pain in his knee and screamed. The burst of light behind his lids
was the first light since they'd made him put on the glasses. The
light slowed to a swimming motion and he fought not to vomit.

"Dedito," Fausto said scoldingly. "Time out, Dedito."

"Just one more. The other knee."

Fausto clucked. "We'll go have a smoke." Main realized he
was speaking to him. "Let Dedito cool off."

They both laughed and squeezed out of the little chamber,
through the opening in the rocks. Main felt an intense relief. The
next kick, push, fall, wouldn't be for... for what? A minute, an hour,
a day? The relief was only temporary. What difference did it

make? They'd be back. In a way knowing that was worse than actually being inside the violence and the panic started again. At first it was like something filling his chest and making it hard to breath.

He thought: an hour, a day. Or if they never came back? He'd end up an arched-back skeleton. How long could he be tied like that without going insane? The sensation in his chest was changing. It felt hollow and black wings were beating in the empty cage. He was in a racing, suffocating panic.

His imagination threw out images: Leopoldo Sanchez bent over his wheel with his eye on his cheek, the photo Huerta had shown him of the body with the brown lump on the stomach — the boy's heart. He was covered in cold sweat and fighting for breath...

He had to stop. He told himself he had to stop. He didn't know whether he'd said it out loud or just thought it. He knew he was hyperventilating and forced himself to count five slow breaths.

It would help to *do* something. He rubbed the side of his head on the rock floor, trying to catch the fisherman's glasses on something. After a couple of tries he was able to get them up onto his forehead. He waited for sight to come back but it didn't. He thought he knew where the opening in the rocks was but he couldn't make anything out. It was pitch black, darker than the darkest bedroom with the darkest curtains on the darkest night, like the idea of black because nothing in the real world could be so absolutely black.

The pressure in his chest was starting again. He had to find something else to do, if there was anything he *could* do in his new shrunken, immobile world.

He stretched his fingers out behind him and moved his wrists the little bit he could. With his thumb he was just able to touch a bit of the cord between his wrists and his ankles, but he couldn't do anything with it. He could strum himself with his thumb.

What else could he try? He was strung so tight he could only move his hips an inch or two. He tried it a few times and moved a few inches across the floor. But what for? He had to find a reason to inch around the floor. Perhaps if he could find a rough spot, he could fray the rope on his wrists. He inched across the floor on his side, feeling the rock with his fingers....

There was a change, a slight diminishment of the blackness, then light and sounds: they were coming. For a split second he was almost excited, someone was coming, then the panic started again: the someone was *them*.

The flashlight came through the opening first, blinding him with its light. When he opened his eyes Fausto was bent over him with the flashlight pointed away from him.

"Shit," Fausto said with exasperation. "He took off the goddamned glasses."

"Damn," Dedo said.

Fausto located the glasses with the flashlight and went to get them. He came back with them and knelt next to Main. He said, "Calvin, the glasses are part of it. Don't fuck with the script. I put a lot of thought into these things." He dangled the glasses in front of Main, holding them by the athletic band.

Main watched light glint off Richard's gold watch. The fisherman's glasses reminded him of the consul, the great fisherman. The consul wouldn't have a clue where to look for him. If he would want to. For all he knew the glasses were the consul's. He imagined Fausto and Dedo and the consul all out on a boat, fighting marlin and arranging heroin shipments. Anything was possible. It was something he'd never know.

Fausto got the glasses on him again and tightened the band in back. The absolute darkness came down again. There was a moment's silence, then Fausto said, "I don't know," as if he'd been examining a problem from every angle and didn't know what to make of it.

"I don' know," Dedo said, sounding as tired as Fausto.

"So, Calvin, what exactly do you want?" Fausto asked.

Main hadn't expected a question, hadn't expected to participate, didn't see how he could. "Isn't it obvious?" he managed, in a voice that didn't sound like his.

"Well, I suppose you want Richard and little, uh, what's her name" — he snapped his fingers — "ah, yes, little Josefina. Is that it?"

Main didn't say anything.

"I guess I got that part, right Calvin? But here's the part I don't get: what's in it for us? You're not in a very strong bargaining position, tied up on the floor there, know what I mean?"

Main didn't answer and Fausto continued the conversation with Dedo: "You know what I mean, Dedo? I suppose if he had Richard and Josefina he'd leave us alone but I can't help thinking he'd leave us alone too if we just killed him. Know what I mean?"

Dedo grunted. He knew what he meant.

Main wasn't really listening any more. He was concentrating on his chest and his breathing

After another pause Fausto said, "So what do you think, Dedo? Kill him or let him go?"

"Well, you know me, Fausto."

"I sure do, but you know, it's almost easier to let him go, 'cause if we kill him we have to decide *how* and there's *so* many ways..."

"Un sacrificio?" Dedo suggested enthusiastically.

"That was great but we already did it. Unless..." He paused to think. "Nah."

"Come on, Fausto, what is it?"

"Well, you know that shaft full of water, with the steep sides. How long do you think he could swim around in there before he went under?"

"Long time, don't you think?"

"We could do that, like a Mayan sacrifice. You know, how they'd throw a virgin in a cenote."

"You think he's a virgin, Fausto?"

"You work with what you've got, Dedo." There was a long pause and Main listened to the wings beating in his chest. Fausto let out a sigh. "Decisions, decisions. You know, when I was a kid," he said dreamily, "my mother used to have this book about saints. I used to love that book. You can't believe all the ways they had to kill those saints. The thing was they had all this technology we don't have. Big rotisseries, winches, pulleys. Not to mention the animals, the horses and lions. You know where we can get a lion, Dedo?"

"Uhhhhhhhhh...."

"See what I mean. On the other hand, you don't really need all that stuff. It's incredible what you can do with a simple knife, you use your imagination."

"A knife!" Dedo said, admiring Fausto's brilliance.

"Just takes a little imagination is all. Right Calvin?" Fausto nudged his foot with a toe. "But I don't know." He sounded tired again, back at square one. "Maybe what we really need to do is think on it some more. What do you think, Dedo? Give it a little more thought?"

"Yeah, more thought."

They went to the opening in the rocks. Dedo must have squeezed through first because Fausto had the time to mutter thoughtfully, "Just a knife," mulling it over.

Main wasn't going to think about it. He began inching across the floor looking for a rough spot. Finally he found a section of wall where two pieces met unevenly and positioned himself so he could rub the rope against the tiny ledge. He couldn't move his arms enough to do any good and had to make a jerky movement with his whole body to rub the rope on the stone. He couldn't feel it with his fingers to see if he was making any progress. Each movement hurt the stretched muscles and tense joints but he kept going until he collapsed, drenched in sweat.

As he caught his breath, he remembered things. Being a few minutes or hours from dying changed the proportions of his life. His years with Ingrid collapsed into a moment. His hour with Carmen that week seemed to fill up a lot of his life. He remembered things he hadn't remembered for years and wasn't sure why they came back to him now.

When he caught his breath and the sweat began to cool, he began again. As he was beginning to work up another sweat he heard them coming again and stopped rubbing. They were talking and then they laughed. One of them was squeezing through the opening, then the other one squeezed through.

"Well, Calvin." It was Fausto. "Guess you're wondering what we've decided."

The question was followed by another detonation of pain — the same knee again. He screamed and then, as soon as he could draw a breath, gasped and then moaned. What difference did it make? Who was there to be a hero for in this black hole?

"Goddammit, Dedo."

"Fucker shouldna hurt me."

Fausto made a disgusted sound, then said, "Anyway, Calvin, I guess you're wondering." He paused for Main to say something but he didn't. Fausto said, "Well, we've decided to let you go."

Before he could say anything, before he could even think anything, Dedo came over to him and bent over to the bit of cord between his wrists and his ankles. He was lying on his side with his wrists to the stone wall. Dedo grabbed the cord and yanked up on it, dropping him onto his belly, like a rockinghorse. He screamed again at the pain in his shoulders but in a way it hardly registered. It was just more pain. They'd do something, he'd scream, but it was losing meaning.

Dedo went to work on the knots on his hands, sending minor

jolts of pain down to his shoulders, then the cord went slack. But his arms and legs stayed up behind him, frozen in their positions. Dedo pushed down on his hands and he cried out again. When Dedo kicked his legs down he managed not to make any noise. He gritted his teeth and lay still getting used to the new circuits of pain Dedo had opened up. Dedo undid the knots on his ankles.

"That better?" Fausto asked solicitously.

"Why," Main said, "are you letting me go?" He couldn't believe he was saying it.

"Why! You never heard about gift horses?"

"Where's Richard?"

"Where's Richard? Hey, Dedo, this guy's a regular bulldog." He made some growling sounds.

"He alive?"

"Guess so, I dunno. Look, you find out, hunh. You're the fucking detective, right. Should be easy for a detective to find. Big fucker, curly hair, jeans and a teeshirt with an artichoke on it, packing a big fucking gun."

They grabbed him by the armpits and hoisted him to his feet. One of them checked the glasses again and tightened the elastic in back.

Main said, "That's a nice watch you're wearing, Fausto."

"Yeah, great watch," Fausto said.

One of them hit him across the mouth. He sucked in the blood. Predictably it was Dedo, who said, "Shouldna hurt me *pinche puto.*"

They got him out of the mine the way they'd got him in, tripping and stumbling.

They went up the last few stairs and into the warm outside air. They stood for a moment catching their breaths. Then they walked and there were sounds: leaves and soil crunching beneath their feet. It was still dark behind the dark glasses but it was almost bright compared to the blackness of the mine pit. He hurt in so many places he could hardly keep them straight, but now each pain seemed like a sign of life.

He was alive. He didn't know why and he'd think about it later, some other time.

He heard the car door open and they pushed him inside. He fell into the seat and got his legs in. The seat was soft. The air was warm and full of smells he hadn't noticed before.

They drove back. He concentrated on his breathing, keeping it even, and counted the breaths as they drove down out of the mountains to connect with Nacional 15. One hundred and sixty-eight breaths. He could use that.

Once they were on 15 again he didn't pay attention. He didn't think. He didn't feel glad to be alive or anything else. Now that he had time he could put things off. Maybe it was shock.

Eventually they stopped and Dedo turned off the engine.

Main said, "Where's Richard?"

"You're a helluva guy, Cal," Fausto laughed. He got out of the back seat and opened Main's door for him. "You going to get out or what?"

Main got out and heard Fausto get in the front seat. He felt something touch his hand and he took it: it was his camera bag. The engine started and the car pulled away.

He stood there for a moment in the black glasses, then took them off. He immediately squeezed his eyelids shut against the blaze of light. The sunlight flared behind his lids like a film of the sun: yellows, oranges, purples, dark spots.

Why was he alive?

THIRTY-THREE

He walked through the lobby, slowly and stiffly, vaguely aware of the desk personnel in guayaberas watching him. He went straight to the gardens and limped past the pool to the cabana bar just above the sand. He got himself up onto a high stool and the man and woman next to him moved away. The barman was down at the other end of the open-air bar, talking to a couple with lobster complexions. Everyone seemed bright red and was making a lot of noise. He looked at his watch. It was six thirty — happy hour.

The barman saw him and quickly looked away. Main aimed a "Pssst," right at his ear. Everyone at the bar looked at him: that wasn't the way tourists did it at happy hour. The barman reluctantly came down to him.

"Tequila, lime, salt," Main said.

"Are you all right, sir?"

"Had an accident, nothing serious."

The barman nodded impassively and went to get the tall shot glass, the lime, salt and the bottle of tequila. Main tried to do some arithmetic. It was about six-thirty. Allowing for driving time he couldn't have been in the mine for more than about two and a half hours. Time hadn't held up. The experience in the mine had seemed endless, timeless, out of time. He couldn't have said how long it had felt.

The barman came pack and poured him his drink, then watched him try to get it to his mouth with a shaky hand. He spilled some of it, threw the rest down and set the glass on the counter, pointing at it for a refill.

"Are you a guest of the hotel, sir?"

"Lazarus, room 666." He pointed at his glass again.

"You're hurt." The barman pointed at his own chin, his own lip, his own forehead. "Perhaps you would like to wash up?" He pointed at the palm thatched restrooms a few yards from the bar.

Main started to tell him just to pour but realized the man was being helpful and thanked him. He got himself down from the stool and went to the men's room. He stared at himself in the mirror, leaning on the sink. No wonder people had moved away from him and the barman had suggested he wash up. The cuts on his lips and chin had bled down onto his neck but the rest of his face was a powdery gray, covered with some kind of mineral from the mine floor, except for his eyes, which were immaculate and outlined in red where the fisherman's sunglasses had pressed into his skin. His face looked like a primitive mask, for use in some odd ceremony. Maybe that was one way to describe what had happened.

Suddenly he thought: Ingrid couldn't call *this* face uneventful. He laughed and it sounded too loud, like a bark. He shook with a violent tremor as if he'd just thrown down a shot of strong drink.

He took off his shirt which was smeared with the same gray as his face and threw it in the waste basket. He'd fit in a lot better at the bar barechested than wearing a filthy shirt, even though his skin was white compared to the vacationeers outside.

He turned on the tap and washed his face and hair as well as he could. He dried himself with paper towels and combed his hair. He took another look and had another uncontrollable shudder. He thought he'd better get back in the sun, though he knew the temperature wasn't the problem.

When he got back to his stool he picked up his camera bag and climbed up again. The barman, who had filled up his shotglass, nodded at his improved appearance. He picked up the tequila and got most of it to his mouth again. He pointed to the empty glass again and the barman came over to fill it. He asked for a pack of Delicados too. The man went off for the cigarettes.

He opened the camera bag. His gun was still there. He checked and they hadn't even taken out the clip. He wondered if it was some kind of insult but didn't really care.

The barman came back with the cigarettes and matches. Main picked up the pack and tried to get the little strip of red cellophane between his thumb and forefinger but they were shaking and he couldn't. The barman did it for him and tapped a cigarette loose, then lit a match for him. He probably figured he was a far-gone alcoholic.

He said, "What kind of accident did you have?"

"Fell."

Main raised the oval cigarette to his mouth. The trembling seemed to have gotten worse. The sweetened cigarette paper stuck to his lips. He drew a lungfull of the sweet-acrid smoke that was different from any other. The barman set the box of matches down and went to help another customer. Main looked at the box. This one showed a hacienda. No, he never *had* seen a landscape painter in Mexico.

He knocked back the tequila and got the barman's eye again. He seemed to hesitate so Main got out a bill and laid it on the counter to show this would be his last one. The man filled it up again and picked up the bill.

Main took a sip and turned his back to the bar, leaning back against it. He tried to relax but it wouldn't come. He wasn't relaxed, he was tense, exhilarated — alive! And he was shuddering every minute or so. He sat straight again, smoking and watching the sun, which was huge and orange and would hit the water in another half hour or forty-five minutes. The light was getting softer. It didn't sear his eyeballs the way it had when he got out of the car.

He was alive. Fausto was wearing Richard's watch. He refused to think about it for a few more minutes. He was alive and not fit for grief yet. He would get to it, he didn't doubt that. He would enjoy being alive for a few minutes more.

On the beach below him the last few vendors were trying to make a last sale. They had to stand outside a rope that marked off the public beach from the strip of hotel beach. The last sunbathers and coco loco drinkers ignored the vendors, who stood there silently raising and lowering their wares in a dumb show of poverty.

Main finished the tequila and got off the barstool. His knee didn't hurt as much as before, or if it did it didn't matter: the nerves were sending the message but his head didn't care any more. The tequila was working. Was he still shaking? He wasn't sure, maybe it had stopped.

He walked down to the beach and asked a couple who were drinking coco locos if they could watch his camera bag for a moment while he had a swim and they said they'd be glad to. He took off his shoes and his pants and the couple quickly looked away. He didn't try to explain that after spending an afternoon getting ready to die, he didn't see any really important reason not to swim in underwear.

He dove through the first row of breakers and swam to the second, diving through the swell. He swam hard for a few minutes until he was far out. He took off his underwear and held them, floating for a while. Being alive.

He felt better when he got out, calmer and some of the stiffness was gone. He put his pants on, went to the desk for his key and — back to being a bulldog and a helluva guy — asked if Richard was back. He wasn't and Main knew he was going to have to face it. He couldn't just go on Being Alive.

He went up, opened his door and threw his bag from the doorway onto his bed. As he did so he realized his shower was running and froze with fear — it all came back instantaneously, the wings, the suffocation. He closed his eyes and took a deep breath. Whatever was going on, it wasn't Dedo or Fausto taking a quick shower. He had to get a grip on himself.

He went to the bed, opened the camera bag and got out the automatic. He went to the bathroom door, turned the knob quietly and opened the door slowly. The shower curtain was solid blue plastic and he couldn't see who it was. He went to the wall next to the shower, leaned his back against it and held his gun shoulder high, as if he was going to burst through a door on a raid. He lowered his gun, he was overdoing it again. No one took a shower with an assault rifle. It was going to be a while before he could trust his reflexes again. He lifted a corner of the shower curtain.

The head was a mess of lather. As the fingers worked in the lather, the muscles moved in the back. He knew the back and the shape and just watched for a moment before he said, "This is a surprise."

She screamed and crouched, covering herself protectively. She looked over her shoulder, then straightened, taking deep breaths, her arms still modestly covering her breasts. "You scared me to death! Who do you think you are, Norman Bates?"

"*What*, Carmen, are you doing here?"

It took another moment for the startled look to fade from her eyes. She let out a long breath and said, "Jesus." She uncrossed her arms and tilted her head back under the nozzle to rinse it. She lifted her hands to her hair and the water and lather ran over her breasts in crazy patterns.

He felt a rush of desire so intense it almost paralyzed him for a moment, swooping down, slamming into place. He smiled as he watched her. It was true, then, what they said: nothing fanned the blood like the wings of death. This was why there were orgies in the shadows of the bubonic plague.

He got his shoes and pants off.

Carmen saw what he was doing and said, "I'm not going to have to seduce you this time."

"I'm alive!"

"What?"

He stepped into the shower, slipping, and she reached out to steady him. "I'll explain later." He pulled her to him. They kissed, slithering against each other and practically drowning under the shower. He got out and helped her out. He put his arms around her from behind and kissing her neck danced her into the room where they fell on the bed and made love.

When they finished his skin slipped over hers with each jagged breath. He paid attention to the breathing, the wet sliding skin, the heat: alive. He realized what he had done and tried not to look at it. He began to feel almost sick.

He lay still on Carmen and she drew some lazy pattern over and over again on the skin of his back. She said, "I decided to come when I got your message on the answering machine."

He lay under a black cloud of guilt and disbelief. He hadn't even thought of Richard from the moment he'd seen Carmen's back in the shower, until he was finished. He'd practically jumped on the dead man's fresh widow. He pushed himself up on his elbows. He had to find a way to tell her.

She was wet everywhere; her eyes were wet. She closed her eyelids and tears squeezed out between the lashes. It stopped him, it made him almost angry. He had to tell her about Richard, tell her how sorry he was, and she was already crying.

He tried to pull off her and she clamped him to her. He said, "I haven't found Richard yet, Carmen... I'm not... I'm not even sure he's alive." He stopped, a coward. He couldn't make himself tell her about the watch, say he knew Richard was dead.

"You can't think like that," she said. She rubbed his spine with her knuckles. "Tell me what you've been doing since the phone message."

Her tone was curious, conversational: grotesquely wrong. It assumed they were in the middle of something instead of at the end of it. He couldn't say what he had to say. He said, "I found Fausto

and Dedo." He stopped: *He'd* found *them!* His choice of words was
an evasion, an evasion was a lie.

"Where?"

"One hundred and sixty eight breaths east of 15 Nacional on
the Durango road."

"You're not making any sense." Her fingers massaged his spine.

"It's a long story," he said, trying to get off her again and
giving in again to her grip around his middle.

He began to tell her as she drew slow pictures on his back. He
told her what he'd done, who he'd talked to, but he didn't quite
come out and say what it added up to. He didn't tell her about the
watch. But he hinted: Richard hadn't been back to his room, it
looked bad, Fausto was unbalanced. His words sounded unreal to
him, like dream words. It was a dream situation, reporting on a
case, and pinned at the groin to his lover, his client, his dead best
friend's widow. A bad dream. And when he got out of it he'd look
worse.

When he finished she said, "You have no proof Richard is
dead. I don't think he is. Richard knows how to take care of
himself."

He gave up — not that he'd tried that hard. But maybe it was
better to give it some time. She wasn't going to hear him even if he
told her about the watch and did his best to convince her. It might
even be better if he let it sink in for the next few hours or days. It
was cowardly, but that didn't mean it wouldn't be better for
Carmen.

She put her arms around his neck and pulled him down on her
again, so tight it hurt. Better for Carmen! Didn't he *want* Richard
to be dead? Could he make himself say *that?*

It had been nice Being Alive, experiencing the explosion of joy.
Now it was coming back to him what his life was really like. Who
he really was. He began to struggle out of her clasp and she
suddenly laughed and put her palms on his chest pushing him
backwards: "You're crushing me."

"Make up your mind." He rolled off her and looked at the
ceiling.

"So what's next?" she asked: another life-as-usual question.

"I can go out there tomorrow and look for them." He didn't
know if he meant it or was just playing along, but the thought
turned his bones to water.

"I don't want you to get killed."

"Me neither."

She seemed sad but not really worried about any of it. She got up and went to the refrigerator and took out a couple of the mini-tequilas, found glasses and messed around with the ice. They were going to have drinks. It wasn't getting any realer.

She set the glasses down and went to the phone. She asked the desk to connect her with Richard's room and stood there while it rang several times. She hung up and said, "Still not back."

He didn't know what to say. He said, "Where are your things?"

"In Richard's room. My room, our room." She picked up her glass and went to the glass door to the balcony. She slid it back and said, "Come on."

"Carmen, you're not wearing any clothes."

"I'm on vacation. Come on." She stepped out onto the balcony.

He got off the bed, got his drink, went to the door and stuck his head out. Carmen leaned on the balcony wall, head and shoulders and breasts facing into the garish sunset like a figurehead on a ship headed into the sun. Main looked in both directions. No one else seemed to be out on their balcony.

He went to stand next to her and look at the hysterical sunset. Carmen said, "The sky is screaming."

He looked at her. That wasn't a life-as-usual sentiment. Maybe she was lining up with reality. He wasn't sure but he thought she was crying again. He would just have to let it take her the way it took her. She was getting it, she was going to get it.

"Are you all right?" he asked.

"No. I'm in love with you."

He put his hand on her shoulder. "That's not what I mean. I mean are you all *right?* Really."

"Yes." She took the step to him and put her hands on his shoulders. She raised herself on her tiptoes to kiss him and he felt the lines her nipples traced on his skin.

"Again?" he asked doubtfully — how was he going to get out of this situation, get her out of it?

She moved her lips from his, to his neck and throat. "Once more," she mumbled. "Yes."

"I don't know...."

"It's very important to me." She looked at him and reached down to take his penis in her fingers, making some slight, coaxing motions. Then she looked down, continuing her motions, watching

him seriously, almost studiously, until he was ready. Then she
squeezed hard and said, "This way."

She turned her back to him without letting go and leaned over
the balcony again. She guided him into her and they made love
into the sunset. He thought they must look like a pornographic
travel poster — Visit Savage Mazatlán — as they made love
slowly and he slipped into a degraded moment of truth: she was all
he really wanted, the rest was just pretending.

When they were finished they sank to the floor. Carmen said,
"We will never forget that one. That's why I wanted it, darling."

THIRTY-FOUR

He was out, on his bed, sleeping uneasily but profoundly. He would awaken from time to time, a bit of the day would come to him, and he would slip under again. He would remember a bit from the cave or a bit from the balcony scene, and go under again with relief. He had a vague memory of Carmen leaving him and once almost formulated the thought that she was in Richard's room — hers too — waiting for the phone to ring or Richard to walk in. He had dreams of physical pain too and during his waking moments would try to localize the pains to parts of his body: the knee, the shoulders, the lip.

He dreamed that someone was knocking on the door and came to the surface. He lay there for a moment, still thinking it was a dream, and wondered how bad his knee was going to be. The knocking continued and he thought it might be real. He sat up on the bed. He looked at the patch of black sky through the balcony door and listened. It was a real knock. He got up and realized he was still naked. He had to go to the bathroom to get his pants and when he got there decided a towel would be simpler. He wrapped it around his waist and hobbled to the door.

He opened the door a crack and saw a room service boy. He was holding a brightly wrapped package in both hands. Main watched him through the crack.

"I'm sorry, sir," the boy said.

He shook his head to clear out the fog and realized he hadn't turned on the lights. He reached to the switch and then opened the door wider. The boy handed him the package. He realized he should give him a tip and told him to wait a second. The boy shook his head — it was all right — and left, leaving Main holding the package.

He closed the door and looked at the package. It was wrapped in birthday paper — Feliz Cumpleaños — and showed balloons. There was a card. He opened it and it said, "Puto."

He was waking up now. The package was getting through the fog. He squeezed it gently; the sides gave, it seemed soft. He lifted it and listened; no sound. He was being paranoid. Fausto had made him paranoid. So be it. Better paranoid than sorry. It wasn't his birthday and the last time he had seen the word "Puto" it had been on the knife in Leopoldo Sanchez's neck.

He took the package into the bathroom and set it in the sink. He dropped the plunger and turned on the tap. When the sink was full he turned off the tap and waited for some water to seep into the package. He began slowly unwrapping the package underwater. He got the top open and a rust-colored cloud floated in the water. He braced himself and reached in. There was something wrapped in cloth. He lifted the cloth out and something fell back into the package, silently in the water.

He pulled the cloth out of the water. It was a teeshirt. There was a picture of an artichoke on it and underneath it said, The Edible Thistle. The picture looked like an engraving in an old book and the parts of the artichoke were labeled in Latin. He held it above the sink and blood-stained water ran off it.

He stood there staring at Richard's teeshirt and then forced himself to look back into the box. He dropped the teeshirt on the floor. He was shaking again and the wings were beating in his chest. He plunged his hands in. The only way he could make himself do it was abruptly. He grabbed it and held it in his hand and threw it back in the water, turning from the sink and rubbing his hands on the towel around his waist. The frantic movement undid the towel and it fell to the floor with the tee-shirt. He forced himself to turn and look in the water again. The water was gently rocking from side to side. Richard's heart was a darker color than the rusty water. He pulled up the plunger and watched the water drain.

He picked up the teeshirt and threw it over the heart. When the water was gone he reached in again and took out the heart, keeping it wrapped in the teeshirt. There was another sound of something else falling into the sink but he didn't look as he quickly opened the door under the sink and put away the shirt and the heart. He closed the door and straightened up to look in the sink again.

Richard's Stanford ring was in the bottom of the sink.

He set it on the top of the sink and turned on the water to wash the blood stains out. Then he took the bar of soap and washed his hands several times.

He put Richard's ring in his pocket.

THIRTY-FIVE

He shut the bathroom door behind him and stood for a moment in the bright room. He went to his things on the low bureau under the mirror and got a cigarette out of the pack of Delicados and got it lit. He smoked and looked at himself in the mirror. It was funny how normal he looked. The trembling was almost imperceptible. The wings in his chest didn't show in the mirror. There were cuts on his lip and chin but no other signs of his time in the mine. His torso was unmarked and strong. His penis showed no signs of Carmen.

But he didn't feel there was much left of what he'd been not very long ago.

He got a mini-Tequila out of the refrigerator and went out onto the balcony. Fausto had taken him apart with incredible efficiency. He was very, very scared. He never had been before, really. It didn't come up much working on insurance fraud and waiting for people to come out of motels, but he had always had a kind of unexcitability — what Ingrid called his uneventfulness — that he might have thought was courage if he really thought about it.

Ingrid, I'm trembling naked on a balcony under a starry sky.

He couldn't think about the mine, he couldn't think about the heart under his sink. He couldn't even think about them. He blocked the images almost before they appeared. At the same time he knew he'd decided to go to the mine the next day. He couldn't even think about it and he'd made up his mind to go back. He had a lot of ground to cover that night, in his mind.

But there was a lot of night in front of him and he went back into the room for another tequila and another cigarette. He could give himself a few more minutes before facing up to things.

He went back out onto the balcony. He felt cold from the inside out and was still trembling. He reminded himself it felt worse than it looked. It just felt like he was coming apart at the seams. He leaned on the balcony and finished the drink and the cigarette.

He went back into his room and then into the bathroom. He closed the bathroom door behind him again. The light was harsh and even and the glare off the bathroom tiles was brutal. He went to the sink and opened the door under it. He made himself take out the teeshirt and set it on the space next to the sink. He undid it and looked at the heart. He was able to do it but it was not enough to accomplish what he had to accomplish.

For his primitive therapy he had to touch it, to make the thought one he could live with, to undo what Fausto had done. He picked it up and held it in front of him. His fingers registered the surface, smooth but almost sticky, and transmitted the revulsion. There, he could do it: he looked at it, stared at it. The famous heart. It didn't look much like in his textbooks, let alone Valentine's cards.

He held it longer than necessary, to be sure. Then he wrapped it again and put it back under the sink, and washed his hands, only once and slowly. Then he went back into the room.

He turned off the light and went to draw the curtain to the balcony to make the room as dark as possible, as much like the mine as possible. He went to lie on the bed and thought of the heart — Richard's heart — he had just held. He was able to do it; there was room for the image in his mind; he wasn't afraid of it. The next step was to remember the mine and that would be harder: that was real fear, it had happened to him. But even more than that it would be hard to even recall exactly; the person that had happened to already seemed another person in another lifetime.

But he kept at it like a sick spiritual exercise, trying to make the fear real again and hold it the way he had held the heart and make it his. And he made it a good part of the way. The physical pain was easy to bring back and from there it was easy to remember the fear of waiting for the next delivery of pain, which was much worse than the pain itself. He remembered the panic of the immobility, and made himself get on to the fear of the knife. This time, more than when he had been in the mine, he thought of what you could do with a knife, as Fausto had suggested.

He was making real progress with that one and stayed with it until the images became less vivid. He decided to move on to the next stage.

His purpose. He was going to go back to the mine...; why? To avenge Richard? Yes, he would love to kill them, but that wasn't it exactly. To take revenge for what they had done to him? That was getting closer. He would have to fantasize about it for years if he didn't do it. But there was more: it was his only chance to find out about Josefina and it would be easier to face Carmen, when she knew — accepted — that Richard was dead, if he had Josefina. And it would make it easier for her to love him. Now he was getting closer to it. It was a mixture of high purpose and low calculation.

He'd done his work. He'd let up and was letting his thoughts follow their own momentum when he heard a key inserted in the door. He practically fell out of bed, reaching for the camera bag. Carmen breezed in and he fell back on the bed, to deal with the latest panic rush.

"I was hoping I wouldn't wake you," she said apologetically and began taking off her clothes in the dark.

He realized she'd taken his key with her, planning to return. He groaned groggily as if he was still half asleep and rolled over. He wasn't up to talking about Richard now. He hadn't been able to tell her about the watch; he wasn't going to tell her he had his heart under his sink. And he wasn't up to making love. They would talk about Richard — would have to — after he went to the mine. And then, after that, could make love again. If she wanted to.

But she didn't seem to plan on anything more than getting into bed with him. She pulled up behind him, kissed him on the neck and then pulled back. He opened an eye and made out his watch. It was only eleven-thirty. He still had a lot of night to get through. But before long he knew he was going to sleep again: he was reconnecting with some of the dreams he'd been having before the nightmare of the giftbox.

The next he knew he was sitting up again, his legs tangled in the sheets, trying to figure out what it was. Carmen put her hand on his shoulder and pointed at the phone on the low bureau. He got up and stumbled over to it, forgetting momentarily to go easy on the knee. He picked up the phone, looking at his watch again. It was just after three, enough time to be completely lost in sleep again. "*Bueno,*" he mumbled, somehow picking Spanish.

"Mr. Main," a voice said urgently in English.

"Yes."

"This is Jaime Sanchez."

"Yes." The cloud was lifting again.

"I have Josefina."

"You do!" He shot a look at Carmen, who understood that something significant was going on.

"I need your help. Can you come get me?"

"Where are you?"

"I'm in a farm house right now but I can't stay here. Do you know where Concordia is?"

"Yes." It was a town he had passed on the road to San Ildefonso.

"Exactly two kilometers past the sign saying to turn off for Concordia is a dirt road. Go two hundred meters up that road."

"Stop, explain."

"I can't, I really can't. Just be there. If you're not...." He let the question hang for a very brief moment and hung up.

Main ignored Carmen and limped to the bathroom to throw some cold water on his face. He went back into the room and began gathering his clothes.

"What is it?"

He didn't know how high to get her hopes up. "I may be able to get Josefina."

"Was that Richard!"

"No."

"I'm coming too."

"No you're not."

"Of course I am."

"I'm not sure this is not a trap, and I don't have time to have a conversation about it." He had his clothes on and was getting his running shoes on without socks.

"If it's a trap, you shouldn't go."

He decided he could do the laces when he'd escaped from Carmen. He found the camera bag. "I have to go. That's what I'm supposed to be doing here. Looking for people, not...." He made a gesture at Carmen, the rumpled bed. He left the room as quickly as he could with his bad knee and hurried down the hall to the elevator. He looked back to the room as he waited for it. Carmen didn't seem to be coming after him.

The elevator came and he made his escape. He wandered around for a couple minutes in the parking lot trying to remember where he'd parked the Caribe the day before. His knee seemed to be working better with the walking. He found the car. The top was down and he left it down. He drove fast and was on the freeway heading south in a couple minutes. He was in his shirt sleeves and it was cool as he drove. He was almost chilled and it was an exotic feeling to be chilled on the outside, after two days of Mazatlán heat, instead of on the inside. He was reviving. He'd probably slept four or five hours altogether. He couldn't be sure — he didn't know what time he'd conked out the first time after coming in from the balcony with Carmen.

And the sense that something was happening was invigorating too. Even if he didn't have a clue what was going on, like what Jaime was doing in a farmhouse. But it was the kind of problem you couldn't think through, you just had to go and see what happened. It might even be true, he might have Josefina tonight.

He caught a glimpse of headlights on the road behind him, at quite a distance. There was no reason someone shouldn't be on the freeway at three-thirty, but.... Every so often he'd catch a glimpse of the lights, neither gaining nor falling behind. He slowed down for a bit but the lights didn't get any closer.

When he saw the sign to Concordia he checked his odometer and slowed down, looking for the dirt road off to his left. At exactly the two kilometer mark he saw it, as Jaime had said, and braked to pull into it. He turned off his lights as he was pulling in and immediately got out, taking a few steps away from his car. If it was a trap he wasn't going to make it any easier for them than necessary.

He watched the hardtop road, waiting to see the headlights that had been behind him go past. In a minute or so a Jeep or some other squarish four-wheel drive vehicle went past, a man driving. So it wasn't Carmen following him in a taxi and he could concentrate on the dirt road.

Waiting for the Jeep to pass, his eyes had become accustomed to the dark and when he looked back up the dirt road he could make it out better. It was on a slight uphill grade. On the left of the road the shapes were indistinct — natural vegetation; on the right were orderly rows of trees — an orchard. He remembered the mango orchards he'd passed when he'd driven out to San Ildefonso to look for Richard. That hadn't even been twenty-four hours ago.

He stared up the road. It wasn't as dark as the mine, or even his room with the curtains drawn, but it was dark enough to remind him, and this wasn't practice. He stood absolutely still, holding his breath and straining to hear anything. Crickets and toads were raising a field of sound but he couldn't make out anything else.

He had instinctively trusted Jaime but he wasn't going to trust that instinct. He was going to go into that orchard exactly as if he were going to meet Fausto and Dedo. And how would that be? On foot? Making it harder for them to see him but leaving him defenseless. Or in the car? Announcing his arrival but giving him a fighting chance of escaping? The choice was easy. He'd drive: He'd rather be shot than taken alive, if it came down to that.

There were lights on the freeway again, coming the other direction. The Jeep went by again.

He got back in the Caribe and got his automatic out of the camera bag. He leaned forward to read the odometer without lights. Two hundred meters, two tenths of a kilometer. He started slowly up the road without lights, hunched forward to present as little target as possible. He saw nothing at the two hundred mark and went another hundred meters, where he still saw nothing: scrub and low trees to the left, perfect rows of mangos to the right.

He made a U-turn and went back down to the two hundred mark, turning the car so it faced the rows of mangos. He climbed out of the convertible, gun in hand, without opening the door. He reached back in and turned on the headlights, at the same instant running away from the car and diving to the ground. He grunted as his knee hit the dirt and clenched his jaws. He rolled over slowly and almost noiselessly three times.

He lay with his gun in his hand, looking down the rows. The headlights, like spotlights in a theatre, created the expectation that something would happen, but nothing did. He did a belly crawl to get to the first row of trees in the orchard. He kept his jaws clenched and tried to keep his bad knee from digging into the clods. When he got to the first tree he knelt on his good knee, getting what protection he could from the tree in front of him.

The crickets and toads raised a sheet of sound that hovered a couple of feet above the ground. The orchard was a grid. He could make out about ten trunks before it became too dark. He tried to count down each row one at a time — method. One of the trees, three rows down and five trees in, was much thicker at the base than the others. He watched it for a moment, then continued counting down the next rows as far as he could see.

Nothing but that thickness stood out and he came back to it. The shape didn't seem human but he supposed it could be if the person were slumped in just the right way. The person or the body. Was it Richard's body? Were they baiting a trap with his heartless corpse? But it wouldn't make any sense. Why would they let Main go in the afternoon to shoot him ten hours later in an orchard? It was another one of those questions you couldn't think through.

He stood up, leaning sideways against the tree trunk. He took a deep breath and dashed — if that was the word for his run — back to the Caribe, barely stopping to turn off the lights, and ran back into the orchard. He leaned sideways against the trunk of another tree. He waited for his eyes to adjust to the dark again, listening to the toads and crickets.

When he was ready he zigzagged from tree to tree until he was one tree away from the shape. He paused again and looked at the form at the base of the tree. It was still not clear whether it was a man but he supposed it could be if he was sitting with his arms and legs around the tree trunk, embracing it, with his head dropped forward. If it was a man, it was a dead man. There was no movement whatsoever.

No movement, no sound, no sign that there was anyone in the orchard besides himself — and the shape at the base of the tree. He got ready to dive over to the tree. The commando-style stuff probably wasn't necessary but it couldn't hurt. If there was no one watching, it wasn't necessary. But if someone was watching, it was the right thing to be doing.

He dove over toward the lump, twisting so he'd land on his side rather than the bad knee, and belly crawled the last couple of feet to it. Still lying flat he reached up and shook it. It moved with his hand but didn't seem to have any life of its own. He got up on his good knee, reached over, found the head and pulled back. The head fell grotesquely back, its weight pulling the slit throat apart, like a bloody scream under the curly beard. At the exact moment the throat opened, a muzzle flashed almost straight ahead of him, a chunk of bark flew off the tree above his shoulder and the sound of a shot registered.

He threw himself back from the body, rolled until he hit another trunk, jumped up and leaned his shoulder against it to present the narrowest target in the direction of the muzzle flash. He held his automatic at his shoulder, trying to see anything in the darkness.

Two more shots rang out from a different direction, off to his left. He turned too late to see anything. Nothing had landed near him. He had only a rough idea where Fausto and Dedo were but they knew almost exactly where he was. Neither of them was between him and his car, so if he could get back....

He was about to make a dash for it when there was a barrage of shots off to his left again, but not from the same spot exactly, and certainly from a different gun, this one automatic. Again nothing landed near him.

There was more shooting but he didn't pay any more attention. He zigzagged back to the Caribe, timing the zigs and zags irregularly, and jumped over the door into the driver's seat. His knee was responding beautifully to the adrenaline treatment. Leaning below the dash, he started the car and shot back into the dirt road. He raised himself so he could just see over the top of the dash and raced down the dirt road in the dark. After about fifty yards he sat up and held on so he wouldn't bounce himself out of the Caribe. Guns were still firing behind him in the orchard.

He skidded as he turned onto the highway and accelerated out of it. He turned on his lights and shifted to second. Just as he shifted to third he passed the Jeep on the shoulder of the road.

THIRTY-SIX

He slammed on the brakes, looking for a spot to park the Caribe out of sight. He found one, parked and ran back to the Jeep. It was empty. He squeezed into the space behind the driver's seat, crouching on the floor and waiting for his knee to get used to the new position. He had his gun out — the only one not fired in the orchard — and caught his breath. He was tense, getting ready to take a more active role in his life, wondering whose Jeep he was in.

He heard footsteps coming at a run and tensed tighter. The driver's door opened and someone threw himself in. Main shot up, grabbed a handful of short hair and pulled the head back against the headrest. He jammed his automatic behind the ear where the skull met the neck. He took a couple even breaths: he didn't even know who he had and he wanted to pull the trigger. The door was still open and the man was holding a rifle by the barrel, the stock resting on the dirt next to the door. Main could see a bit of the man's profile, which looked vaguely familiar....

The passenger door opened and she got in.

He tightened his grip on the short hair. "What the fuck is going on Carmen! What the fuck...!"

She spun around, letting out a cry. She fell back against the headrest when she saw it was only him.

"I mean it goddammit, what's going on?" He relaxed his grip on the head in front of him, then let go. He took the gun off the neck.

John Newkirk turned to face him.

"This just gets better and better," Main said.

"What's going on," Newkirk said, "is we just saved your life."

"Thanks."

"Believe me, there was nothing in it for me," Newkirk said.

Carmen finally spoke: "He offered to help and I thought it was a good idea. He's just proven it was a good idea."

"A terrific idea."

Newkirk said, "We haven't got time for this. What was that in the orchard? A body?"

"Jaime Sanchez."

"Oh Christ," he said and Main remembered he knew Jaime.

Carmen was staring at him with a look of shock. Newkirk said, "They're taking out everyone, first Leopoldo, now Jaime."

And Richard, Main thought.

Newkirk got his rifle in and closed the door. He set it between the bucket seats so the muzzle was pointing past Main's right shoulder. It was an M-16.

Carmen said in disbelief: "Jaime?"

Newkirk said, "Unless we hit them, they'll be coming down this road. I'd rather not be sitting here."

"They'll probably be going the other way, towards San Ildefonso," Main said. Towards the mine.

"Still."

He put the Jeep in gear, asked him where his car was and dropped him at it. Carmen said, "We've got to talk."

Main laughed sourly. "Yeah, I'd say so. Uh, your room, or mine, or his?"

"Yours," she said, ignoring the sarcasm.

The sky was starting to change from black to charcoal as he drove back. It only took about half an hour but it was plenty of time to feel sick, to think about Richard, and Leopoldo, and Jaime. And about Carmen and Newkirk. And Fausto and Dedo got in there too. But none of the feelings were as strong as they probably would be some other time. He mainly felt a little sick and told himself his immediate goal was just to get through the conference in his room with a little dignity, to drop the sarcasm, to stop showing.

They got to the hotel and rode the elevator together. Newkirk had the M-16 in a camouflage rifle bag and Carmen had a large L. L. Bean bag over her shoulder. When they got to his room he went in first and pulled the cover over the bed. There was a tiny table with two chairs. He gestured to them and sat on the edge of the bed himself a couple feet away from the table. Carmen set her L.L. Bean bag on the night table with a clunk.

"What have you got in there?" Main asked. "The hand grenades? The mortar?"

"Not funny," she said.

Newkirk set his rifle bag against the bureau. Main remembered the picture of the young lieutenant and his men in the jungle on the wall of Newkirk's study, from the pre-begonia period of his life. "The M-16 from Vietnam?" he asked.

Newkirk nodded.

"What does Mexicana say when you check through an M-16?" he asked, remembering the dash he'd made to the Mexican consulate to get a firearms permit.

"We didn't take Mexicana," Carmen said. "John flew us down."

"Oh I forgot," Main said, meaning he'd forgotten about the photo of Newkirk getting into his jet. He remembered watching the jets land at the Salinas airport a few hundred yards from where Leopoldo Sanchez had been murdered. If there was a connection he couldn't put it together.

Newkirk and Carmen had taken the chairs. He got up from his corner of the bed and went to the phone to call room service for coffee. Then he went out on the balcony to smoke a cigarette. He wasn't ready to get down to business, and unlike them, knew there was nothing to rush for. Not with Richard's heart under the sink in the bathroom. He smoked. Cigarettes hardly seemed to be the main threat to his life expectancy these days.

The sky was gray now and the sea was a darker gray. It didn't seem it could be the same balcony Carmen had bent over the night before. He finished the cigarette quickly. He didn't want to get onto that line of thought.

He went back into the room. "Where do we start? Who starts?"

"I do," Newkirk said.

Main sat on the edge of the bed again and looked at Newkirk. He didn't look like the same tense, uncertain man he'd seen at Carmen's and followed to his home. He was flushed and clear eyed, a man living life. "You enjoyed that, didn't you," Main said. "Like being back in the jungle again."

"Yes, I enjoyed that," Newkirk said unapologetically. "I can't let my life be run by a psychotic."

"What do you mean, *your* life?

"That's what we have to talk about," Carmen said, and looked at Newkirk to begin.

"I'm not just along for the fun of it," Newkirk said. "I came because I felt partly responsible."

"Because you put Carmen and Richard in touch with Jaime's agency?"

"No. Because I got Dedo out of prison."

"You what?" Main said. Newkirk had his interest but there was a knock on the door and he got up to go get the coffee. He came back in with the tray and set it on the table without pouring. He took his seat again.

Newkirk explained himself: "Fausto came to see me about six weeks ago. He'd heard about me from Jaime and knew I was a lawyer. He told me if Dedo didn't get out on his parole hearing he'd kill my family." He poured everyone a cup. "He was very... convincing, I did what he said." He drank some coffee and looked thoughtful. He shook his head. "Believe me, I wasn't proud of myself but I didn't think I had the right to play the hero with the lives of my wife and children."

He paused and Main nodded. He was beginning to understand the man and didn't really want to. "And when Josefina was kidnapped you put it together?"

Newkirk nodded. "Fausto and Dedo were very fresh in my mind when Josefina was kidnapped. I figured they had to have something to do with it. It was too much of a coincidence. And I was in it."

Main picked up his coffee. "Now what?"

"Kill them," Newkirk said without hesitation. His introspective mood was gone and he was warming up to the pleasures of the jungle again.

"The important thing is to find Richard," Carmen said. Main looked at her but she wouldn't let him catch her eye. He couldn't tell if she really believed what she was saying.

"If they can tell us where Richard is before we kill them, so much the better."

"Christ," Main said with disgust. "You make it sound so easy."

Newkirk said, "One hundred sixty-eight breaths east of 15 on the Durango road." He held his hands out in a nothing-could-be-easier gesture.

"No!" Carmen said, looking first at Newkirk, then, guiltily at

Main.

"So much for confiding in Carmen," Main said.

"I'm sorry, Cal."

"What's your plan?" Newkirk said.

"I need time to think."

"What about?"

It was true. His only plan was the same as Newkirk's but he wanted Newkirk to disappear. He gave him a disgusted look, like he had lots of things to think about and said to Carmen, "Could I talk to you alone?"

He went out to the balcony with his Delicados, leaving it up to Carmen to get rid of Newkirk. It didn't work exactly the way he had in mind — Carmen and Newkirk both got up and left his room.

She'd probably be back. And if she wasn't he'd probably get more thinking done without her, if he could just think what to think about. He finished his cigarette and she wasn't back. He went back in for his coffee and went out to the balcony again, sitting on the cement, as he had, exhausted, after making love to Carmen. He was exhausted again but it was different. She still didn't come back. He began to wonder if she would. He had another cigarette and looked at his watch. It was six-thirty; already it wasn't cool any more. He wasn't getting any thinking done.

He had his head against the balcony wall and his eyes closed when he heard her come into his room again. She came out to him on the balcony and sat across from him. To give her credit, she seemed dejected too.

He tapped out a cigarette and offered it to her. He would have to forgive her anything, knowing he still had to tell her about Richard. "Why did you bring him?" he asked.

"He wanted to help. He came over to the house just after you left...."

"Oh, I'll bet he came *right* over when the coast was clear."

"Cal, we have more important problems right now."

"My point, Carmen, is if you have to have two lovers, you're supposed to keep them apart."

"I spent the night with *you*, didn't I?"

"How do I know where you spent the night? You leave, I fall asleep, you come back. What do I know?"

She got up and moved across to him, putting her hand on his shoulder. "Not now. Please."

He wasn't doing a very good job of forgiving her anything. He nodded.

"Seriously, Cal, what are we going to do?"

"I'm going out to the mine. If you can, stay with Newkirk and keep him away."

"No, Cal."

"You've got to keep him here, you understand?"

"No, listen, don't go" — she was squeezing his upper arm — "I don't want you to get killed."

"It's the only move we've got and I don't want to — I can't — work with Newkirk."

She was opening her mouth to protest and the phone rang. They both looked at it like it was radioactive. He got up and went into the room and she followed.

He picked it up. "Hello. *Bueno.*"

"Main? Fausto."

"Yes." Carmen was crowding his shoulder.

"I have to talk to you."

"I haven't got anything to say. I'm tired out after the mine and the mango orchard."

There was a silence. "Look, this is important. I want to give you Josefina."

"Get a new line, Fausto."

"Meet me at, uh, the aquarium."

"No. Give me your phone number and I'11 call you back in exactly one hour. I'm picking the meeting place this time."

There was a pause, then Fausto said, "This is some real petty shit, Main."

"Give me your number," Main said.

He gave Main a number. He had to look for a pencil and paper and told him to repeat it. Then Fausto said, "I got 6:58."

"What do you mean?"

"Synchronize our fucking watches, mon." Fausto hung up.

Main looked at Carmen. She probably hadn't heard the part about Josefina but seemed to have the jist of the conversation. It wasn't that complicated.

"I'm coming," she said.

He nodded and she looked surprised. He didn't explain that he was afraid she'd end up going out to the mine with Newkirk if he didn't have her with him.

She went to the table where she'd left her L.L. Bean bag and picked it up. It made a heavy clunking sound again when she moved it.

"What do you have in there?" he asked.

She opened it and took out a huge ivory-handled Colt .45, the other half of the brace on Richard's study wall. Richard had the other one. She put it back in the bag. "Where do you want to meet him?"

THIRTY-SEVEN

He didn't know. Not in the hotel.

They went to the Caribe and Main asked her to drive. She gave him a look but he got in the passenger seat and asked her to drive south.

He looked at the hotels as they passed on his right. It was already hot and overcast with the haze holding in the heat. The sun made a polished spot in the dull gray sky.

Carmen tried to start talking but he leaned back against his seat and closed his eyes. He felt heavy and overcast on the inside. Nothing special was going on: no anger, pain, fear, love, jealousy. Too much had happened and he hadn't caught up. He knew he still had to tell Carmen about Richard. Dread was some kind of emotion, but even that was dulled.

"You still thinking?" she asked, almost teasingly.

She couldn't know how wrong the light tone sounded. "Yeah, thinking." He didn't open his eyes.

He felt her hand on the inside of his thigh. She squeezed a handful. "It will turn out all right."

The hand was much worse than the light tone. "Let me think," he said roughly. He could imagine her giving him a look, wondering what had gotten into him. Compared to this he'd been fairly civilized back at the hotel, with Newkirk. She removed her hand.

"Where am I going?" she asked, annoyed.

"Just keep driving."

"*Sí señor.*"

When he opened his eyes they were passing hotels that had been the best there were in about 1970. He closed his eyes again and wondered why Fausto had become obsessed with killing him. He didn't know.

When he opened his eyes again they were much further south, approaching the lighthouse. A piece of time seemed to be missing and he wondered if he could have slept. Was it more disturbing, under the circumstances, to think he'd fallen asleep, or to think a piece of time had just dropped out? He didn't know.

Carmen was watching him as he looked around. He could meet Fausto at the lighthouse, for high drama. They passed the lighthouse, curved east and were entering the industrial port area. She turned away from the docks and cranes. After a few blocks of warehouses and junkyards, they were on a causeway crossing an estuary. It was black in places where the mud was exposed and steel gray in others where slicks of water caught the sky. It was dotted with gorgeous egrets and flamingos.

"Jesus, what is this place?" he said.

"I don't know. I'm just driving, remember?"

He could meet Fausto in the desolate mud slick, shoot it out with him, their shots sending the magnificent birds into the lead sky, with the slums and industrial junk in the background. Slipping, sliding, falling, all in slow motion of course.

Was he serious? "Incredible place," he said.

"Yeah, fascinating. You, uh, still thinking?"

"Yeah."

"You okay, Cal?"

"Yeah."

"Look, Cal, if you're still upset about John...."

"Nothing to do with Newkirk," he said almost angrily. "Carmen, we've got to talk about Richard." He turned to look at her.

She looked straight ahead. "I know about Richard," she said softly. "I think I do." She looked quickly to him to see if he would contradict what she thought she knew. When he couldn't say it wasn't so, she looked back to the road. "If Fausto will give us Josefina, sell her back to me, okay. If not, it's all over. We go back." She drove looking... he didn't know exactly how she looked... determined.

He looked away. He didn't know when it had sunk in. Had she already known Richard was dead when they made love on the balcony, when she came back to his room that night? When she went out to the orchard to blast away with Newkirk? Men were always saying they didn't understand women, but... he sure didn't understand her.

After the mud estuary they went through a couple streets of auto shops and into a slum which became by degrees less miserable as they continued. The buildings were getting older and smaller, then they started getting bigger again. They were almost downtown, the downtown that was too far from the beach for most tourists to visit, where Mazatlán seemed like part of Mexico.

Carmen pulled into a parking place. Main looked at her.

They were at the zócalo. "There's a public phone," she said, pointing. "Call Fausto. Meet him here, or at the post office" — she pointed at the building across the zócalo — "or the cathedral" — she pointed to the left — "but meet him somewhere."

Determined was the right word. He got out and went to the phone which, to his surprise, was in working order. He dialed.

"Dígame." It was Fausto.

"Fausto, we'll meet in the mercado."

"The mercado? Why?"

"In fifteen minutes. In the witchcraft area."

"You have an hour to think about it and you want to meet in the fucking mercado at the fucking brujo's?"

"I know you like that kind of stuff. Sacrifices and all."

"Yeah, I just love ethnic shit. Okay." He hung up.

He went back to the car for Carmen. She got out and said, "Where?"

"At the mercado."

"The mercado?"

He smiled. He didn't know why he'd said that. Because it was there, just up the street. He took her hand and they started walking fast, past the cathedral, a department store, stepping around the beggars on the sidewalk.

The mercado took up a block. They went in a corner entrance and down a long aisle with purses and knee-length teeshirts. At the end of the teeshirts they turned into the florists' section and walked between hundreds of gladiola stalks. There didn't seem to be any other flowers. After the flowers they were in the fruits and vegetables and then seafood: turtles, shrimp, fish. They took a random turn and ended up with the butchers: pink and lavender tripe, red meat, dark organs, all neatly arranged, assorted into piles. There was a sweet pervading odor in the heat. He went to stare at a pile of hearts. He picked one up.

"What are you *doing?*" Carmen said.

"Find out where the brujo is, Carmen." He examined the heart in his palm.

"Put that down." She took his elbow and turned him to her. "Are you sure you're all right?"

"Never been better. Find out where the brujo is."

"The guy with the love potions and the hexes?"

"Yep."

There was a butcher down the aisle from them, standing behind a little pyramid of skinned calf heads, tender pink and glassy eyed. She went to him, he pointed and gestured, she came back. She took his hand and led him off through a maze of aisles until they were approaching a corner of the market where the aisles got narrower and there wasn't as much light. He began to like his unpremeditated choice of meeting places.

At the dead end of a narrow aisle they got to an old man in a small booth. A string of dried toads and bats hung next to him and behind him were rows of small wooden drawers. The man was tallying up piles of coins and looked up at Main and Carmen. This section wasn't for tourists and he just watched them without saying anything.

In the space in front of the booth sacks of herbs were set out on the concrete floor. Just beyond the bags a huge concrete pillar rose to the roof thirty feet above. The sacks were labeled: liver trouble, bad eyes, evil eye, bedwetting, impotence, blood, diarrhea, dizziness, *el espanto* for the generic "fright."

"Well stocked," Carmen said.

She still had his hand. He led her back down the alley about fifteen yards and turned left into another aisle. They went a few more yards past the nuts and into the chilis. There was a little space between two women selling every kind of chili imaginable. He pulled her into that space and kissed her, then pulled back.

"Can I have your gun?" he asked.

"I guess so." She stood still while he undid the zipper on her bag and got the Colt out. He put it in his camera bag.

"Don't worry," he said, "this part isn't dangerous."

"Are you all right, Cal?" She grabbed his elbow and squeezed hard to get his attention. "You seem strange."

"Things are strange, don't you think?"

She looked concerned. His eyeballs felt hot and he remembered to blink. He let out his breath.

She said, "I'd rather help than just stand here. Let me have your gun if you're taking mine."

He shook his head.

"Then why did you want me to come?"

"So you wouldn't go out on maneuvers with Newkirk and get yourself killed."

"We're the ones who saved *your* life, remember?"

"If you want to save it again, just promise you'll stay here out of sight. If I have to worry about you, then I'm in danger. If I can just concentrate on what I'm doing, it's easy."

"Women and children stay behind?"

"This is not the time to raise my consciousness. Promise me you'll stay here."

She nodded doubtfully and he left. He went back down to the brujo's booth. He went to lean against the concrete pillar. From there he would see Fausto as soon as he turned into the alley, about fifty feet down from him. He unzipped his camera bag and stuck his hand in. He had a minor decision to make. He'd rather shoot him with his automatic, but the Colt was a lot more impressive. He put his fingers around the cracked ivory of the Colt. He wanted to talk to him first and the Colt would be more of a deterrent. He kept his hand on the ivory grip inside the camera bag.

The brujo was watching him but looked away when Main looked over to him. He swept all the coins he'd been neatly stacking into a messy pile and pushed the pile into a bag he held under his counter. He seemed to know something was going to happen. But he probably didn't need to be a brujo with special powers to figure that out.

Main didn't have to wait long before Fausto turned into the alley, walking fast, his leather shoes beating out sharp time on the concrete floor. Main raised the Colt straight out in front of him. Fausto stopped cold, then raised his hands to his chest and kept coming. When he was a few feet in front of Main he turned his back to him so Main could search him. Main didn't move. Out of the corner of his eye he had seen the brujo going down behind his counter.

"Well?" Fausto said over his shoulder.

"Let's do it right," Main said, nodding toward the brujo's counter.

Fausto went over to it, put his arms out to the counter and took a couple steps back, spreading his legs. It looked like he was doing a pushup against the counter. Main went up and searched him carefully and stepped back four paces. He raised the gun again.

Fausto straightened up and turned to face him. "I think there's an old man behind the counter."

"There is."

"Well, anyhoo...."

"I got the teeshirt. I got the heart." Saying the words he saw them again. He saw the bloody water dripping from the shirt and the dark shape of the heart under the cloudy water. He remembered holding the heart, making himself get ready. There was nothing he wanted to talk about now. The "case" was over and they were onto something else.

It must have shown. Fausto went serious and said, "I see."

It was unbelievable how heavy the gun was. It was a strain to hold it at arm's length with one hand. He could feel the weight along his arm, into his shoulder, all the way down to his leg braced under the weight. The weight seemed right, matching the weight of what he was going to do. When he pulled the trigger his life would be out of his hands. No more Fausto, or Richard, or Carmen, or Ingrid, or Newkirk. No more questions. A clean slate. The shot would wipe out the past. No more Calvin Main.

It wasn't revenge he was going to feel, it was relief. He changed his stance slightly and reached with his left hand to his right wrist. The gun would have an Old West kick....

Fausto looked to his left and Main saw something out of the corner of his eye. He tried to ignore it, reluctant to look away from Fausto. There was a pink speck in the corner of his eye. He looked. A woman with a pink bundle was coming down the alley. She hesitated, then stopped cold. Fausto nodded briskly and she started coming again. Then Main saw Carmen come into the alley and follow behind the woman. Fausto kept nodding her on. When she got to the area with the sacks on the floor, he nodded at a clear spot and she set the bundle down.

It began moving and crying. Fausto nodded again — the woman had done what she had to do — and she turned around and walked back down the aisle, squeezing past Carmen who was still coming. Carmen rushed to the bundle

Main lowered the gun.

Fausto smiled. "That's Josefina. That's all I can do. Richard is, how can I say? Out of my hands."

He started to leave and Main said, "Stop," raising the gun.

Carmen had got the baby girl out of her blanket and was holding her to her chest and rocking her.

Fausto stopped just long enough to shake his head. "The moment is past." He turned and walked out.

There was the baby crying, and the sounds Carmen was making to calm her, and the sound of heels on concrete.

THIRTY-EIGHT

It wasn't adding up any better but they were getting somewhere. He drove, dividing his attention between the road and Carmen, who held Josefina tight. Carmen's head was bowed to the baby's black curls; her eyes were closed and her cheeks glistened with tears. She was smiling and every minute or so she held the baby up in front of her face, looked at her for a moment and kissed her violently on the cheeks, before squeezing her protectively to her again. Main could almost feel the glow from Carmen on his skin.

Carmen raised her head from the curls and gave him a glorious smile. "We've got to get things." She held up Josefina as if he might not have noticed her.

She was a beautiful baby and Main admitted to himself he was planning to raise her. After a decent interval he would ask Carmen to marry him... why pretend? And they would raise the beautiful girl. And have others. And live happily ever after. Appropriately, bits of blue were breaking through the gray sky.

They found a Centro Commercial which turned out to be a sort of K-Mart and supermarket combined. They filled a cart with diapers, powdered milk, pabulum, Gerbers, bibs, rattles, dresses, talcum, pajamas, two dolls. Main picked out a stuffed tiger for her.

When they got back to the hotel one of the hotel men in a guayabera helped them up to Carmen's room — Richard's room — with all the new family equipment. He didn't seem concerned that tourists would arrive with a baby and then have to go out and buy every single thing a baby would need.

In the room, Carmen lay Josefina on the bed and undressed her and cleaned her. New diaper, powder, lots of legs kicking in the air and gurgling and smiling. Then she picked her up again and held her out in front of her and bounced her up and down.

"She remembers me. I can see she does."

"Of course she does."

Carmen held Josefina close to her again and looked at Main. She smiled and walked over to him. She leaned forward to kiss him with Josefina in her arms between them. "Cal, I need an hour alone with Josefina." She smiled again: He would understand.

He smiled. He understood.

Back in his room he poured a cold cup of coffee from the pot still on his table and slowly smoked a Delicado. This time he really did have some things to think about, and even knew what they were. Even so it took a few minutes to get started. The image of the happy Carmen kept intruding.

Why did he find it almost disturbing, as well as delightful? Had he expected her to grieve more ... more, fully? But her marriage hadn't been good. She'd spoken of loyalty to Richard, not love. Couldn't she be relieved — though no one would ever say it — that Richard was dead and she was no longer responsible for keeping her life in a certain shape? And how could he know what she was really feeling? Shock could take so many forms.

He stubbed out his cigarette and decided to get down to the more immediate questions. The first was whether to call the consul. He should, it made sense: If anyone could begin to straighten out Josefina's adoption it was the consul. But he'd never been certain it wasn't the consul who had put Dedo onto him. And the fisherman's glasses they'd made him wear. Just a coincidence, surely, but he hadn't been able to shake the suspicion. It occurred to him now he had even more reason to wonder about the consul: It didn't make any sense for Fausto to just hand over Josefina, who was worth money. It just wasn't him. But if he was taking orders, working for someone with a cooler head, it would make sense. The investigation would cool off with Richard dead and Josefina safe.

No, he wouldn't call the consul just yet. The next question didn't require much thinking. It required doing. Fausto had been wrong. The moment wasn't past, just postponed. He had to kill Fausto and Dedo. He owed that much to Richard. And the primitive symmetry would help him, with his grieving, or whatever it was.

Next problem: Newkirk. If even Fausto was starting to do things that made sense — giving Josefina back — wasn't it time for him, Main, to start being logical? What made sense was to take Newkirk — the man who knew his way around the jungle — out to the mine with him. His solo fantasy had been... stupid. He had to live. To marry Carmen, raise Josefina.

He had the desk ring Newkirk's room, where there was no answer. Which wasn't surprising: He was probably already out at the mine.

He went to Carmen's room again — he'd be surprised if she didn't know where Newkirk was — and knocked.

"*Adelante*." Carmen, speaking Spanish, thinking he was hotel staff.

"It's locked."

"*Momentito*."

He heard Carmen fumbling with the lock and then the door opened.

But it wasn't Carmen. It was a hotel employee, a woman wearing a dress with the hotel's name stitched above her breast. She was holding Josefina.

He asked the hotel babysitter where Carmen was.

She didn't know. The Señora hadn't told her where she was going.

THIRTY-NINE

He tore through the traffic then slammed on his brakes to stop in front of a corner store full of beer, suntan lotions, things to float in. He found a flashlight and batteries and raced back to the car.

He drove as fast as he could until he got to the turnoff to San Ildefonso, then slowed down a bit: he'd have to drive at the same speed Dedo had driven — whatever that had been — and breathe at the same rate he'd breathed — whatever *that* had been. The only thing to do was check every dirt road between, say, one hundred and fifty breaths and one hundred and ninety. That should cover it, even if Dedo had been driving, and he had been breathing, a little faster or a little slower than he was today.

There wasn't much traffic on the Durango road. He passed a taxi with no passenger coming down out of the hills and wondered if that was how Carmen had got there. He couldn't think of any other place she might have gone

At one hundred and fifty breaths he saw a dirt road and turned into it. But it went on and on into the hills and he remembered that the dirt road he'd been on, in the black glasses, hadn't seemed to go more than a hundred or a hundred and fifty yards. He found a place to turn around and raced down the road again.

When he got back to the hardtop road he drove as fast as he could again. He was in the target area and would check every dirt road without worrying about driving at the same speed as Dedo.

He pulled into a second road and after twenty-five yards went around a bend and saw the black Riviera parked ahead of him. He didn't see Newkirk's Jeep but figured it would be hidden somewhere. He hoped it was hidden somewhere, that Carmen wasn't in the mine alone.

He stopped and ran up the road, pausing next to the Riviera. The mine was another thirty yards ahead. The opening was a black square in the scrub covered hillside, a cool mouth in the side of the hill. He had his automatic in one hand and the flashlight in the other. Carmen had jokingly taken back the Colt, saying she didn't suppose he'd be needing it any more.

He stood still, remembering. It wasn't a good idea to remember what had happened in the mine the last time. It would just make it harder to go in and he had to go in no matter what; ignore it since there was no choice. Living pretty much consisted of ignoring death anyway. It was just that the timeline was radically foreshortened and death might be right behind that neat black square.

He went to the entrance and stood to one side so he wouldn't be backlit in the opening. He slipped around the edge into the cool darkness and stood still, waiting for his eyes to get used to the dark; it was hard not to remember. The light from the opening reached in a few feet and beyond that there was nothing.

He couldn't see without turning on the flashlight. He'd have to hope they were in another shaft or one of the chambers because if anyone was watching he'd be a bright target when he turned it on. He held it as far from his body as he could and turned it on. Nothing happened. He listened but he didn't hear anything.

He played the beam of light around the shaft in front of him. The path slanted sharply down in front of him. That was where he'd slipped the other time. He went down carefully, trying not to make any noise. At the bottom of the incline the shaft made a jog to the right. He pointed his beam down it. Twenty yards ahead a piece of rock hung low. That was where he'd smacked his head. It didn't seem like such a big deal now that he could see.

He made his way quietly along the shaft, listening. He ducked under the low rock and in another ten yards found the ledge he'd walked off, spraining his ankle. This time he sat on the edge and was just lowering himself when a tremendous explosion rocked the mine.

He threw himself to the ground and covered his head, thinking the mine would cave in. The explosion bounced back and forth through the shafts and a sharp scream pierced the receding echoes. Then there was a roar of laughter like crashing surf, rolling back and forth, crashing and crashing.

"No!" It was a woman's scream, a new scream he thought, or

maybe the same one bouncing back.

He jumped up and ran down the shaft until he got to another shaft crossing at a right angle. The laughter was still rolling around, seeming to come from both directions. Then there was a new whoop of laughter and a "Stop!" They both seemed to come from the right before they returned from the left.

He hurried to the right and went around a bend in the shaft. There was a semicircle of light on the ground in front of him, coming from an opening in the wall. He turned off his flashlight and stepped quickly to the edge of the opening, putting his back to the flat wall, then rolling and dropping flat into the opening, gun arm extended.

A blood-smeared figure wheeled on him with a gun. The hole in the barrel seemed big enough to disappear in. Main held his own gun steady. Neither fired.

Main said, "Richard." He said it very softly.

"Richard, please, darling," said a woman's voice, behind Main. He didn't turn. It was Carmen.

Richard slowly lowered his gun. His eyes were shorted out. He gave a violent shudder and roared with laughter, squeezing his eyes shut and rolling his head from side to side.

He was barechested, splashed with blood. The blood beaded in the matted blond hair on his chest.

Main slowly got to one knee and lowered his gun. He took in the chamber, moving his eyes without moving his head. It was lit by a Coleman lantern. The light was hard and colorless.

A body lay on a cot against one wall: Dedo, with the top of his head gone. Blood was still dripping down the wall, the same blood beading on Richard's chest. This was the shot that had rocked the mine just seconds before.

They'd brought a cot into the mine; there were boxes of diapers on the floor. This was their hideout, where they'd kept Josefina.

On the other side of the chamber John Newkirk lay sprawled on the floor, a huge red hole in his chest.

Fausto was tied with rope to a straight-back a chair near the center of the chamber, to Main's right. He was alive. His hands were loose at his sides beneath the rope. The gold watch Main had been sure was Richard's was on his left wrist. His eyes were wide and alert, without their mocking light, but his nostrils were still tense with disdain. There was a red welt on his forehead.

How had Richard found them?

There was no time to answer questions. Richard was directly across from him, sobbing with laughter. Carmen was somewhere behind him.

"Richard," Main said again, as if handling a verbal bomb.

In his peripheral vision Main was aware of Fausto nodding over his shoulder in the direction of Newkirk's body. Fausto said clearly: "He fucked Carmen too."

Main didn't say anything and kept his eyes on Richard.

Richard wasn't hearing anything but his own voices. He was quieting down and nodding at the floor with his eyes still closed.

Fausto was melodramatically swinging his head, trying to get Main's attention, trying to signal something: the gun hanging loose at Main's side. "He's going to shoot you too *machito.*"

Main ignored him, watching Richard.

"You dumb fuck," Fausto hissed. "Take him *out.* I got a lot of money. You get it and you get her." He shot a glance over Main's shoulder.

Carmen didn't say anything behind him.

Fausto nodded urgently towards Main's gun. "Your buddy's a fucking psycho. I don't get it. You can die or you can live. With her. What's the big fucking dilemma?"

Main finally looked at him. Fausto locked his eyes on him. Main shook his head.

"Oh fuck it," Fausto said with disgust. He seemed to shrink in the ropes that held him.

Richard opened his eyes. They were exhausted. He took a deep breath and slowly began to raise his gun in the direction of Fausto.

Main raised his gun again.

"Richard, please, *please,*" Carmen pleaded.

"It's not over, Carmen," Richard said. "It's not over. It has to stop."

"I'll shoot," Main said. His gun was on Richard, Richard's was on Fausto.

Richard didn't react. "He fucked with my daughter," he said.

Fausto filled out against the ropes again. "I gave her back." His voice was steady, still not begging.

"It has to stop," Richard said again.

Main knew he couldn't pull the trigger but he was frozen with his gun on Richard.

"We have Josefina, darling. She's in the hotel. We'll go home.

It *is* over."

"He fucked with my family." Richard's face twisted with pain as he tried to focus on Fausto, as if he were miles away.

"But I didn't fuck your wife. He did." Fausto looked at Main, smiling grimly.

The diversion didn't work. Maybe it hadn't registered. Richard raised his other hand to the wrist of his gun hand.

"Richard!" Carmen screamed.

Fausto gave a barking laugh and strained forward in the chair. "I'm the only one who *didn't* fuck her!"

The shot was a concussion in the rock vault. The chair flew back. Fausto lay in the upended chair, his back on the floor, his knees bent over the edge of the seat. There was a hole in his throat. One foot twitched but his eyes were wide and empty.

Richard stood with his gun still pointing at Fausto. He said something but Main was still deafened by the shot that rolled like waves of pressure in his brain.

Main lowered his own gun and dropped it to the floor. He'd never use it. He was still on one knee. He lowered his hands to the rock floor to steady himself. He had the vague idea that he might tackle Richard, take off at him like a runner off the block.

Richard said something again, to no one. Maybe he was just mouthing words. Main heard nothing. But he heard Carmen behind him: "It's over, Richard."

Richard looked at her, and down at Main, as if he'd momentarily forgotten who they were. He lowered his gun.

"God, Cal, why did you *come?"*

"What do you mean?" Main said.

"You fucked her too," Richard said sadly.

"That's not true!" Carmen said. "You're not going to believe what Fausto said?"

Richard looked from Main to Carmen, confused. "What did Fausto say?"

"He said... nothing, never mind. Richard, darling. It's over."

"This has nothing to do with Fausto." He looked back down at Main. "This is different."

Main thought: Just spring at him.

Richard said, *"Corazón malherido."*

"What?" Main whispered.

"You remember that poem, Cal?"

"No."

"I do. Funny things have been coming back to me. Carmen taught you that poem" — he looked at Carmen — "you remember it?" He looked back at Main without waiting for an answer. "You drove me nuts with that poem, Cal."

No one said anything. Richard's eyes filled with pain again and he squeezed them shut, slowly shaking his head.

Just spring at him.

Suddenly Richard shouted: "Why did you do it? Goddammit Cal, I tried.... I tried to look the other way. I gave you a reprieve, sent you my fucking heart. You *hear* me?"

Main didn't know what to respond to. He shook his head.

Carmen said, "God, Richard, what are you *talking* about?"

"Sent you my heart," he sobbed.

Richard raised his gun on Main. The hole was huge. Richard's knuckles on the grip were torn and purple. His own gold Philipe Patek glinted on the wrist behind the gun.

"Why did you have to *come?*" he wailed. "I swear to God, Cal, this is the only one that is going to hurt...."

There was a flash of pain and a bank of lights went off. There was a final awareness of cold rock on his cheek.

FORTY

When he opened his eyes he lay absolutely still and looked straight up at the white ceiling, some kind of fire retarding building material, modern. He was lying absolutely flat. He moved his fingers and found sheet and covers. He heard a groan off to his right and then another. He was getting the idea. He was in a hospital.

He moved his eyes until they were sighting down his nose and saw a curtain at the foot of his bed. The curtain was framed with metal poles. A clip board with an x-ray of a skull hung from one of the poles. His eyes were tired from the angle and he let them float straight up again. In a moment he strained his eyes to the right, still without moving his head, and saw another curtain, and then to the left — an I.V. stand and another curtain. He focused on the writing on the I.V. bottle. Spanish.

He relaxed and closed his eyes, then looked down to the x-ray again. A hospital equipped with a memento mori? There was a crack in the skull, he could make that out from where he was, and he remembered the crease in Leopoldo Sanchez's skull. But this one was his. The crack was maybe an inch and a half long, a memento Carmen.

He drifted out or thought he did. He couldn't really tell. He was looking at the same bit of ceiling and wasn't sure if it had been a second or an hour since his last thought. He heard the groan off to the right again. He was in a ward, partitioned off from the others.

He was starting to remember what had happened in the mine. It was still in bits and pieces but it was enough for him to understand that nothing was the same as before. He would have to think it all through again, but he wasn't able to do that yet. As he began to drift off again he realized there was no hurry. He knew that now he would have all the time in the world.

When he woke again the light was different and he realized he must have been out for longer. The light was richer and there seemed to be a lot of it. He found the source of the light: a high window fifteen or twenty feet from the curtain at his feet. Perhaps there was a corridor and a window in the corridor. The light was pouring in, so it was morning or evening. It was yellow. He thought that made it afternoon. He would find out pretty soon if it turned to a sunset.

A Mazatlán sunset blaring through the window. Carmen bent over the balcony in front of him. He would have that image of Carmen to bring out. Savage Mazatlán. What was it she had said? Once more. She'd wanted to make love once more, but she hadn't meant once more that evening, she'd meant once more, ever. She'd been decent enough to have tears in her eyes, the tears he hadn't understood, thinking she was perhaps remembering Richard as she leaned over and pulled him to her.

Everything would have to be rethought, working backwards from the mine, when he wasn't so tired....

Some time had passed when he floated back in. The window was a brassy yellow now, so it was the sunset beginning. Perhaps, probably, it was the same day. The mine in the morning, the hospital in the evening. He remembered another light, a steady glare, the emergency room or an operating room. The bits were coming back and he'd have it all sooner or later. He put his fingers to his head: a mushroom of bandages. He tried turning his head slightly. It didn't hurt but it probably wasn't a good idea.

Bandages, and he remembered Richard's bloody teeshirt and the heart. It would all come back, one thing suggesting another. He forced himself to stay awake and see the thought through: since Richard wasn't dead, it was Richard himself who had sent the bloody package. What kind of heart had it been? A sheep heart? A calf heart? He wondered at what point exactly Richard had gone mad.

Richard had said something about a reprieve. The teeshirt and the heart had been the reprieve, his chance to figure it was all over and go home.... He drifted out, exhausted by so much consecutive thought.

He was awakened by male voices above him but kept his eyes closed. The conversation seemed to be part Spanish, part Latin. The

Latin parts must be what happened to his skull. Doctors. One doctor did all the talking, reporting to the other, who made noises to show he was following. When the talking doctor got to the end of the official part of what he was saying, he said, "We have no idea who he is." Main kept his eyes closed. "No wallet, no I.D."

Main hesitated for a moment longer, wondering if there was any advantage to seeming amnesiac. No, they would think he had brain damage and keep him longer.

He opened his eyes, wondering if he did have brain damage. A young doctor with serious black eyes and steel-framed glasses that pinched his fleshy nose stood above him. He held the clipboard with the x-ray of his skull. The other doctor was older. Perhaps the younger one was a resident, the older one a staff doctor....

"Where am I?" he asked in English.

The younger doctor looked at the older one and back at Main. "Norteamericano?"

"Sí." Spanish was going to be too hard. "Where am I?" he asked again in English.

"In the IMSS hospital in Mazatlán," the older one answered in good English.

Main smiled slightly — or at any rate imagined he was smiling — at the irony of finally ending up in an IMSS hospital after looking so hard for the clinic in San Ildefonso. "How badly am I hurt?"

"You have a fractured skull," the older doctor said. He took the clipboard from the younger doctor and showed it to Main, tracing the line of the fracture with his finger. "The fracture itself is not so serious but we will have to do tests tomorrow to see if there is any damage to the brain."

That was blunt. At least they were going to hold off on the tests until tomorrow. He wasn't ready yet to count fingers or remember series of numbers or whatever it was they did.

"Who are you?" the younger one asked in halting English.

"My name is Calvin Main, from San Francisco. I've been staying at Hotel Los Sabalos on vacation."

"What happened?"

"I was hit." He tried to look agitated. "My bag, my camera bag with my wallet, my camera...

The young doctor shook his head. "It must have been robbery. We'll have to call the police and the American Consulate."

He didn't want them yet. He had to think. "Yes," he said and let out a tired sigh. "What time is it now?"

"About seven o'clock."

"P.m?"

"Yes."

"I'm so tired. Can that wait until tomorrow?"

"The law is clear," the young one said.

"But medically it might be best to wait," the older one said. "No one would know that he gave us his name this evening and not tomorrow morning."

The younger one nodded uncertainly.

"We could do the tests early, before they wear him out with questions," the older one said to make his case stronger.

The younger one nodded and Main thanked them. The older one left and the younger one began filling out a form now that he had a name for the patient. Main closed his eyes again before the doctor could change his mind. But he opened them again when a question occurred to him: "How did I get here? I was attacked near the mercado."

"Someone dropped you off." The doctor finished what he was writing and hung the clipboard back at the foot of the bed. "Someone dropped you off on the sidewalk in front of the hospital. Didn't even bring you in." He shook his head at what people did. Main started to ask another question but the doctor told him it would better for him to rest and left.

The window above him was running to lewd pinks now.

The doctor had shaken a vital piece loose: He had a clear memory of Carmen helping him out of the car and setting him down on the sidewalk. There had been people there and someone had run over to hold him under the armpits. Carmen had hurried back to get behind the wheel of the red Mercedes. Richard had looked at him from the passenger seat, not with crackling-crazy eyes but from far, far away.

The red Mercedes, Richard's red Mercedes. The pieces were coming and wouldn't stop, even the ones he didn't want to have. He felt himself floating again. Maybe it wasn't too late to get some amnesia.

When he awoke again later the sky was dark except for some streaks of bruise purple and a nurse was changing his I.V. She joked, saying it was time for dinner as she attached a fresh bottle to the tube.

He was clear for a little longer than the other times and got some thinking done.

FORTY-ONE

A hand rubbing his cheek woke him. Carmen was standing over him, her hand on his cheek. She bent over and brushed her lips over his. The lines of fatigue and worry had bitten into her face again — she'd been so happy that morning! There were dark smudges under her eyes and her eyelids were rimmed in red.

He closed his eyes again. There it was, etched into her features, all the tragic stuff that was always just beneath the surface with Carmen. From the very first time, when, within minutes of meeting her, he'd been repeating phrases of tragic-romantic poetry after her. "The cups of dawn are broken... monotonous wail, like the wind over the snow... hot sand begging white camellias." He'd never had a chance with that stuff, whatever it meant.

He opened his eyes again. Her eyes were lustrous. Naturally, what else? He said, "Richard was right, Carmen, I do remember that poem. *Corazón malherido,* etcetera, etcetera."

She rubbed her hand on his cheek. "Darling, it's not your heart, it's your head." She laughed from nerves but the laughter was grotesque, cracking the perfect tragic lines of her face.

He closed his eyes: if he was going to be left with memories, he would try to pick the ones he liked.

When she stopped laughing he opened his eyes again. She said, "I can't stay, it's dangerous, but I had to see you, to... to tell you why I did it, I couldn't just...."

"Slow down. The police don't know about it yet, so you've got all the time you need. There's a lot I need to know before you leave. I think I can ask that much. Since I won't see you again."

"I'll see you again." The fingers on his cheek. "What do you mean?"

Maybe she thought she was telling the truth. He didn't know how much she knew. "No you won't," he said.

She looked baffled and changed the topic: "You do understand why I had to hit you?"

"Yes."

She explained anyway: "Richard was going to kill you. I thought if I could just remove the... the provocation, and get some time to talk to him."

"Yes."

"He... you see, he didn't *want* to kill you, really, so if I could just get you out of the way...."

"Yes, I understood. But did you have to get me out of the way so thoroughly?" He pointed at the x-ray of his skull hanging at the end of the bed.

"My God!" She went to the end of the bed and took the clipboard off its hook. "I did that?"

"They're going to give me tests for brain damage tomorrow."

"Cal, I... I'm so sorry. I never did that before, I was panicked, I didn't know how hard you had to swing to knock someone out."

"How would you?" He smiled generously. "It's all right. After all, you saved my life again."

She smiled, relieved at his smile, and put her hand over his hand on the cover.

He removed his hand. He didn't feel *that* forgiving. "Of course, my life wouldn't have needed so much saving if you'd let me in on the game."

"What are you talking about, Cal?"

"You used me," he said, surprised at his own bitterness. "I played the fool."

"What do you mean?" she asked again, but this time weakly, afraid of what he'd say.

He looked at her. He had to ignore his feelings and focus. How much did she know? He said, "How did it work? Did Richard call you from Mexico?"

She hesitated and nodded.

"You'll have to help me with the details," he said. "How did he call you if your phone was tapped?"

"He called his secretary. She came over to the house with a number where I could reach Richard."

She put her hand over his again and he let it stay there.

She'd answered his question, she seemed to be cooperating. And she'd given him another piece. "You had got my message on your answering machine and told him I'd found his hotel."

"Yes."

"That explains why he never came back to the hotel. I was the last person he wanted to see. He knew I'd try to stop his rampage."

"I don't know." Maybe she didn't. She squeezed his hand.

"He asked you and Newkirk to fly down."

She went white. "Just me. John came because he wanted to, just like he said." Her voice was thick-throated. "His family...."

She couldn't go on. He had almost forgotten Newkirk was dead. It hadn't mattered to him. Perhaps he could have stopped him from going out to the mine.... "I'm sorry," he said.

She was holding his hand tightly. She closed her eyes. "It's my fault."

He didn't say anything for a moment. The next question was the hard one. He returned some of the pressure she was putting on his hand. She opened her eyes again. "He told you to come to the hotel and find me, didn't he?"

She nodded miserably.

"He told you to find out what I knew. Such as one hundred and sixty-eight breaths east of fifteen. He told you to stay with me until I learned something."

She didn't say anything.

"I'm right, aren't I?"

"How did you know?"

"It's the only way it makes sense." He laughed bitterly. "Richard's whole plan was to find Fausto and beat it out of him. Torture him until he found out where Josefina was. That's why he didn't want me in on it. There was only one problem — a major problem. He couldn't find Fausto. He thought with me — the *pro* — on the job, I might be able to help him. But he didn't want to show his face. Enter Carmen."

She nodded weakly again, then stared off, then rallied: "The police never would have found Josefina. He was right about that, wasn't he?"

"Yes, but I might have."

"But you wouldn't have... have done what was necessary to get her back from Fausto."

"Tortured him?"

She shrugged. She wasn't going to get involved with that word.

"But we did get Josefina, didn't we?" he said.

She stopped looking blank and defensive. "Why? Why did Fausto bring her to us?"

He laughed his bitter laugh again. "Ah, that one had me confused. Everything Fausto did had me confused. To start with, why the hell would he let me go when he had me in the mine? But when it came to me, staring at the ceiling here, that Fausto wanted to find Richard as badly as Richard wanted to find Fausto, it made sense. It's good, if you like black humor: these two guys wanting to tear each other apart except they can't *find* each other." He laughed again.

"What are you talking about, Cal?" She looked worried. He didn't know if she was worried about him or what he was going to say.

"I'd only been in Mazatlán a few hours and Dedo is trailing me in the Riviera. I wasn't sure why but now it's obvious: They wanted me to lead them to Richard. But I lost Dedo and they never found out about the hotel, or at least not until I told them where I was staying." He paused, remembering the histrionics in San Ildefonso, firing the gun in the air, throwing down the gauntlet to Fausto. "Then they had me in the mine and it was obvious I didn't know where Richard was. They let me go to try again. But I still couldn't find Richard and Richard wasn't coming to me. So they gave us back Josefina."

"I still don't understand."

"Richard would come out of hiding when we had Josefina. That's what he was after, right? And when he came out, they would kill him. They were trying to flush him with Josefina. The go-between — me — hadn't worked out."

"Why would they want to kill Richard?"

The question seemed oddly innocent, considering Richard had blown Dedo's head all over the mine and put a gaping hole in Fausto's throat. And it was a question he wasn't ready to answer until he'd got a few more details.

"Where is Richard now?" he asked.

"I got him to a private sanatorium," she said. "Well, really it's just a doctor's house. But I am paying him very well and Richard is under heavy sedation. When he is better, we'll go home and get real help."

She seemed to mean it. She seemed to think they were going home. "Carmen, I don't understand. Didn't you know Richard had gone... was out of control? Couldn't you *see* it?"

"I never saw him. I just talked to him on the phone. He didn't want to see me." She got out a cigarette and offered him one.

"No. A hospital, with a picture of my skull in front of me, is a good time to go cold turkey." It did smell good though. "Let's go back a bit. You got to the hotel, found me, I told you where Dedo and Fausto were. You phoned Richard and told him about the mine, the hundred and sixty-eight breaths. Told him *and* Newkirk."

"Yes," she whispered defenselessly.

"How did they get Fausto and Dedo? Go out to the mine, wait for them and conk them on the head when they came in?"

"I don't know."

She wouldn't: Richard wasn't in any shape to talk about such practical matters.

Another thought hit him and the bitterness welled up again. "Did Richard tell you to wait in the shower and *fuck* me? Was that your idea or his?"

She looked as if she'd been slapped. "Cal... what are you... my God." Her eyes filled with anger. "The *fucking* was all my idea."

"I'm sorry," he said.

"The only reason I ever made love to you," she said, hurt, "is because I love you. You should know that."

"I'm sorry, Carmen." He wanted to know things that were more knowable: "How did Richard know we... made love at the hotel?"

She tensed and drew on the cigarette. "When I went back to your room, to spend the night with you...."

"After you'd left me asleep to phone him with a report, and talked to Newkirk too."

She grimaced. "After I came back to your room he phoned me in his room — his and mine — several times but I wasn't there to answer."

"That's all?"

"That's all. You were right, Cal. He'd always suspected, and he was not... healthy... by this time."

He wasn't healthy but he was right.

"When you were out of my room Richard sent me a... package. The contents were supposed to make me think he was dead. Did you know about that?"

She looked surprised then shrugged. "No, but he did tell me not to be worried if you thought he was dead."

"The idea was for you to convince me to go back to California, once you'd passed on the information about the mine."

She nodded.

"But then he tried to get you on the phone for half the night and decided to get me out to the orchard to kill me instead."

"What!"

He studied her. She really didn't seem to know the rest. He would have sworn. But his track record with judging Carmen wasn't very good. It was terrible.

He shrugged, meaning maybe he had it wrong. "What are you going to do now?"

She squeezed his hand again and got up looking for an ashtray. Naturally there wasn't one in the hospital. She dropped the cigarette to the floor, stepped on it and slid it under the bed. She sat down again. "No one knows about the bodies in the mine, Cal, except us."

He gave a tired laugh and relaxed into the mattress. "Is that why you came here? To make sure I wouldn't say anything?"

"No," she protested, watching him anxiously. "But... what is done is done. I can take him back for proper care."

"What about Alison Newkirk?" he said meanly. "Doesn't she get told?"

"Yes, of course. I... I don't know... of course I'll tell her."

Without moving he tensed on the mattress to get through the rest. "You can't take him back, unless you want him in a psyche ward with bars on the windows, at best. Or on death row at worst."

"Please, Cal. It's over. We can't bring them back. You don't have to say anything."

He couldn't watch her. He looked straight up at the white tiles. "Carmen, Richard isn't just having a mid-life crisis. We can't just be understanding and forgiving."

"Justice, you mean? Isn't that a little abstract? Richard is your oldest friend. And — whatever you think — I do love you." She paused but he kept looking at the ceiling. She leaned forward into his peripheral vision. "I'm *asking* you, Cal. Me."

"There are *five* bodies, Carmen." He looked to her finally — he had to know.

"Five?" It didn't seem to add up for her. But it was as if she hadn't heard, she didn't seem to be hiding anything. Then her eyes changed and she drained to a very sincere ash color. "Five?"

"You really don't know, do you?"

"Cal, what...." She was watching him, waiting.

"He killed Leopoldo Sanchez, and Jaime Sanchez." She shook her head and ran her fingers through her hair. He hesitated, then finished: "Leopoldo Sanchez was... roughed up. Richard did it. He thought Sanchez could tell him where Josefina was. But all Sanchez knew was the general scheme — Mazatlán, the orphanage, San Ildefonso. The hideout in the mine would have been a secret from him. It was enough though to point Richard in the right direction. And when you got here you told him where Jaime was, another bit of information I'd passed on. Richard decided to try again."

She watched him for a moment longer, then her face sank into her hands.

An enormous fatigue settled onto him, a fatigue that felt like a physical sickness. He'd said everything he had to say. It was over. He closed his eyes again.

He heard her say: "Richard wasn't there. He couldn't have killed Leopoldo. He'd already caught a plane."

He didn't open his eyes. He opened his mouth. The weight was so heavy he had to make a special effort to speak. "Please don't lie to me any more, Carmen. It's too late. You are driving his red Mercedes. You know he didn't fly down."

She drew a sharp breath. He wondered if she'd actually put her hand to her mouth in a gesture of shock. He heard her chair scrape back and felt the bed give as she sat on the edge of it. He felt her hands on his shoulders. "Please, Cal," she whispered. "No matter how many people are dead, we can't bring them back."

Eyes still closed, he said, "No doubt you could convince me to be quiet, or maybe not — it doesn't matter though. I think Huerta is way ahead of me on this. You can't go back."

He opened his eyes for one last look, one exact image: her full lips were pressed tight refusing to accept what she would have to accept; slightly arched nose, nostrils flared with tension; the sharp lines, the sharp cheekbones, the slightly tilted eyes. Black, black eyes. Hair pulled back. He remembered it loose in the sunlight, copper tipped, fiery ended.

"And that's why I won't see you again." He tried to smile. "Love of my life."

"*Mi corazón.*" She leaned forward until her head rested

lightly on his chest.

    Malherido. His eyes rolled up or his lids drifted down. An undertow of sleep was pulling him down. Her head seemed to float on his chest. She would be gone when he awoke. He went down slowly like a weight just slightly denser than water.

FORTY-TWO

He awoke again, but in a different bed, with different plaster on the ceiling. Still flat on his back but in the hotel. He'd passed his brain damage test, the consul had signed him out and got him back to the hotel, two hotel employees had helped the consul get him up to his room. He'd immediately fallen asleep again.

He decided he was feeling better, just very weak. He looked slowly around the room. He was alone. The consul had told him he'd come by the following morning to check on him and assured him he'd arranged for the hotel staff to check on him every couple of hours. Two pillows were off to his side. He carefully sat far enough forward to work them behind his head and eased himself down on them. Pillows: one more step on the road to recovery.

His head was hurting a lot now and they'd given him a supply of codeine but he put off taking another pill. He looked around again. The doors to the balcony were open but the curtains over them were only open a couple of feet. They bellied into the room in the ocean breeze and for a moment a hummingbird hung absolutely still between the blur of its wings and then darted off. He propped himself up a little higher until he could see himself in the mirror over the low bureau. The white bandages around his head were startlingly white; underneath them he was haggard and unshaven. He had taken the x-ray of his skull as a souvenir and someone had stuck it in the corner of the mirror. There was a large vase of salmon gladioli, the long stalks leaning lopsidedly out of a vase that was too low for them.

He worked his feet to the floor and rested on the edge of the bed. He stood up and felt dizzy for just a second, then felt fine. He took a few careful old-man steps over to the balcony and stood between the curtains. It was late afternoon again and the light was piercing. He closed his eyes, took a step back and closed the curtain. It would be sunset time again in a couple hours and he didn't want another Mazatlán sunset. He made it back to his bed. He supposed the weakness was normal.

He lay against the pillow, tired from his hike across the room. He took the codeine and looked at the plaster some more. Sleep was coming to his rescue again.

When he awoke again he knew he'd been having ugly dreams. Codeine-cushioned but ugly nonetheless. He kept his eyes closed to try to remember them but couldn't. When he opened them a school of dolphins seemed to leap by his right eye. He was startled in a slow sort of way and turned his head slightly to the right.

"Jesus." His tongue was thick and stupid. "Vic."

The school of dolphins were leaping across Vic Huerta's sportshirt, across the expanse of his chest. Huerta was on a chair, leaning over close to the bed.

"What happened?" Huerta said.

"I got hit on the head."

"I mean the rest."

"You're awfully blunt, Vic, anyone ever tell you?" He worked himself a little higher on the pillows. "You're supposed to start with something like 'how are you feeling?'"

"How are you feeling?"

"Very thirsty." Huerta didn't seem to get it so he added: "Could you get me something from the refrigerator?"

Huerta got him a 7-Up and a Carta Blanca for himself. He watched Main sip the 7-Up and took a couple swallows of beer.

"I didn't know you drank, Vic."

"I'm on vacation," Huerta said, and put the beer on the floor, done with having a good time. "What happened?"

He was ready for all these questions. He just needed some time to come to. As if he'd just remembered where he was, what was happening, he anxiously asked, "Any sign of Richard and Carmen yet?"

"No."

He lay more heavily into his pillow and let his eyes close.

"What happened?" He didn't answer and Huerta said, "According to the consul your story is this: You and Carmen and Richard and Newkirk all went out to a beach way up the coast with a briefcase full of money to meet Dedo and Fausto and get

Josefina back. You went ahead of the others to make sure they had Josefina. You got knocked out, left for dead, and the next thing you knew someone had dropped you off at the hospital. That the story?"

"It's not a story, it's what I know. Little as it is."

Huerta had his broad blank face on him for what seemed like an eternity. He finally said, "So that's the way it's going to be?"

"I don't know what you're talking about."

Huerta kept watching him, though "watching" made it sound too active. He was looking in his direction; he had his face toward him — something like that. Huerta said, "I just don't know for sure. I usually know if someone is lying but this time I'm not quite sure. I think you are...."

"Look, I've got a fractured skull, I'm full of codeine, I'm not lying, so why don't you cut the bullshit." He thought he was doing a fair imitation of tired indignation.

"Your story doesn't make sense. Why would they want to kill you and not the others? Wouldn't they kill Richard and Carmen and Newkirk and take the money? Or if the others got away, where are they? And why didn't they help you?"

"I don't know." He sounded too tired to think about those things.

There was another long silence, then Huerta said, "I'll be back tomorrow for the details. We'll have a long talk. But for now, just in case you don't know it, I'd better break the bad news."

Main slowly rolled his head to face Huerta.

Huerta said, "Richard killed Leopoldo Sanchez and presumably Jaime Sanchez."

"What!" He thought he sounded surprised. "He couldn't have. He was in Mexico."

"He had plane reservations and he even picked up his tickets. But when we checked the boarding manifest the next day — he was never on that flight." Main started to protest but Huerta raised his voice and kept talking: "And remember that motel across the field from where Sanchez was killed? Richard was there the night of the murder, calling a taxi. It's solid."

It was Main's turn for a long silence, as if he was struggling with the idea. He frowned at the ceiling, looked at it as if there was a message to read there, closed his eyes as the idea sank in.

He opened his eyes again and rolled his head to Huerta, looking at him accusingly. "When did you learn this? Before I left?"

"I knew about the tickets before you left. I didn't have the I.D. from the hotel clerk yet." Huerta's honesty was disarming, especially compared to his own total dishonesty.

He let out a long sigh. "That's why the first time we talked about my coming the idea was to find out about the baby smuggling and not worry too much about Richard and the second time you told me to concentrate on bringing Richard back. That it?"

"Yes. By the time you left I had good reasons to want to talk to Richard." Huerta picked up his beer again and took a swallow.

There wasn't anything he could say unless he wanted to whine about how Huerta had used him. It was getting to be his tune.

He thought he'd better protest some more to make it seem real: "But why would Richard do that?"

"His adoption was illegal. He couldn't tell us everything and he thought he could get Josefina back by himself. I had mentioned Leopoldo Sanchez to him. Stupidly. He thought he could beat it out of Sanchez. Remember, he'd been tortured."

"Torture? Come on, Vic."

Huerta put his beer down again and looked at him. There was no way to draw him into an argument. Huerta said, "Where are Richard and Carmen and Newkirk?"

"I don't know. You want me to say it? If they're not around, they must be dead." He closed his eyes again at the idea. It wasn't hard to fake: they were dead to him now.

"That's going to be the story?"

"Stop calling it a goddamn story. I don't know. You tell me where they are."

"They're dead. Or they're hiding out. I'm afraid you're going to have to be the one to tell. Maybe tomorrow." Huerta heaved himself up.

"What are you going to do now?" Main asked.

"I don't know. I'm on vacation. Until tomorrow evening."

"The hotel puts on a show of Mexican folk dancing."

Huerta went to the door. The joke fell flat. Huerta didn't have a sense of humor. Or the joke wasn't funny.

Huerta said, "See you tomorrow," and left.

Main waited for more sleep but he was wide awake and much too clear.

It would be a long convalescence.